Frederick William Waldebrand Pattenden

Verses by F. W. W. Pattenden

Frederick William Waldebrand Pattenden

Verses by F. W. W. Pattenden

ISBN/EAN: 9783337252403

Printed in Europe, USA, Canada, Australia, Japan

Cover: Foto ©Andreas Hilbeck / pixelio.de

More available books at **www.hansebooks.com**

VERSES

BY

F. W. W. PATTENDEN.

COLLECTED

AND

PRIVATELY PRINTED.

London:

JAMES CLARKE & CO., 13 & 14, FLEET STREET.

—

1891.

CONTENTS.

Verses for or to Children.

Miscellaneous Verses.

VERSES BY F. W. W. PATTENDEN.

Prize Poems at the Grammar School, Boston, Lincolnshire.

PERSIA.

HAIL Iran! ancient Iran! sacred name
  To every heart that Ayran blood can claim!
What land can boast the imperial renown
That decked the lustre of thy former crown?
Ah! could the annals of thy pristine might
Unfold their wonders to the astonished sight,
What records of the long-forgotten dead
Would rouse the warrior from his earthy bed,
To fight his former battles o'er again,
And reap the glory that he died to gain?
Once more great Cyrus beats his rivals down,
And treads the bloody path that gives a crown.
Again his warriors, nursed in victory, scale
The cliffs that frown o'er Hermus' rugged vale,
Where Sardis nestles 'mid its guardian rocks,
That seem to brave or time's or battle's shocks.
Again he fells Belshazzar's tott'ring throne,
And gains the brass-capped walls of Babylon;
Subdues the unsubdued, and adds a gem
To the bright frontlet of his diadem.
  But see! Darius arms his myriad host
To pour their living flood on Hellas' coast.

See how the Persian dreads the wild career
And crushing onset of the Athenian spear!
See how Darius' craven hirelings bend
And cower 'neath "freedom's best and bravest friend";
And deluging with war a land of peace,
Win Grecian graves instead of conquered Greece.
Ah! hapless Iran! thine it was to mourn
Thy sons who fought and fell at Marathon;
Reft of thy bravest children, thine to see
Thy legions baffled at Thermopylæ;
Where Spartans in their death wrought deathless deeds,
And falling fell 'mid heaps of slaughtered Medes.
There in the bosom of that reeking pass
Died Sparta's noblest son, Leonidas.
No victor's garlands Sparta's brows shall grace,
For cypress-wreaths the laurel-crowns displace.
Mourn for him, Hellas! Iran, mourn, for know
Ne'er warrior fell beneath a nobler foe.
No need a short-lived monument to raise:
He has a living tomb that ne'er decays.
No need of bards his glory to attest:
He lives enshrined in every Grecian breast.
Ah! Salamis! thou too hast heard the roar
Of Freedom battling round thy sea-girt shore;
When Greek and Persian mingled seas of blood,
Purpling the glutted, still insatiate flood;
When haughty Xerxes' vanquished armament
Back in a surge of their own gore was sent.
Ah, hapless Salamis! thy conscious wave
Still sighs and moans o'er many a hero's grave.
   See, Persia, see where Philip's warlike son
Triumphant leads his conquering legions on;
Spurns the fair flowers of Peace with iron car,
And crushes her beneath the heel of war.

As o'er the rocks the avalanche thundering down
Whelms with colossal mass the helpless town,
So, Iran, like a thunderbolt on thee
Rushed the avenger of Thermopylæ.
Granicus felt the bloody hand of war,
Its waters glowing with its children's gore.
Then trampling down the dying and the dead,
To Issus' stream the laurelled phalanx sped.
Onward again they urge their deadly way,
And swoop like vultures on the writhing prey;
On fair Arbela's plains they deal the blow
That lays the pride and power of Iran low.
Cumbered by myriads fell that huge array,
And in their very strength their weakness lay.
The vanquished Persian urged his wild retreat,
And Asia bowed at Alexander's feet.
High o'er his helm the avenging eagle stood,
Its weary pinions steeped in Persian blood.
Yet he who conquered on the embattled plain,
Who fought no bloodless victory to gain,
He sears the laurels of a deed like this
In the charred ashes of Persepolis.
Yes, fired by Thais' charms, his maddened hand,
Trained to the sword, now wields the flaming brand.
Mourn thy lost beauty, Iran, curse the feast
That marred thy child, " the glory of the East."
    Weep, Iran! darker days are yet in store,
When fierce Mohammed o'er the world shall pour
The flood of Moslem zealots nought can stem,
Pagan to us, a Demigod to them.
From Beder's field of blood and Ohud's plain
Sweeps the Impostor-Prophet's conquering train.
Ambition leads the way and blinded zeal
And back their faith with arguments of steel.

The sword their God, they yoke the steeds of war
With gory chains to fair Religion's car.
On come those fiends of fight, that wolfish horde,
Their battle-cry, "The Koran or the Sword."
Is there no patriot in all the land
For Mithras' sake to raise a Gheber's hand?
Shall Iran leave the faith its sires adored,
And cringe before a self-created Lord?
"Islam or Death!" the frenzied Moslems cry.
Well, better far that every Gheber die,
Than see his country writhing 'neath the heel
Of those accursed votaries of the steel.
What men could do they did, but all in vain,
They fell entombed in heaps of Moslem slain.

Where, Iran, where are now such hearts as those
That scorned to yield them to their country's foes,
Welcomed in Mithras' cause a patriot's death,
And cursed Mohammed with their dying breath?
Alas for Iran, childless and forlorn,—
Her laurels trampled and her banners torn,—
Islam—her faith,—her people—slaves,—proclaim
Iran is Iran now in nought but name.

DECEMBER, 1873.

PRINTING.

O FOR the power to build the loftier rhyme
   That graced the poesy of former time,
When fancy mantled with a golden dress
The forms she conjured out of nothingness!
Just as the sculptor—whose deft hand can give
Breath to the stone, and make the marble live,

God-like can bid a mortal form to be,
And rear the ideal of humanity :—
When at his feet Carrara's wealth is strown,
Where others see a shapeless mass of stone,
He dreams of shadowy forms that wait his art,
Beneath his magic chisel-stroke to start
Into the half-immortal form and face
Of perfect symmetry and perfect grace.
Here, frowning thunder, lowers Olympian Jove,
There Venus smiles with all the power of love :
Here Ares stands, and here the huntress Queen,
With sage Athene's classic face between :
There childless Niobe pours the stony tear,
While next her towers the perfect " Belvedere."
  With such a master-mind the poets brought
New creatures from the untrodden realms of thought,
Embodied all the shadows of their dream,
And in the wild caprice of power supreme
Clothed their creation with ideal grace,
And spurned the vulgar world of common-place.
Thus in their Paradise a stream, they told,
Poured its bright waters over sands of gold,
So pure, the sun half-seemed to pause awhile,
Upon its dancing portraiture to smile,
Ling'ring to gaze upon its golden beam
Gilded anew in bright Pactolus' stream ;
And the wild swallow loved to plume her breast
And glossy wings, o'er this the loveliest
Of all the mirrors Nature wrought to enhance
Her children's forms with pictured radiance.
Such and so bright the stream of Knowledge flows,
Tracing a golden path where'er it goes :
Its healing water knows but how to bless,
And makes a garden of a wilderness.

The fabled stream, how broad so e'er it rolled,
With greedy waters hugged its useless gold,
But Knowledge showers abroad its precious store,
And only hoards it to bestow the more:
Like Salem's pool, it lifts the weakly up,
Honeys the lips to sorrow's bitterest cup,
And o'er the sinking mind, with solace fraught,
It waves the wings of Hope, the lovely after-thought.

Fourteen long centuries the Gospel-light
Had but half-made the gloom of ignorance bright;
So long had Knowledge wrestled with her foe;
So loth were men her priceless boons to know;
Still Ignorance clung to her degrading sway,
Still found she priests her mandates to obey.
As far-off stars, tho' robed in heavenly light,
Scarce lend a glimmer to the shade of night,
So Knowledge, high o'er all things worldly rear'd,
Scarce pierced the darkness of the common herd,
Till loud to heaven she cried against her foes,
And, heaven-sent helper, GUTENBERG arose.

Far from life's busy whirl, by Main's blue stream,
He nursed with secret love his hope, his dream.
Many a long, long day of toil passed by
In the slow train of dull monotony,
And still the earnest brow, the hollow cheek,
And distant look, that thoughtful labour speak,
And the firm mouth, where suffering graves her trace,
Still marked the student severed from his race.
As the skilled pilot in a sheltered bay,—
Where, weary of their all too boisterous play,
The wanton billows fain would sink to rest,
And lay their heads on peaceful Ocean's breast,—
Looks fearless from his silver-cradled spot,
Sees the mad tempest rage and heeds it not,

So to the student passed unnoticed by
The cares and pleasures of humanity;
And life with all its duties, all its calls,
Dwarfed to the limits of his chamber's walls,
Showed him but one idea, his aim, his end,
His only solace, and his only friend.
At length the wondrous work is fully wrought,
The tenfold fruit of all his toil and thought;
And printing speeds on pinions of the wind
To shape the world anew, and change mankind,
    In that fair pile, where shrined in glory rest
Those Britain styles her greatest and her best,
Too late, alas! their clouded sight to bless,
Our English Caxton reared the Printing Press.
    With such quick strides Invention speeds her way
The man of yesterday's a babe to-day ;
The myth to-day, that sober minds would chase,
May haply be to-morrow's common-place.
Born amid kings and bards her fairest child
In the first grace of infant beauty smil'd,
But as the hoar frost chills the opening flower,
As on the waking morn the storm-clouds lower,
With blasting fury on the weakly life
Burst the fierce rolling tide of holy strife.
Religion, maddened with the battle-cry,
Turned her wild arms upon her best ally.
In vain: the influence scatters east and west
Her radiance, ever blessing, ever blest :
And Knowledge, spreading wide from coast to coast,
Pours its full blaze—a second Pentecost—
Raising the dimness of our mortal sight
To the perfection of celestial light.

DECEMBER. 1874.

THE ARCTIC REGIONS.

SEE how yon vessel at her cable strains,
    With quiv'ring sides, to burst her iron chains.
See how the crowds on pier and jetty swell,
To speed their loved ones with a last farewell
Here a proud mother strives to hide her fear,
And checks the weakness of the natural tear;
There a fond wife upbraids with tender voice,
And makes her sailor half repent his choice,
To lose the magic of that warm word "Home,"
In frozen Nature's prison-house to roam;
To go, he knows not where, and come again,
If come he may, he knows not how or when.

    Past is the anguish of the parting tear,
The bitterest pang that life inherits here;
When first the sundered hearts the keenest feel
The maddening wound that time and patience heal.
Still strains the ship, in headlong race to vie
With the proud waves that mocking pass her by:
As, in past days, the generous Elian mare
With trembling petulance snuffed the bracing air,
And neighed and panted past the bar to fly,
That shut the road to fame and victory.
Soon her flushed owner proudly takes his stand,
With Altis' hard-earned palm-branch in his hand.

    The anchor's heaved; she flies—with futile force
The straining eyes of love would stay her course.
Now the far object baulks the dazzled gaze,
Where sea and sky unite in one blue haze.

Soon over floe and iceberg, sea and land,
The Arctic night will fix its withering hand;
Soon the last gleams of the long day will smile
O'er Greenland's glacier-plains and Zembla's isle;
The fiery Sun grow ruddier still and less,
And faster leave the world to loneliness;
Till, like a drowning man, the ocean o'er
It struggles once, then sinks to rise no more.

The helpless vessel in these icy fields
To Nature's adamantine bondage yields:
Loud howls the blast, the quivering timbers creak,
And chafe the shackling ice, but all too weak.
As when a troubled sleeper fain would flee
The weird creation of his fantasy;
The shriek, half-uttered, chokes upon his lip;
His fingers stiffen with convulsive grip.
The grisly horror still pursues amain,
And still the rebel limbs defy the brain.
His helpless knees but mock his frenzied sense,
And cower in agonising impotence.

See, a dark arch of clouds o'erspreads the sky,
Fringed with a halo of pale brilliancy!
Now a bright ray, athwart the chilly night,
Sways, like a wind-tost ribbon clothed in light,
Then fades before a thousand coloured beams,
That sparkle forth in ever-varying streams;
While, in the zenith, pours serenely down
The silvery splendour of the Boreal crown!
Till the dazed eye beholds the etherial frame,
A cupola of scintillating flame.
Faintly distinct a mystic rustling sounds,
Thrills the crisp air, and frights the cowering hounds.

Round the beleaguered vessel slowly grow,
In frozen heaps the battlements of snow.
Yet can they make the ice some warmth supply,
And have a friend in their chief enemy.
Though loud without the baffled tempest's din,
Louder the answering notes of mirth within;
While peerless Shakespeare sways the listening throng,
Or Handel melts with all the power of song.
Now round the hearth the eager listeners come—
Their sole memento of the hearths at home—
Whilst one, on whose grey locks and storm-beat face,
Hardship has furrowed her recording trace,
Tells of the time when Franklin led his crew
O'er ice-bound plains, a faint and jaded few;
And how that hardy child of Lincoln's soil
Faced every peril, hardier still in toil;
The while his fainting sailors fell around,
Nor grudged their way-worn bodies to the ground.

Thus they deceive the night, till o'er the sea
The waking Sun throws off his lethargy.
As bees reviving at the breath of Spring
Flit round the hive with busy murmuring;
Or like the fabled ghosts that midnight calls
To the grim banquet-war in Odin's halls:
Thus the bold seamen wake to seek their goal,
To scour the ice, and gain the wondrous Pole.

That spot no human eye has lived to see,
Mysterious Nature's great anomaly:
That spot where circling suns nor set nor rise,
And stars stand motionless in constant skies:
Where'er the eye may rove is South alone:
The card forgets its points and knows but one.

There, 'mid the ice, the ancient legends tell,
Apollo's Hyperborean favourites dwell,
Dowered with Spring eternal, cloudless skies,
Immortal youth, an earthly Paradise.
Nor, sceptic, call it vain, that Science deems
Those snow-clad wilds once felt the torrid beams.

Once and again has Nature barred the way,
And baffled human art must needs obey.
Back have our Vikings turned their prows again :
They did what men could do, and did in vain.
Yet live there still, who such a task will dare :
Still Albion's sons know not the word—despair :
Warm English hearts frights not the Arctic cold :
Peril, that scares the coward, lures the bold.
Forth sped the summons, and not one, but all
Rose as one man, at Queen and country's call.
One vacant place a hundred suppliants ask :
Not levying, then, but choosing was the task.

Now first the vaporous force its aid has brought,
With all that hardly-won experience taught.
To Britain's sons again the work is given,
And Honour leads the van—so speed them Heaven !

JUNE, 1875.

VISIT OF THE PRINCE OF WALES TO INDIA.

HUSHED is the house : no voice of mirth, no sound
of laughter peals,
And through the halls with chilling power a sombre
silence steals,

And children look with wond'ring eyes, and speak with
  bated breath,
While none dare say, yet all can feel—it is the house
  of death.
Around his couch a sorrowing throng of silent mourners
  stand,
Where, flushed and haggard, lies our prince, the heir of
  all the land.
'Tis sorrow's court; and there he lies stretched on that
  ghastly bed,
Where fever fires the throbbing veins, and racks the
  aching head.
Even hope, long sojourner, deserts the cheerless
  threshold now—
And yet how well a diadem would sit upon that
  brow!
Ay, so it shall! for God heard then a mourning
  nation's voice,
Baulked the grim tyrant of his prey, and bade the
  land rejoice.
Time rolls away, and Albion bows in common prayer
  again,
That Heaven may watch around her prince across the
  angry main,
And God, who from the jaws of death has plucked
  that precious life,
Will guard it through the boisterous clash of elemental
  strife.
The waves that back from Cæsar's skiff in baffled
  terror poured,
Will shrink where good *Serapis* bears a mightier
  empire's lord.
So speed thee well through all the storms of many a
  fitful sea:

Good ship, thou hast a golden freight, a nation's heart,
    in thee!
Yet never in the fiercest rage of beating tempests
    wince:
Be this thy safeguard through them all—thou bearest
    Albion's prince.

    Land of the snow-girt mountain-chain, land of the
        tangled wood,
Where fertile plains and arid wastes bathe in a golden
    flood;
Where streams of silver softly thread the jungle's
    inmost maze,
And fresh from snowy couches love to shun the garish
    blaze.
The gaudy parrot pours its cries from all but human
    throat,
The timid ring-dove answers back the bulbul's mellow
    note,
Mount, vale and plateau, mead and waste, all teem
    alike in thee
Thou sample-pattern of the world, the earth's epitome.
Where all is one fair printed leaf, just fresh from
    Nature's press,
Of all God's works, man's soul alone is gloomy
    wilderness.
Yet Superstition's noxious hand, that tyrant of the
    soul,
With foulest blots has soiled the page, and marred the
    beauteous whole;
With coarser thoughts and things of earth debased the
    once refined,
And as with Circe's witching rod, has brutalised the
    mind.

Human in passions are their gods, ay, worse than
    human too:
All Pandemonium could not send to earth a viler
    crew.
Here Siva with his river-crown and ghastly necklace
    frights
The sensual crowd that bends the knee to his revolting
    rites.
There Doorga's votaries implore their queen with
    beaten breast
To reign within her image-form and grace her holy
    feast;
" Descend, celestial queen, enshrined in every Hindoo
    heart,
To this cold stone the ambrosial breath of heavenly
    life impart.
She comes, she comes: then speed the dance, enwreathe
    her sacred brow,
No age so weak, no heart so chill, but glows with
    fervour now."

Now peals that ill-named worship, hideous revelry
    from far,
Where Vishnu tops the carven bulk of Jaggernauth's
    dread car.
No organ's solemn incense breathes around the
    heavenly throne;
But shrieks and yells, fit harmony to soothe the ears
    of stone.
Crashing, the sacred chariot drags its ponderous
    weight along,
And leaves a mangled trail of death amid the frenzied
    throng.

As measured music's varying tones in blended
    cadence roll,
Each without other incomplete: combined, a perfect
    whole;
Still winding in the harmony, yet ever softly clear,
One key-note breathing through the rest speaks to the
    practised ear,
Even so the Babel-voices hum from out the maddened
    crowd,
While ever and again above the clamour rises loud
A shriek, the key-note to the rest, " To thee, to thee,
    my god,
The offering thou lovest best, I give my life, my
    blood."

Ah! where is that pure worship of the bygone days
    of Ind,
Ere bloody conquest swept the land, like a Sirocco
    wind?
When man in gloom benighted toward the glimmering
    beacon trod,
When, Nature's God unknown, he made Nature herself
    his God.
When Agni's fire and Marut's blast, and India's
    cloudless blue,
And Surya's beam, and Ushas' blush were all the gods
    he knew.
When purity was still untouched by the rough hands of
    vice,
And Soma's mystic essence was his only sacrifice:
When in his soul Genasa breathed the Veda's holy
    page,
And Vishnu showered Armita down the immortal
    beverage.

But as in stagnant waters, be they ne'er so fresh and
    clear,
Ere long unsightly forms pollute, and noxious weeds
    appear;
So men would fain these harmless rites with coarser
    orgies stain,
And pay the ruthless homage of the human victim slain.
That men should their Creator glut with feasts of
    creature food,
And soothe the Almighty Father with His slaughtered
    children's blood!

Then sped, like fire o'er pampas-plains, the infuriate
    Moslem horde,
And India lay a wounded life 'neath Mahmoud's
    conqu'ring sword.
Then Islam and the Koran with the zealot warriors come,
And Vedas, scorned by victors, with the vanquished
    find a home.
In vain the Mongul raised his spear the Moslem power
    to shake,
In vain the foreign tide upon the imbedded granite brake,
Worthy the soldier-prophet's name, a new Mohammed
    rose,
And dying stemmed the torrent of his god and country's
    foes:
Brief respite this: the Crescent-light, long flickering
    on the wane,
Now dim and paling sank before the star of Tamerlane.

Yet, India, thou again beneath a foreign yoke shalt
    bend,
In bonds, but bonds of love, shalt own thy conqu'ror
    and thy friend.

Commerce, a mightier power than arms, lays the
    foundation stone
Of a far wider empire than Aurungsebe called his own,
On that a Clive, a Wellesley reared the tower of
    Britain's sway,
Cemented with the out-poured blood of Plassy and
    Assaye.
No province this for Roman lords in slavery's chains
    to hold,
To grind the poor and scare the rich, in their mad
    lust for gold;
No tyrants now of Timur's house the groaning land
    oppress,
But India, ruled for India's good, tastes peace and
    happiness.
No more fierce Kali's vassal-bands for the doomed
    traveller lurk,
In impious hope that heavenly bliss will crown their
    murd'rous work ;
No more the mourning widow mounts her lord's
    funereal pyre,
And thinks celestial glory lies beyond that road of fire.

Speed thee, *Serapis;* bold thy task and high thy
    mission now :
No sacred Delian bark had e'er a holier end than thou.
What stronger pledge could Albion send, what more
    could India crave ?
For lo! we give her here the best, the dearest pledge
    we have.

December, 1875.

2

WELCOME TO THE PRINCE OF WALES ON HIS RETURN FROM INDIA.

SONS of Britain, shout the greeting!
   Loud the joyous welcome raise!
In a choir of triumph meeting
   Peal the echo of his praise!
Long in foreign climes a stranger
   Albion hails her eldest son:
All the hardship, all the danger,
   All the dark foreboding done.
Angry billows fell before him,
   Shrank the jungle's teeming brood:
Mightier powers were watching o'er him,
   Guiding him o'er land and flood.
Well has India kept the treasure,
   Given her loyal heart to prove,
Filled to overflow the measure
   Of a grateful nation's love.
Many a time have Kings victorious
   Won the immortal bay ere now;
None more worthy, none more glorious
   E'er has won his meed, than thou.
Home at last! the note of gladness
   To the wanderer's heart has come;
Now put off your boding sadness,
   Britons, shout his welcome home!

No more the Indian wonders now
   At abstract rule and powers unseen,
That give him laws, he knows not how,
   But vaguely asks what all may mean.

'Tis hard for human hearts to love
 A name, but now 'tis theirs to see
Embodied in their presence move
 The form of Britain's sovereignty.
Not vain the work that he has done,
 Nor light the perils he has past;
But the brave soul within has won,
 And victory crowns his toil at last :—
Not victory got with blood, as erst,
 When Timur broke his deadly way,
Or when the British handful burst
 Upon the myriads of Assaye.
But grows the tree without the knife?
 What stone uncut its brilliance showers?
Not far the time when India's life
 And India's strength shall rival ours :
When that fair jewel of our crown,
 No more the rough, the uncut gem,
Polished by British arts has grown
 The glory of our diadem.
And who shall say the Briton's heart
 Has lost the vigour of his sires,
That his chilled soul is slow to start
 To the pure blaze of patriot fires?
That England's pulse is cold and dead,
 And true-born English hearts are rare
Faith, Courage, Truth, all, all are fled
 And Britons are not what they were?
Defiant Albion still may rise,
 If such a whisperer vile there be,
Cast in his teeth the traitor's lies,
 And, Albert Edward, point to thee.
The generous stream that throbbed of yore
 In the blue depths of Alfred's veins,

That fired a Richard's soul, and bore
  The Norman lord to Albion's plains:
The blood that nerved an Edward's arm.
  And spurred him through the battle's shock.
That blood flows still as pure, as warm,
  In every scion of his stock.
Whate'er their task, that Kingly stem,
  Nor faint their heart, nor slow their hand:
No Briton e'er need blush for them,
  The pride, the glory of our land.
And we for Fatherland and fame
  Can still the patriot's laurel woo;
Our English sires we dare not shame,
  What they have done we still can do.
The Lion sleeps perchance, but still
  His teeth are no less sharp to-day,
Than when let loose from Brussels' hill
  He rushed upon the shrinking prey.
Their country's call, whate'er the task,
  Ne'er strikes unheard on Britons' ears:
They go to life or death, nor ask
  What toils or dangers may be theirs;
Whether on Alma's battled rock
  To buy with blood the victor's wreath,
Or startled worlds with wonder shock
  In Balaclava's vale of death;
Or Nature's secrets from her wrest,
  Where Nile once hid beneath his sand,
Or where in ice-bound armour drest
  She frowns upon the adventurous band.
Then, India, join thy heart and voice,
  Wreath him a crown of Eastern flowers,
Bid all thy swarthy sons rejoice,
  And let thy triumph equal ours!

And, Britons, bear ye not to hear
  His glory dimmed, his laurels torn!
What prince or monarch, far or near,
  Could bear the toils that he has borne?
Then welcome, Britain's princely heir,
  The fairest branch of England's vine.
No venal burst of praise we bear,
  No British heart but beats with thine.
From tower and cottage, high and low
  In loyal love united come,
And with triumphant rapture show
  How England bids thee welcome home

JUNE, 1876.

Verses written on various occasions during a Trip Round the World.

~~~~~~~~~~~~~~

·ONE MORE RIVER.

Sung by the Zealandia Minstrels, June 6th, 1883.   Written for the occasion by Ned Nettap.

JOHN ELDER built a ship one day,
　　　　　There's one more river to cross,
And called it the *Zealandia*,
　　　　　There's one more river to cross.

CHORUS—
One more river, and that's the river of Jordan,
One more river—there's one more river to cross·

The officers came in one by one,
　　　　　There's one, etc.
With Captain Webber so full of fun,
　　　　　There's one, etc.
　　　CHORUS—One more river, etc.

The officers came in two by two,
　　　　　There's one, etc.
Tyler the Chief, in a coat of blue,
　　　　　There's one, etc.
　　　CHORUS—One more river, etc.

The officers came in three by three,
> There's one, etc.

With Morris—a handsome man is he,
> There's one, etc.

> CHORUS—One more river, etc.

The officers came in four by four,
> There's one, etc.

With Williams, a careful navigator,
> There's one, etc.

> CHORUS—One more river, etc.

The officers came in five by five,
> There's one, etc.

With smart little Robb, who's all alive,
> There's one, etc.

> CHORUS—One more river, etc.

The officers came in six by six,
> There's one, etc.

The Purser, whom I've seen up to his tricks,
> There's one, etc.

> CHORUS—One more river, etc.

The officers came in seven by seven,
> There's one, etc.

The Doctor who helps us off to heaven,
> There's one, etc.

> CHORUS—One more river, etc.

The passengers came in eight by eight
> There's one, etc.

The girl who at breakfast's always late,
> There's one, etc.

> CHORUS—One more river, etc.

The passengers came in nine by nine,
>> There's one, etc.
An elegant, eloquent Argentine,
>> There's one, etc.
>> CHORUS—One more river, etc.

The passengers came in ten by ten,
>> There's one, etc.
That scurrilous scribbler, Pattenden,
>> There's one, etc.
>> CHORUS—One more river, etc.

The passengers came in quite a number,
>> There's one, etc.
Old Nathan who loves in his chair to slumber,
>> There's one, etc.
>> CHORUS—One more river, etc.

The passengers still came trooping in,
>> There's one, etc.
The ladies' darling, Benjamin,
>> There's one, etc.
>> CHORUS—One more river, etc.

The passengers came in a mighty throng,
>> There's one, etc.
The German whose coat is a mile too long,
>> There's one, etc.
>> CHORUS—One more river, etc.

The passengers came in all that day,
>> There's one, etc.
The pair that frequent the companion-way,
>> There's one, etc.
>> CHORUS—One more river, etc.

The passengers came in a motley crew,
　　　There's one, etc.
A lovely girl from Honolu*lu*,
　　　There's one, etc.
CHORUS—One more river, etc.

There came the veteran, gay and skittish,
　　　There's one, etc.
Maccabe, the foe of tyranny British,
　　　There's one, etc.
CHORUS—One more river, etc.

The man who repeats a nursery rhyme,
　　　There's one, etc.
And knows how to give you enough at a time,
　　　There's one, etc.
CHORUS—One more river, etc.

The *glowing* Major, a gay young *spark*,
　　　There's one, etc.
Who wickedly doesn't believe in the *arc*,
　　　There's one, etc.
CHORUS—One more river, etc.

At last there came a handsome group,
　　　There's one, etc.
The great Zealandia Minstrel Troupe,
　　　There's one, etc.
CHORUS—One more river, etc.

JUNE, 1883.

BIRTHS.

A T Woodburn, Bucks, England, on March 25th
(Easter Day), the wife of Edwin Thomas, of the
Harmonious Table, of twins—boy and girl. [By
Telegraph.]

>   Poor Thomas even in this life
>   Is punished for his sins:
>   By way of Easter eggs, his wife
>   Presented him with twins!

June, 1883.

A TRIP ON THE "ZEALANDIA."

By an "Alphabetical, Every-day Young Man."

A   IS the Agent so civil and spruce;
    B is the Berth he reserved for my use;
C is our Captain, the jolliest of boys;
D is the big D he never employs;
E's a young Englishman, fussy and mannish;
F is our Friend who harangues us in Spanish;
G is the German who has on his best coat;
H is the Hebrew who won't wear a waistcoat;
I is the Ice—I'm so glad they have taken it;
J is the Jump that the passengers make on it;
K is the King of the fathomless ocean;

L is the Line where he makes a commotion;
M is the Mariner always athirst;
N is the Novice who's shaved and immersed;
O is the Ordeal he has to go through;
P is the Pleasure it gives to the crew;
Q is the Qualm that I hardly need name;
R is the Roll that produces the same;
S is the Steward we foolishly trust in;
T is the Terms we express our disgust in;
U's the United States' thrice welcome shore;
V is the Vow that we'll voyage no more;
W's the Way that the said vow we break;
X the 'Xcuse we invariably make;
Y is the Yankees, we'll shortly be greeting;
Z's the *Zealandia*, record time beating.

NED NETTAP.

JUNE, 1883.

~~~~~~~~~~~~~~~~

NONSENSE VERSES.

A YOUNG man on board the *Zealandia*,
  When his hind legs grew bandier and
  bandier,
 Said: "For giving more purchase
 Whenever she lurches,
They're certainly very much handier."

A lady on board the *Australia*
Tried to grow in her cabin a dahlia
 But the Steward, in sport,
 Threw it out of the port,
And so the thing turned out a failure.

A passenger on the *New York*
Was uncommonly partial to pork,
    His knife was of use
    For collecting the juice,
And he never ate peas with a fork.

A man on the *City of Sydney*
Was fond of a nice devilled kidney.
    Now, seeing each sheep
    But a couple can keep,
He soon cleaned out the *City of Sydney*.

June, 1883.

AN ACROSTIC.

Captain Webber.

CAREFUL commander, genial man, the weary voyage
    througH,
All hail! thou gallant captain of a brave and gallant
    creW.
Patient in hardship and in toil, in friendship staunch
    and truE,
To thee the Poor box owes, I ween, full many a
    handsome suB,
And in thy bathroom oft I've had a most delicious
    tuB.
In games and sports athletic thou art ever to the
    forE,
Nor strange is thy " fantastic toe " upon the dancing
    flooR.

June, 1883.

THE GALLANT SKIPPER.

Air—"Golden Slippers."

Written for the Complimentary Dinner to Captain Webber and Officers of the "Zealandia," by Ned Netlap.

I.

OH, our gallant Skipper he has brought us through
From the land of the rabbit and the kangaroo,
Though the seas they roared and the winds they blew,
    On board of the good *Zealandia.*
Now he's landed us upon the "golden shore,"
And too soon we'll see his merry face no more,
But we'll sing again as we have sung before
    To the Skipper of the good *Zealandia.*

CHORUS.
Oh, the gallant Skipper! Oh, the gallant Skipper!
    Henry Webber, a health to thee, a bumper toast
    we'll fill.
Oh, the gallant Skipper! Oh, the gallant Skipper!
    Henry Webber, a health to thee we'll drink with
    right good will.

II.

Oh, our gallant Skipper he is fond of chaff,
And we love to listen to his merry laugh,
So let every man of us a bumper quaff
    To the Skipper of the good *Zealandia.*

From the time we sailed from Auckland's port
He was always foremost in every sport,
And we wish there were many of the same old sort
    As the Skipper of the good *Zealandia*.

                       CHORUS.

III.

Then we'll toast him, boys, with a hearty cheer,
For he knows no favor as he knows no fear;
And long may he prosper in his bright career
    As the Skipper of the good *Zealandia*.
So with heart and soul and with voices free,
Try to crack your lungs along with me,
And shout the chorus with three times three
    For the Skipper of the good *Zealandia*.

                       CHORUS.

JUNE, 1883.

YOKOHAMA AMATEUR REGATTA,

OCTOBER 2, 1882.

———

Four-oared Race between representatives of the Tea, Silk, and Banking Interests.

———

BRIGHT was the day and keen the strife that
    marked the great Regatta,
My muse forgets the winners' names—nor does it
    greatly matter;

For mine it is to sing the race, when forth the rival
  Three
Stepped boldly, Yokohama's pride—the Silk, the Bank,
  the Tea.
Black was the Silkmen's trusty boat that foremost
  braved the seas,
While at her prow a Hank of Silk courted the ev'ning
  breeze.
Next in the Bankers' azure bows floated a flash Bank-
  note—
Or, rather, *would* have floated, but no note was there to
  float.
Last in the Teamen's snow-white prow was set the
  fragrant plant,
Dear to the pig-tailed Chinamen, dear to the maiden
  aunt.

First to the starting-point there came the boat of sable
  hue,
And up and spake the Silkman Chief unto his gallant
  crew :
"Silkmen of Yokohama, best that ever *sat in*
  boat,
To-day let men your sterling worth, your priceless
  value *quote ;*
And, steersman, if to victory you'd bear the flowing
  hank,
Be sure to *thread* your way with skill and do not *foul*
  the Bank,
Forget the office desk, and careful *writer* though
  you be,
Remember when you're *right in* 'front,' you must not
  cross *the Tea.*"

Next to the starting-post there came the boat of azure
tint,

And up and spake the Banker Chief, with many a
useful hint:

"Steersman! mark well the *rising wind*, the *current
note*," said he;

"*Advance* with caution, and make sure of *good
security*.

Preserve your *balance*, and maintain your *credit* safe
and sound,

That still your name may *honoured* be wherever banks
are found;

And, Bankers bold, remember this, and struggle till
you drop,

Whate'er the *checks* that we receive, the Bank must
never *stop*."

Then up and spake, with counsel brief, the Captain of
the Teamen:

"Comrades, to-day you change your name—be bold
and lusty *Seamen*,

Fill well your *chests*, and heed it not if men should call
you *green*,

For when the water boils around, your *strength* will
soon be seen."

Now at the post they sternly wait the signal for the
fray;

Then forth with straining oars they shoot—the
Teamen lead the way.

But soon on equal terms creeps up the Bankers' boat
of blue,

While Silk is struggling in the rear, a length behind
the two;

Now neck and neck they race amid the shouts of all
    the throng,
" Eyes in the boat ! "   " You're gaining, Tea ! "   " Well
    rowed, Bank !   Keep it long ! "

And now the winning post is near, still neck and neck
    they speed,
But slowly inch by inch the Tea is *drawing* out a lead
Till, rowing gamely to the end, by dint of " stay " and
    strength,
The Teamen catch the Judge's eye—a quarter of a
    length.
And now the drooping hank of silk no longer proudly
    floats,
And, all too confident before, the Bankers *change their*
    notes.
While taunting speaks the Teaman chief : " Whene'er
    you race with me,
The prize can ne'er be yours, because the *Pot* is for the
    Tea."

Japan Gazette, OCTOBER 4, 1882.

ON AN AMATEUR PERFORMANCE OF

" A SCRAP OF PAPER,"

Yokohama, Sept. 30, 1882.

'TIS said that certain dames of Yokohama,
  Who love not dress, but quite adore the drama,
To save expense, perhaps, or spite the draper,
Appeared in public in " A Scrap of Paper " !

Hiogo News, NOVEMBER 2, 1882.

THE NEW YORK ELEVATED RAILWAY.

THE "L."

THERE once was a man who in life began
   In a somewhat humble way;
But in ways that are dark he was amply schooled,
And soon over railway lines he ruled,
And he wasn't a man who was easily fooled,
And his patronymic, I ween, was Gould,
   While his previous name was Jay.

Now this artful man, he devised a plan,
   And the same to a friend revealed;
"A railway," said he, "I propose to lay,
Through New York City—d'ye tumble, eh?
I think it's a pretty good thing," said Jay
   To Cyrus W. Field.

"But how can we buy the ground?" said Cy.;
   The money how can we raise?
It's easy enough to lay our hand
On tracts and tracts of the Western land,
But New York City would hardly stand
   Such very irregular ways."

"Why, no," said Jay; "but I've found a way—
   Elevated our road shall be;
Right through the streets, but ever so high,
So never a foot of the ground we'll buy."
"Oh, that's a different thing," said Cy.,
As he playfully winked his dexter eye;
   "You're a pretty smart man, J. G.,"

So they went to the Cor-poration for
   Authority signed and sealed ;
And the City allowed them right away
Their road through the principal streets to lay—
For capitalists must have their way—
And never a cent. did it make them pay
" I told you how it would be," said Jay,
   To Cyrus W. Field.

They didn't devise the enterprise
   For personal gain or profit ;
For millionaires and railroad kings
So frequently do unselfish things
For the pleasure a noble action brings,
    Though you wouldn't suspect them of it.

So now o'erhead, like a phantom dread,
   It broods over New York City ;
And some people call it quite immense,
Some talk of its great convenience—
But nobody yet possessed of sense
   Has ventured to call it pretty.

For over the street, some thirty feet,
   It spreads its gruesome pall ;
And its hideous outlines darkly loom
And make the Avenue like a tomb,
Imparting a general sense of gloom
   Wherever its shadows fall.

And its pillars are right in the driver's light
   As he nimbly speeds along ;
And hence collisions and " jams " ensue,

And struggles to force a passage through,
And personalities, not a few,
   From the hackman's lavish tongue.

No words can tell how I loathe the " L,"
   As if it were aspirated;
For the *employés*, as a rule, are rude,
And the use of tobacco is quite tabooed
(Unless it is put in the mouth and chewed)
   On board of the Elevated.

And every time you must pay a dime—
   They'd charge you more if they could;
The conductors hurry the folks about;
They hustle you in and shove you out;
And as to the station—if you've a doubt—
You can't distinguish the names they shout,
   And they don't intend you should.

"And how does it pay?" I asked of Jay;
   " And does it a profit yield?"
"Well, I should snigger!" the Gould replied,
By which remark (I am notified)
A strong affirmative is implied—
And he laughed as he nudged the adjacent side
   Of Cyrus W. Field.

The Judge, NEW YORK, DECEMBER 1, 1883.

THE ELEVATED RAILWAY.

Dirge of a Sixth Avenue Householder.

RUMBLE, rumble, railway car !
　Strangers wonder what you are,
Up above the street so high,
Shutting out the light and sky.

Rumble, rumble, railway car !
Yet you would be better far
Underneath the ground so low ;
There you'd not annoy me so.

Elevated railway car,
What a horrid bore you are !
You allow the curious eye
In my third-floor rooms to pry.

Elevated railway car,
What I most distinctly bar
Is the nightly noise you make,
Keeping me and mine awake.

You provoke, O railway car,
Phrases most irregular
In the early watches, a.m.—
Other times I never say 'em.

Then the pillars under you
Wholly spoil the Avenue ;
Block the way, obstruct the traffic,
Sour the temper most seraphic.

They are also fraught with danger
To the unsuspecting stranger;
When to jump he takes a notion
From a horse-car while in motion.

Rumble, rumble, railway car !
Some day, with a nasty jar,
Down into the street you'll tumble—
Then you will no longer rumble.

NEW YORK, NOVEMBER 20, 1883.

SHERMAN AND SHERIDAN.

General Philip Sheridan succeeded General Sherman as General-in-Chief of the United States Armies, Nov., 1883.

" SAY, General, what do you contemplate ?
    And what is the change to be ? "
I ventured to say to Phil one day ;
    And thus he replied to me :
" Why, Sherman's methods are out of date,
    His notions are old, you see ;
So the Army's about to turn 'em (M) out,
    And take up a new *idee* (ID)."

NEW YORK, NOVEMBER 1, 1883.

NIGHT THOUGHTS.

———

A Sapphic Ode.

———

WHEN more favoured mortals are wrapped in
　　　slumber,
Dreamily forgetful of care and cumber,
Round my pillow hover in countless number,
　　　　　Beastly mosquitos.

Chiefly when I'm feeling a trifle seedy
Do I hear thy voice piping shrill and reedy;
If I could, how fain would I slaughter thee, de-
　　　　　tested mosquito!

" Hither, sweet-voiced minstrel, awhile, I pray thee,
In mine outstretched hand for a moment lay thee;
Deem not I would foully deceive and slay thee,
　　　　　Foolish mosquito!

" Come ye all, dear friends, on my right cheek cast your
Hungry eyes—you'll find it a juicy pasture;
Leave that dry old blanket, it's surely nastier,
　　　　　Gentle mosquitos.

" Wherefore linger ?　Think ye, forsooth, I am a
Gay deceiver telling an awful crammer ?
Fear ye, lest this hand like a Nasmyth hammer
　　　　　Crush ye, mosquitos ? "

" Nay," they sing, "but small are our wants, and
  therefore
Such delights just now, Sir, we do not care for;
Juicy cheeks are far too *recherché* fare for
                    Humble mosquitos.

"And besides, it's well to be somewhat wary;
Therefore, though this blanket is dry and hairy,
Yet we deem it wholesome and salutary
                    Food for mosquitos.

"But we'll take a snack on your outstretched toes, if
You do not object to our bite corrosive;
As for closer neighbourhood—not for Joseph!"
                    Say the mosquitos.

Flocking to the feast with their buzzing tuneful,
Of my vital fluid the brutes are soon full,
And I'm losing blood by the table-spoonful,
                    Drawn by mosquitos.

On my inaccessible parts they light, and
Fill their greedy carcases, nothing frightened
By the distant threat of my vengeful right hand,
                    Wily mosquito.

On my face some venture when I am dozing,
And my hand is cautiously on them closing,
Till with one swift motion I smash—my nose, in-
                    stead of mosquitos.

So my rest by sundry remarks is broken,
Some discreetly murmured, and some outspoken;
And the mildest form that they take is—" Oh, con-
                    found the mosquitos!"

He shall rank as one of the world's great teachers,
Whoso shall checkmate the obnoxious creatures,
And secure our nasal and other features
> From the mosquitos.

All in vain you fix up a stuffy curtain;
There are always some little holes, for certain,
Through the which to squeeze doesn't even hurt an
> Airy mosquito.

Vain the far-famed powder of Mr. Keating,
Which, the fleas all say, wants a lot of beating;
Even it must take a distinct back-seat in
> View of mosquitos.

Wherefore were mosquitos at first created,
Only by mankind to be scorned and hated,
And, as far as may be, annihilated?
> Hapless mosquitos!

They are but productive of rage and passion
And profanity, which is out of fashion,
For a man *will* swear when he fails to smash an
> Artful mosquito.

If that with the rattlesnake, wasp, and hornet,
This ignoble insect had ne'er been born, it
Seems to me that no one would deeply mourn it,
> Friendless mosquito.

Let it roam the realms of the non-essential,
Or enjoy the sweetness of life potential;
So the future, happier stock of men shall
> Love the mosquito.

IN THE ROCKY MOUNTAINS, AUGUST 12, 1883.

Published Verses on Various Subjects.

~~~~~~~~~~~~~~~~~

SKETCHES AT THE "INVENTORIES."

WHAT a terrible crowd at South Kensington
    Station!
Why, what in the world can have come to the nation?
What pushing and squeezing! What hurry and bustle!
How fiercely they struggle! How madly they hustle!
Such rushing and crushing, such knocking and banging;
Such dashing and clashing, such shouting and slanging,
As some clumsy wretch blindly onward is borne,
And plants a huge foot on his neighbour's pet corn.
What a numberless throng! it would almost appear
As if all the people in London were here;
Such crowds have assembled from east and from west—
One is tempted to ask oneself, "Where are the rest?"—
They gather from every point of the compass,
And raise all together a terrible "rumpus."
A stream of humanity onward they go,
For this is the great Opening Day of the Show.

And I with the others am fighting my way,
And pushing ahead in the thick of the fray,
But thanking my stars, as I struggle along,
That Nature has fashioned me sturdy and strong.
For I have a very particular mission
On the Opening Day of the great Exhibition;

No idle spectator to see the Inventions,
I go with much higher and greater intentions.
To tell you the truth, I am here with a view
Of describing the whole thing, dear reader, to you!

I refrain from comparing the relative claims
Of the three Exhibitions with curious names;
They christened the "Fisheries" that which came
    first,
And no one would venture to call it the worst.
In the year '83 it was clearly the best,
For Time had not yet given birth to the rest.
Then, second in order, the "Healtheries" came,
With a borrowed, but very felicitous name.
And though in the order of time it was second,
Yet second to none it was properly reckoned.
And now by one more is the number increased,
And we've come to the third, which is last, but not
    least.
Let us hope, of the three Exhibitions, the latest
Will be known—till next year—as the best and the
    greatest;
The thought and experience and labour of centuries
All gathered together and called the "Inventories!"
Thus Fate by a strange and most happy decree
Has allotted one common surname to the three;
So a right noble family they shall be styled,
And as each coming year brings another new child,
We shall try by the aid of ingenious speech
An appropriate name to discover for each;
And no matter how many there be, they shall claim
A right to the use of the family name.
You come to the entrance, and there you must wait,
And struggle to keep in the line for the gate.

At last when you're lucky enough to get through,
A mass of bright flow'rs and sweet plants meet your
     view;
And there in the midst an equestrian statue,
That seems to look fiercely and haughtily at you.
We'll leave the proud horseman to stare at the rest,
While we hurriedly pass through the halls to the
     west.
We come to the street of Old London at last,
As it was, more than two hundred years in the past,
Before the Great Fire swept Old London away,
To make room for the London we look on to-day.
How strange in the quaint little street, as you stand,
That seemed to our forefathers spacious and grand!
So crooked and jutting, so narrow and small—
However could people have got on at all?
Yes, there are the shops and the houses of wood—
They stand just as once in Old London they stood.
And there are the 'prentices, just as of yore,
In the very same dresses they formerly wore.
But what are they working with? Are those the tools
That were used in the days before Steam and Board
     Schools?
And what are they saying? Is that the quaint tongue
That was spoken in London when Milton was young?
Oh, if from his grave we could stealthily raise
Some craftsman or 'prentice of those ancient days,
And, still in his sleep, bring him carefully down
To the great Exhibition in Kensington Town,
Set him right in the midst of "Ye Olde London
     Streete,"
And suddenly wake him—it *would* be a treat!
How the good man in stupid amazement would stare,
And wonder if 'twas but a horrid nightmare!

How he'd gaze at the busy, bewildering scene,
At the 'prentices working the latest machine !
How he'd prick up his ears at their Cockneyfied twang
In the newest and choicest edition of slang !
And how he would stare, if he lingered till night,
At the street all ablaze with the Edison light !

But noon is approaching, and so we must go ;
For the Prince will be coming to open the Show.
Yes, there in the entrance-hall distantly loom
The officials rejoicing in plenty of room ;
The Executive Council we envy so greatly,
The Foreign Commissioners haughty and stately.
But we are poor nobodies out in the cold,
And meekly and humbly must do as we're told
By a few big policemen so fussy and proud
Of their short-lived authority over the crowd.
They jam us together—a regular squeeze—
And then they expect us to " pass along, please " !

But, see! here's the Prince with his good-humoured
    face—
The type of our true British manhood and grace ;
And not much resembling his statue up there,
Which gazes at *him* with the same haughty stare.
And there's the Princess, with the sweet sunny smile,
That won many a heart in the Emerald Isle !
Sir Frederick Bramwell now reads the address,
Which every one thinks a decided success.
And the Prince makes a speech in his happiest way,
And declares the Show open to all men to-day.

But if I don't hurry I'll never be done.
For I haven't yet told you a tenth of the fun ;

The "Milkeries," "Hatteries," "Tailories," "Boot-
    eries,"
The "Glasseries," "Potteries," "Cutleries," "Shoot-
    eries,"
The "Indiarubberies," "Printeries "—all
The departments, in short, of this wonderful Hall.
See, there is the Welsh girl, whose work never fails,
In the curious dress that finds favour in Wales;
And her hat! If a candle you want to extinguish,
You couldn't, I'm sure, for a handier thing wish!
And there are the guns, both for land and for
    water,
That men have invented to simplify slaughter;
The patent machine-guns of these latter days,
That kill you in dozens of different ways.
Such an ugly collection! You think the whole place
In a minute or so will be blown into space.

But I fear that you'll never have patience to read
If I scribble much longer; so now we'll proceed
To the dining-room, where you're substantially fed
At the moderate figure of sixpence a-head.
Then we pay to the Aylesbury Dairy a visit,
And drink some fresh milk, and on asking, "What
    is it?"
We're puzzled to find that there's nothing to pay,
For they tell you, "We're making no charge, sir,
    to day."
And then, before leaving, we'll just take our stand
In the gardens, and listen awhile to the band.
What beautiful music! Hallo! What is that?
Why, it's raining, and I've got a brand-new top-hat.
We must rush under cover, and yield to the weather,
For music and rain don't go nicely together.

And now, gentle reader, I think it is time
To shut up the ink-pot and finish my rhyme.
" I've had quite enough of this doggerel," you cry,
And to tell you the plain honest truth, so have I ;
So I'll make no apology now, for I know
You don't want to hear any more of the Show ;
And I'm certain you'll be rather pleased than irate,
    if I've
Done with the great Exhibition of '85 !

The Family Circle, MAY, 1885.

THE COLONIES.

THE fourth Exhibition is one that we know   ·
        As the " Colonies "—so men have christened the
    show.
    And for weal or for woe,
    By that name it must go.
I'm aware *Mr. Punch* wants it called the " Colindcrics,"
But one thing, that e'en *Mr. Punch* cannot hinder, is
People just calling the show what they please,
The name that's pronounced with the greatest of ease.

We enter the grounds by the eastern door—
A place where we've frequently been before—
    Then we turn to the right,
    And start with affright
At the great hunting trophy revealed to sight.
    Let us pause ere we pass,
    And look through the glass,

Where the tigers crouch in the jungle-grass;
Where the leopard, the bear, and the panther roam,
And appear on the whole to be quite at home;
    And see over yonder
    A huge anaconda,
That seems on its next little meal to ponder,
And other big snakes in the forks of the trees,
    Looking quite at their ease
    And ready to seize
The passing stranger and calmly squeeze
The life from his body by slow degrees.
    And here in the front
    Is a tiger-hunt,
To the "Colonies" specially sent from afar
By His Highness the Rajah of Kooch Behar.
    Who wouldn't be willing
    To put down a shilling
To witness a tiger-hunt—minus the killing?
    The elephant's there
    With his trunk in the air,
    And there's really no knowing
    How loud he is blowing
His trumpet in rage, or, it may be, despair.
Of course he's entitled to feel in a funk
When the teeth of a tiger are tight in his trunk;
    It must really be horrid
    To feel in your forehead
    Two powerful jaws
    And a handful of claws;
If he kicks up a row, then, it's not without cause.
It's certainly lucky for him that his hide
Has nothing but stuffing and sawdust inside;
So it doesn't quite hurt him so much as it would
If the stuffing were flesh, and the sawdust were blood.

Let us hope in the end that the poor beast tosses
  His enemy dread
  Right over his head
With a mighty sweep of his huge proboscis.

  To the Indian section,
  If you've no objection,
We'll pass and examine the fine collection;
  Where the products of art
  From every part
Are neatly arranged to be easily seen,
Each district behind its appropriate screen.
Bombay and Baroda, Cashmere and Bengal,
Lucknow and Benares, Assam and Nepaul,
Karauli, Jeypore, Madras and Mysore,
Coorg, Hyderabad, and a great many more.
There are muslins and silks from Orissa and Dacca,
While Hyderabad sends us " bidri " and lacquer;
  There's marble inlaid,
  That at Agra is made,
  And quite on a par is
  The brass from Benares;
  There are shawls from Cashmere
  Most awfully dear,
And beetle-wing muslins that look very queer;
There are bangles and earrings and rings for the
    nose,
And rings for the fingers, and rings for the toes;
There are carvings in ivory, metal, and wood—
But to try and enumerate all is no good.
  Suffice it to say
  That the wondrous display,
Examined in merely a cursory way,
Will take you at least the best part of a day.

We pass through the Indian Palace, a place
Where there's little of furniture, plenty of space.
In quaint little shops round the spacious courtyard,
The natives are working—apparently hard;
There are goldsmiths and silversmiths, carvers,
      engravers,
And dyers, productive of horrible savours,
And four little boys weaving carpets, who drone
A queer sort of song in a queer sort of tone:
It may be to help them to lay the threads straight, or
Perhaps just to humour the British spectator.
We go through the archway presented by Scindiah,
And so with reluctance bid farewell to India.

Then on through Old London, deserted and bare;
For the curious workshops no longer are there;
   And so to the Cape,
   Where we stand agape
To see how a diamond's knocked into shape.
   And here is the mine
   Of the Bultfontein,
An elegant model of clever design,
With a railway of wire down a steepish incline.
   It can hardly be jolly
   To sit in a trolly
And whisk through the air on a sleeperless line!
At least it's a trip I should firmly decline.
   Here they wash the "blue earth"
   To see what it's worth,
And of diamonds somehow there's never a dearth,
Which suggests an old saw to the sceptical mind:
" For him who has hidden, it's easy to find."
   Far be it from me
   To assert that you see

More jewels than Nature intended to be ;
  But still there are found
  To be lying around
Such a number of stones in that dirty " blue ground,"
That it really might make one suspect for a minute
That they first of all bury the diamonds in it,
  That the " blue ground," in fact,
  Has been carefully " packed,"
Or " salted," I should say, to be more exact.
  At any rate when you in-
  Quire if it's genuine,
Every one tells you it's quite *bonâ fide*,
And so says the threepenny guide-book, *quod vide*.
  Be that as it may,
  I have only to say,
  You may see the blue clay—
Nothing extra to pay—
And the men in a thoroughly business-like way
Just churning out diamonds every day.
  Hard by is the place,
  In a great glass case,
Where they cut and polish the stones apace,
  On a circular plate,
  Which revolves at a rate
That I really am almost afraid to state :
I believe I'm correct when I say that it's reckoned
To make twenty-four revolutions a second.
  Of natives too
  You may see a few,
Great muscular creatures of dusky hue.
Just look at that fellow as dark as pitch,
A Zulu or Kaffir—I don't know which—
Arrayed in a blanket, a curious whim,
And an old straw hat with a wonderful brim—

It must have been specially made for him—
And a wholly inadequate crown a-top,
That you never yet saw in an English shop;
  You can hardly call
  It a crown at all,
For the size of his head's so absurdly small.

We pass by New Zealand, alas! for the hour is
Too late for inspecting the land of the Maoris;
  But we peep at a few
  Of the portraits on view
Of chiefs with their faces of curious hue;
For the higher their station, the more they tattoo—
Perhaps as a sign that their blood is so blue.

As we enter Australia, lo and behold!
  An archway of gold,
  Imposing and bold,
Though if you imagine it's real. you're sold.
  Gold, gold,
  Riches untold,
And all from a country just fifty years old:
  Nuggets and quartz,
  Gold of all sorts,
Some of it just as it leaves the retorts.
  Gold, gold,
  Nothing but gold,
All that the stores of Dame Nature enfold
Before us in lavish profusion is rolled.
And there is a real native hut, that was bought
(For a very diminutive sum it is thought)
From a genuine bushman, and hither was brought;
And with it are figures so skilfully wrought,
  A man and his wife,
  So exactly like life,

That if you don't look at them close you'll be caught.
  The wife has a baby
    Abaft of her shoulder,
  A year old it may be,
    Or possibly older;
The man holds a boomerang ready to throw,
  And because of the heat
  His attire's incomplete
And rather adapted for comfort than show.

  But our time is run out:
  We must turn right about;
Though we haven't seen all, there is no sort of doubt
That the sights we have missed we must e'en go without.
But if this of South Kensington shows is the last,
Although I've no wish for a moment to cast
  A slur on the rest,
  Yet it must be confessed,
Of the four Exhibitions the last is the best.

   The Family Circle, JULY, 1886.

~~~~~~~~~~~~~~~~~~

THE EGG MACHINE.

[Published with Twenty-one Illustrations.]

THERE once was a man, as I've heard it said,
  In a humble walk of life,
Who worked, as he might, for his daily bread
  Unencumbered by child or wife.
His nature was crafty, his heart was hard,
And he kept a few fowls in a small back-yard.

But his hens wouldn't lay, and his lot was sad,
　For with poverty he was stricken;
So as food was scarce and the times were bad,
　He was forced to subsist on chicken.
They wouldn't supply him with eggs to eat,
　So he fed upon *them*—which indeed was *meet*.

Till only one mate for the lordly male,
　One only was left alive;
And she strutted about with her haughty tail
　At an angle of ninety-five.
For she was no chicken of low degree,
A thorough-bred Hamburgh hen was she.

The very perfection she stood confessed
　Of gallinaceous beauty;
And strange to relate it—this hen possessed
　A remarkable sense of duty.
She felt she was morally bound to lay
An egg for her master every day.

Yet he thought that she didn't lay eggs enough:
　He coveted more, this man.
It really would seem to be rather rough
　On a hen who does all she can.
But his nature was crafty, his heart was hard;
And he mused as he walked in his small back-yard.

Till at length this ingenious-minded man,
　In the solitude of his hovel,
Evolved from his masterly brain a plan
　Which at least was extremely novel.
" I'll have eggs for my breakfast, I trow," said he,
" And eggs for my dinner, and eggs for tea."

So he went and got him an old tea-chest
  For the guileless hen to lay in ;
And made her a nice little cosy nest
  By putting a wisp of hay in ;
And underneath in the treacherous floor
He fixed a diminutive spring trap-door !

And the good hen went to her nest so smart
  To deposit her daily dole ;
And she rose from her task with a thankful heart
  And an unsuspecting soul.
She carefully lifted each dainty leg
So as not to disturb the new-laid egg.

Then she raised on high a triumphant shriek,
  The note of maternal pride—
But suddenly on her parted beak
  The exulting pæan died.
For glancing back she became aware
Of the startling fact that the nest was bare.

She peered into every nook and hole
  In terrible perturbation ;
Till she thought she had been the dupe (poor soul!)
  Of a strange hallucination.
" Well, it only shows," she remarked, relieved,
" How easily people may be deceived."

So she sate her down, to her duty true,
  And another she laid with care,
And eagerly turned the result to view,
  But alas! no egg was there!
" Well, I never ! " exclaimed the bewildered hen,
" I could almost have *sworn* that I laid one then."

" Am I awake ? "—and she pecked her leg—
    " Or is it a horrid dream ?
" 'Tis a night-mare's nest, for it holds no egg;
    " And things are not what they seem."
So musing vaguely she laid a third;
For she was a conscientious bird.

But when a quick backward glance revealed
    The tenantless nest to sight,
Her brain grew dizzy, her senses reeled,
    Her feathers stood bolt upright.
A reckless frenzy inflamed her breast,
And she laid and laid like a hen possessed.

And her crafty owner was soon content :
    His pitiless greed was sated;
So he fastened the little trap-door, and went
    Away to his house elated.
" I've eggs for my breakfast enough," said he,
" And eggs for my dinner, and eggs for tea."

But the good hen turned with a weary glance,
    And there was an egg at last !
And she woke, as it were, from a painful trance,
    And a cloud from her vision passed.
" Why, I've been dreaming, I do declare,
The whole of the time I've been sitting there ! "

Then she went to her mate, and she told her tale
    In a voice with emotion weak;
But just like an unsympathetic male
    He laughed in her very beak.
He chuckled and crowed, and remarked, " I fear
" You're going clean off your head, my dear."

Now this crafty man had his wits all there;
　His talents were only latent;
So he washed his face, and he brushed his hair,
　And went and took out a patent.
Then he bought a frock-coat and a white top hat
And some fancy pants and a silk cravat.

He formed a company there and then,
　And he was the chairman of it;
And all the directors were well-known men,
　And they made an enormous profit.
They traded on a gigantic scale,
And paid their dividends on the nail.

And ev'ry one blessed the inventor's name—
　"What a wonderful man he is!"—
For eggs in a very short time became
　As plenty as blackberries.
And the people feasted and made good cheer—
But the hens had a pretty bad time, I fear.

And if you would know how the thing is done
　You must go to the Exhibition,
That's now being holden in Kensington;
　For there, in a good position,
At the great "Inventories" may be seen
The PATENT PERENNIAL EGG MACHINE!

OCTOBER, 1884.

A DEAD SECRET.

AS wise a man as ever stepped,
   Laid down this golden rule of life:
That if you want a secret kept,
   You musn't tell it to your wife.

For I'm informed that women who
   Have heard a secret seem to languish
For somebody to tell it to;
   And, till it's told, they suffer anguish.

I speak from hearsay, I may state,
   It isn't in my line, for I
Was born and bred a celibate,
   And such I'm pretty sure to die.

But Providence, to make amends
   For lack of children and of wife,
Has blessed me with two faithful friends,
   To cheer my lonely path through life.

If what the poet says is true,
   Of all the gifts of heaven the best is
A friend who'll always stick to you—
   Play Pylades to your Orestes.

Who'll back your bills with faith serene;
   Nor hesitate to put his name on,
As Pythias, if bills had been
   Invented, would have done for Damon.

For such a friend in years long past
   I vainly hunted up down,
Until I came across, at last,
   The man I sought in William Brown.

The closest friends were Brown and I,
  But fearing lest our own society
Should bore us, I resolved to try
  A third companion for variety.

And now, I ween, in all the town
  If there's a soul my spirit owns
As dear to me as William Brown,
  That soul belongs to Thomas Jones.

Three jovial bachelors are we,
  And I believe, from here to Rio,
Search where you may, by land or sea,
  You'll hardly find a jollier trio.

What cosy dinners we have had!
  What glorious evenings passed together!
On such occasions, I may add,
  We rarely talk about the weather.

And in expansive moments I
  Have sometimes made a rash confession;
But each declared I might rely
  Upon his absolute discretion.

And if I doubted, they were pained:
  On secrecy themselves they prided,
And on that subject entertained
  A greater confidence than I did.

    *   *   *   *   *

One morning as I sat me down,
  And o'er *The Times* began to pore,
I saw the form of William Brown
  Serenely sauntering to my door.

" Good morning, Smith!" said he; " I've got
    Upon my hands an hour or two,
And thought I might as well as not
    Drop in and pass the time with you."

" I'm glad to see you, Brown," I cried.
    " Sit down; and now that you are here,
A something bids me to confide
    A secret in your private ear.

" A secret, Brown, that none suspects:
    I found it out the other day;
A thing that seriously affects
    The character of Mrs. A——.

" I kept it locked within my breast
    Until it fairly tortured me.
At last myself I thus addressed :
    ' You must confide in William B.'

" But, William, you must pledge your word,
    And swear it by your father's bones,
You'll ne'er disclose what you have heard,
    Not even unto Thomas Jones."

" My friend, you know me," answered Brown;
    " Discretion is my leading feature,
And I would rather hang or drown
    Than breathe it to a living creature.

" And as to Jones, 'twixt you and me,
    There's not a better fellow living;
But as regards his secrecy
    I've always had a slight misgiving."

"Enough!" said I; "my course is clear."
  And thereupon, without delay,
I pour into his startled ear
  The scandal touching Mrs. A——.

I noticed when my tale was done,
  That Brown grew restless more and more;
I saw him ever and anon
  Cast furtive glances at the door.

A silence, too, upon him fell;
  An anxious look obscured his brow.
At last he rose, remarking, " Well,
  I think I must be toddling now."

" Why, Brown, I really must object;
  You came to spend an hour or two."
" Ah, yes; but now I recollect
  I've got some pressing things to do."

My arguments were all in vain:
  Remonstrance only made him firmer.
He went, and I began again
  The latest telegrams from Burmah.

In half an hour or so, once more
  I heard the bell's distracting tones,
And Susan at my study door
  Appeared announcing, " Mr. Jones."

His breath was quick, his colour high,
  His speech abrupt, his manner flurried;
And to the least observant eye
  'Twas evident that Jones had hurried.

"So glad to find you in," he cried,
　"I've almost walked myself to death."
And to his forehead he applied
　His handkerchief, and gasped for breath.

"Be calm," I said. "Advancing years
　Take youthful strength and vigour from us:
You've walked too fast; your frame appears
　Exhausted—pray be seated, Thomas."

Then when his breathing grew more clear,
　Said he, "My flurry you'll excuse
When you have heard what's brought me here:
　I've come to tell you startling news.

"I know that you'll be sorely grieved,
　And it's a tale you'll hardly credit,
A thing I'd never have believed
　If anybody else had said it.

"But my informant's one who knows,
　I can't divulge his name of course;
But this I venture to depose—
　I have it from the highest source.

"He bound me down to secrecy;
　And most emphatically, too
(I can't think why), he cautioned me
　Against disclosing it to *you*.

"But really it can make no odds
　To tell it *you*, my oldest friend;
But you must swear, by all your gods,
　To keep the secret to the end.

" You mustn't tell a soul in town,
   And even Brown is not exempted :
I don't know why I mentioned Brown—
   I thought perhaps you might be tempted."

" Thomas, I am your friend," I said ;
   " And I am worthy of the title ;
I shall be silent as the dead :
   Proceed, then, with the dire recital."

Then o'er my listening ear he bent,
   And told in a mysterious way—
But not without embellishment—
   The scandal touching Mrs. A——.

The very tale I'd told to Brown,
   When he by all his father's bones
Had sworn that he would rather drown
   Than tell it even unto Jones !

As for the tale, I'll now admit,
   'Twas what the vulgar call a " sell,"
For I myself invented it
   As Brown was ringing at the bell.

The Christian World Magazine, JANUARY, 1887.

WHEN DO PEOPLE MARRY?

THE following figures, extracted by the *Economist* from the Registrar-General's last return, will be found of great interest:—

Marriage Ages of Bachelors in Different Occupations, 1884-5.

Miners ...	23.56	Commercial clerks ...	25.75
Textile hands	23.88	Shopkeepers, shopmen	26.17
Shoemakers and tailors	24.42	Farmers and sons ...	28.73
Artisans...	24.85	Profession and inde-	
Labourers ...	25.06	pendent class ...	30.72

A GIRL'S GRIEVANCE.

I HEAR the wedding bells that chime
   From chapel, church and minster;
But what are they to me, when I'm
   A miserable spinster?

My face, they say, is passing fair,
   My figure most majestic;
My tastes and habits always were
   Decidedly domestic.

And I have been engaged a year;
   Of money we have plenty;
But Harry is an engineer,
   And only four-and-twenty!

So we must wait—but not because
   We want the will to marry;
But certain economic laws
   Condemn us thus to tarry.

The reason why we wait, in short,
  Is one I've scarcely hinted ;
It's in the Forty-eighth Report
  The Registrar has printed.

Though written by a kindly man,
  The good Sir Brydges Henniker,
To me it's far more tragic than
  The tragedies of Seneca.

For there, upon a certain page,
  In largest pica leaded,
Statistics show the proper age
  At which good folks are wedded.

The strange connection you'll descry
  That great things have with small things ;
For marriages are govern'd by
  The *export trade*—of all things.

At twenty-three the miner is
  At liberty to marry ;
The hands employed in factories
  Till twenty-four must tarry ;

The tailor, too, and cobbler wait
  Till four-and-twenty summers;
This likewise is the time to mate
  For carpenters and plumbers.

At five-and-twenty clerks essay
  Connubial relations ;
The counter-jumper needs must stay
  Till twenty-six in patience.

The farmer two more years—poor thing!—
  A bachelor must linger;
At twenty-eight he buys the ring
  For his intended's finger.

But there's a still more luckless crew;
  For sad beyond expression
Is their unhappy fortune who
  Belong to a profession.

They must be thirty years before
  Their wedding bells may jingle;
And Harry's only twenty-four!
  Six years he'll still be single.

Oh, would he were a miner bold,
  However black and dirty!
For I shall be so very old
  Before he reaches thirty.

Why can't the export trade be changed?
  It's such an awful pity:
The thing could surely be arranged
  By people in the City.

O Registrar, most wise and great,
  It's hard on me and Harry,
For we shall have so long to wait
  Before our time to marry.

'Tis true, Sir Brydges Henniker,
  We're powerless as midges;
But *can't* you make it earlier,
  Sir Brydges, O Sir Brydges?

THE ANTI-LUCIFER MATCH.

MESSRS. SULFER and WHACKS of
Fenchurch Street,
Had a frontage of twenty or thirty feet,
  And an office well known to fame,
And a factory down by the London Docks,
Where they made their matches, and every box
  Had Sulfer and Whacks's name.

Messrs. Sulfer and Whacks paid income-tax
  On several thousands yearly;
But business was not what it once had been,
For competition was fierce and keen,
And the prospect anything but serene,
And Sulfer and Whacks long ago had seen
  That matters were looking queerly.

Now it happened one day when trade was flat,
As Sulfer and Whacks in their office sat
  Digesting their mid-day snacks,
That a clerk announced, " There's a man below,
Who's got an invention he wants to show
To the head of the firm, and declines to go."
  " Well, let him come in," said Whacks.

A wizened and weird little man appeared,
With a dirty face, and a fortnight's beard
  On a sharp protruding chin ;
And first having carefully shut the door,
His hat he deposited on the floor,
And produced from his pocket about a score
(There might be less, and there might be more)
  Of match-boxes all of tin.

He passed them across with a careless toss,
  To the partners twain, in batches,
Then drew himself up, and with lots of cheek,
In a voice that was very much like the creak
Of a rusty hinge, he began to speak,
As if he'd been silent for quite a week:
"I think you'll agree that this thing's unique
  In the way of a box for matches.

"P'r'aps, gentlemen, you remember when,
  With a flint and steel and tinder,
They used to beguile the tedious hours,
And waste their tissue and vital powers—
Their time was worth much less than ours—
While the fire descended in reckless showers
  With nothing on earth to hinder
The sparks, which flew about left and right,
From simply setting the house alight,
  And reducing the place to a cinder.

"And many deplored the woful waste
Of time and energy so misplaced,
Till the difficulty was boldly faced
By a man with a scientific taste,
Who the old-fashioned flint and steel replaced
  By a thing that was less uncertain.
Now this was a lucifer, made from the juicy fir,
Still it was likely to play the deuce, if a
Head should detach itself from the match,
And frolicking off at a tangent, catch
  A neighbouring dress or curtain.

"So one of a well-known firm one day—
I can't quite say whether Bryant or May—
  From fire to afford protection,

Invented a match that would only ignite
On the box—and not always on that, despite
The frequent injunction to *rub them light*—
But anyhow this, you'll agree, was quite
   A step in the right direction.

" But, it's not—to quote Cicero—*quantum suff*,
I mean that they didn't go far enough,
   And that's why I reprobate 'em.
Their principle's good without a doubt,
As far as it goes, but to work it out,
With a will that's firm, and a heart that's stout,
   Is the great *desideratum*.

" Now I've brought the principle to maturity :
More security for futurity—
That is my plan in its simple purity,
   That's what my heart desires.
But he who would compass this end must pause,
And make a study of nature's laws,
And he'll see what catastrophes matches cause,
By simply referring to Captain Shaw's
   Reports of our London fires.

" And now you'll allow me, with all dispatch,
To explain the chief points of my patent match
   With diffidence and humility ;
You see I begin by packing them in
A non-inflammable box of tin,
Which renders an accident akin
   To a moral impossibility.

" I know my invention will simply floor
Both Bryant and May and the ·Tandstickòr,'

Though they're '*utan svafvel och fosfor*,'
Which, I take it, is Scandinavian for
  'Without either sulphur or phosphorus.'
I must say, by the way, that when foreigners send
Their wares over here, they should condescend
To a tongue that their customers comprehend;
At least at the end they might append
  A something by way of a gloss for us.

" Now the regular lucifer heads will fly,
But with mine your efforts I can defy ;
All day and all night you may freely try :
They won't come off, and I'll tell you why—
  No head to the match attaches !
They simply consist, as all matches should,
Of nothing but good substantial wood ;
So their name will be readily understood—
  The ' Anti-Lucifer Matches.'

" Messrs. Bryant and May have had their day,
For though their notion, I'm bound to say,
Was highly commendable in its way,
  Mine's happier, simpler, newer ;
For with mine it is immaterial quite
How hard you rub 'em : they won't ignite
On the box, or anywhere else—you might
  As well endeavour to coax a light
  From the end of a wooden skewer.

" So now I am anxious to come to terms
With one of the leading London firms,
  And it's my belief sincerely,
That if you adopt it, your fortune's made,
For the match will do an enormous trade,
The danger from fire will be quite allayed,

And soon it will hardly be gainsaid
That the Metropolitan Fire Brigade
  Is ornamental merely."

He ceased, and the partners answered thus:
" Your idea most excellent seems to us:
  The matter you ably handle ;
But what we have hitherto failed to catch
Is, how you propose, with a headless match,
  To light your bedroom candle."

The confident look of pride forsook
The inventor's face : with a hand that shook
  He picked up his battered hat ;
He simply ejaculated " Eh ? "
And made for the door without delay
In a limp condition : he did not stay
To collect his boxes or say " Good-day ! "
But they heard him remark, as he stole away,
  " Why *didn't* I think of that ? "

The Christian World Magazine, MARCH, 1887.

THE "RATIONAL DRESS" CRUSADE.

By an Unprejudiced Male.

THE Town Hall of Westminster never, I ween,
    Looked down on so strange and impressive a scene,
As when the apostles of Rational Dress
Convened a great meeting of ladies, to press
Their views on their suffering down-trodden sisters—
Excluding, of course, the *irrational* Misters.

A lady of rank in the chair was installed—
The "chairwoman" properly she should be called,
> But the epithet might
> Be considered a slight
On so noble a dame; yet how else it were right
To describe her is not very clear at first sight.

> Then her ladyship rose,
> With an air of repose,
To dilate on the burdens, oppressions, and woes
> That harass and vex
> Her unfortunate sex
From the very beginning of life to its close;
And this is about what she uttered—in prose:
> "From the day of our birth
> "We are victims of Worth
" And fashion, the cruellest tyrant on earth.
"They jealously watch o'er the feminine baby,
" And eagerly seize it as early as may be,
" Subject it to all kinds of torments (the brutes!)
> " And very soon force it
> " To put on a corset,
" A tight-fitting bodice, and narrow-heeled boots,
" While the men see the torture, but, like Mr. Toots,
" Say *that's* ' of no consequence,' if the thing suits.
" But what I am chiefly concerned to subvert
" Is the wearisome load of the vile modern skirt.
" Oh, how can I sum up the skirt of the period?
" Advantages *nil*—disadvantages myriad!
" It hangs like a circle of lead on the hips,
" Into all of the puddles it carefully dips,
> " It prevents the free play
> " Of our limbs day by day,
" And its hurrying owner it constantly trips;

" Yes, for injuring health and for gathering dirt
" And impeding all movement, I boldly assert
 " That nought can compare with it—
 " Why do we bear with it?
" Skirt of the Period, horrible Skirt!
 " To conclude my address,
 " I desire to impress
" The fact that our notions are quite a success
" Both for beauty and comfort, as all will confess,
" When they see some examples of Rational Dress."
So saying her ladyship gave a direction,
And lo! at her bidding a goodly selection
 Of ladies descended
 The platform and wended
Among the assembly for closer inspection;
And all, like the lady herself who presided,
Wore different forms of the skirt that's divided.
 Some seemed quite at ease
 In a costume Chinese,
Some were dressed for the mountains and some for
 the seas,
And some for the parallel bars and trapeze;
In fact, 'twas a Rational " Go-as-you-please "!
And every one voted the thing a success—
But they didn't all vow to wear Rational Dress.

Now, whether the skirt should be severed or whole
Is not altogether for them to control;
For women, in spite of her ladyship's cries,
Have a certain regard for our masculine eyes.
 And they'll wear such attire
 As the men will admire;
They'll submit to discomfort, but won't appear
 " guys."

It may be, indeed, when with ladies we mingle
  We see (so they say)
  "Dual dresses" each day,
And think in our innocent hearts they are single.
  And if it is true
  That to common folks' view
The difference can't be discerned 'twixt the two,
I don't see the ground of objection—do you?
But it's surely their own fault if ladies of wealth
Wear dresses too heavy for comfort or health.
There's a time-honoured proverb that none can impugn :
"*He who pays for the piper can call for the tune ;*"
  And the ladies, at least,
  Can compel the modiste
To see that the weight of their skirts is decreased—
That is, if they do not object to be "fleeced."
They can cut down the measure of fluting and
  frilling,
And plaiting and quilting, provided they're willing
To pay what they're asked to the uttermost shilling.
And for her who's obliged to be saving of pelf,
The remedy's simple—*to make it herself.*

But there's one thing that sensible women and men
Can join in reforming by deed, voice, and pen;
To wit, when with fingers all aching and sore,
Or eke with the help of her maids, one or more,
  A young lady pinches
  To seventeen inches
A waist that Dame Nature has made twenty-four.
The hour-glass she takes for her model, forgetting
  That kinship it owns
  With the skull and cross-bones,
The moral of which would be rather upsetting.

If, leaving the question of flounces and trains,
The ladies to *this* will devote all their pains,
  We may hope that the Fashion 'll
  Yield to what's rational—
That is to say, to what Nature ordains.
And there's one other point that we cannot but mention,
A matter well worthy of ladies' attention,
And that is their fashion of evening costume,
In which for improvement there's plenty of room.
  While the Rational Dress
  Propaganda say "Less"
For the skirt's heavy burden demanding redress,
Here Modesty, Reason, Health, Beauty, all four,
Are always, like Oliver, "asking for *more !*"

The Christian World Magazine, APRIL, 1887.

~~~~~~~~~~~~~~~~~~~

DR. BROWN'S FIRST PATIENT.

THE Lady Mary Vandeleur
    Was fifty-seven and a fraction;
She might be fairly called mature,
    And rather wanting in attraction.

But how much better than the bloom
    Of youth, a house in Eaton Square is!
And no Belgravia drawing-room
    Was crowded more than Lady Mary's.

And then, besides the rank and birth,
    Whereafter every wordling hankers,
She had the noblest thing on earth—
    A handsome balance at her banker's.

She drove about the park each day;
 Went always twice to Church on Sunday,
And worshipped in the strictest way
 The sainted shrine of Mrs. Grundy.

In fact she was in all respects
 The very model of propriety;
As one must be whom fate selects
 To be a leader of society.

Now, as declining years slip by
 (Poor creatures we of circumstances!)
We seem to be—I don't know why—
 More liable to morbid fancies.

And though no race was e'er more pure,
 No blood more blue than Lady Mary's,
The bluest blood is not secure
 From human failings and vagaries.

One morn, as she began to sip
 Her tea with due deliberation,
Quite suddenly her ladyship
 Was conscious of an odd sensation.

It felt as if a wandering hair,
 Or eke a bone from last night's mullet,
Or bristle from her tooth-brush, were
 Securely lodged within her gullet.

First back, then forward, went her head,
 She coughed and choked and gulped and swallowed,
Took pints of water, pounds of bread,
 But no result to speak of followed.

Then Lady Mary sent a note
   In haste to summon her physician,
For even now she felt her throat
   Incapable of deglutition.

Sir Joseph came at her command.
   And made a careful diagnosis,
And, seeing nought, prescribed off-hand
   The most innocuous of doses.

The Lady Mary carried through
   The doctor's orders to the letter;
Did everything she ought to do,
   But never felt the least bit better.

Then, seeing that the doctor's plan
   Had no effect upon the bristle,
She swore—as near as ladies can—
   Sir Joseph for his fee should whistle.

She summoned, then, another leech,
   Who, having used his best endeavour,
Remarked—for he was brief of speech—
   " There's nothing in your throat whatever."

Her ladyship, when she was vexed,
   Was not accustomed to conceal it:
" You say there's nothing there! What next!
   When I have told you I can *feel* it!

" You dare to doubt a lady's word!"—
   Her ladyship was growing hoarser—
" Such insolence was never heard.
   Why, what on earth d'ye take me for, Sir?"

The doctor simply took his hat,
　And left, remarking in conclusion,
"Of course you *think* it's there; but that,
　I tell you, is a mere delusion."

Then all the great M.D.s were brought,
　And closely o'er her lips did hover,
But none of them discovered aught—
　For there was nothing to discover.

Now, in a humble part of Town
　There lived, or rather vegetated,
A youth, by name Leander Brown;
　"M.D." his door-plate indicated.

Although behind-hand in the race,
　For he was brainless as a gander,
When told of Lady Mary's case,
　A brilliant notion struck Leander.

So to her ladyship he wrote,
　Requesting leave to call upon her,
And undertook to cure her throat,
　If she would let him have that honour.

The Lady Mary Vaudeleur
　Was now in such a sad condition,
She welcomed any chance of cure,
　And gave him the required permission.

And when he read, "To-day at two,"
　Leander cut a mental caper;
Then from his tooth-brush deftly drew
　A bristle, which he wrapped in paper.

His case of instruments in hand,
   He called at the appointed hour;
With seeming care the throat he scanned,
   And used a glass of extra power.

" Why, there, of course ! " Leander cried,
   " It's plain enough to see what's in it;
Just keep the mouth, please, open wide,
   And I'll extract it in a minute."

His bristle then he placed with speed
   Between the tweezers, hid from view;
Just scratched the throat to make it bleed,
   Then forth the blood-stained bristle drew.

" A bristle from my tooth-brush ! That's
   Just what I said," cried Lady Mary;
" And yet those doctors, blind as bats,
   Said it was quite imaginary.

" I never can express my sense
   Of all the suffering you've averted:
Be sure that all my influence
   On your behalf shall be exerted."

The Lady Mary kept her word :
   To praise him was with her a passion;
And everywhere his name was heard,
   Till Dr. Brown became the fashion.

And soon he moved to Harley Street:
   His notions grander grew and grander,
And to himself he said, " 'Twere meet
   To find a Hero for Leander."

So he was wed; but (hapless youth!)
 Love made him reckless and unwary:
One day he told his wife the truth
 How he had cured the Lady Mary.

She promised ne'er of it to speak;
 Her efforts really were heroic;
For one whole agonising week
 She bore the torture like a Stoic.

But when the week was at an end
 She felt she'd done enough for glory,
And so she told her dearest friend,
 In strictest confidence, the story.

And then the secret filtered round:
 Of solemn pledges none was chary;
Until a candid friend felt bound
 To tell it to the Lady Mary.

And when she heard the shameful tale,
 A paroxysm of rage she flew in;
When that was over, calm and pale
 She set about Leander's ruin.

The power that gave him fame, she turned
 Against him now without compassion:
Leander everywhere was spurned,
 For Lady Mary set the fashion.

His guineas more unfrequent grew,
 His patients gradually dwindled;
For none would have a doctor who,
 So Lady Mary said, had swindled.

And soon he could not pay his way,
　His income was reduced to zero;
And bitterly he rued the day
　When he confided in his Hero.

* 　　 * 　　 * 　　 *

The handsome house in Harley Street
　Is now the noted Dr. Porter's;
Leander's fame was short and sweet,
　And now he's in his former quarters.

The victim of connubial trust,
　The dupe of female curiosity,
He bows his head in sheer disgust
　And hopeless impecuniosity.

The Christian World Magazine, MAY, 1887.

THE STORY OF A PRACTICAL JOKE:

A LEGEND OF INDIA.

A LGERNON HUGH ALEXANDER CAREW
　　Was a cavalry subaltern, aged twenty-two,
With plenty of money and little to do.
The regiment owning this scion of Mars
We will call, for convenience, the Hundredth Hussars,—
　　I'm aware that, of course,
　　Such a body of Horse
Is unknown in the ranks of Her Majesty's Force.

6

It is needless to state
With precision the date
Of the incident I am about to relate;
Suffice it to say that the regiment had
Its quarters just then at Mofussilabad—
A station that all
Anglo-Indians call
A "hole" in the very worst part of Bengal;
Where the "griffin" an adequate knowledge obtains
Of what's meant by a summer that's spent in the plains.
So Algy Carew
Very speedily knew
What an Indian sun at his hottest can do:
How it dried up his vigour and muddled his brains,
Till he wistfully sighed for the season of rains;
And then when they came, in the soaking cantonment
He gained a good notion of what a Monsoon meant.
And so to the fact that he had to go through
A season or two
In the plains may be due
The queer temper of Algernon H. A. Carew.

Now it ought to be said
That when slumber had fled,
And red ants and mosquitos were present instead,
Carew had a habit of reading in bed
Ghost-stories that stiffened the hair on his head.
If you wish, gentle reader, to clear and dilate your
Ideas on the point, read "The Night Side of Nature";
Or if modern theory and new nomenclature
Your genius fires,
You will find your desires
Fulfilled in the writings of Gurney and Myers;

For the old-fashioned ghosts are quite left in the
    lurch
By the modern apostles of psychic research.
      Carew used to boast
      That although he'd read most
Of the works on the subject, a terrible host,
Yet he wasn't the least bit afraid of a ghost;
      For wherever he slept,
      'Neath the pillow he kept
A pistol, with which he was quite an adept,
And he promised the first supernatural form
That appeared a reception unpleasantly warm.

      Percival Chubb
      Was the senior " sub "
In the regiment we have decided to dub
The Hundredth Hussars, and just there was the rub;
For Percival, being a bit of a scrub,
Took advantage of senior standing to snub
      And score off Carew
      When he'd nothing to do,
For he thought him "a beastly conceited young cub."
      So Algy from Percy
      Expected no mercy,
And when he'd the chance, it was just "*vice versy.*"
Now Percy was one of those imbecile folk
Who think there is fun in a practical joke:
      No mere lover of chaff
      For the sake of a laugh
That nobody minds—no mere genial poker
Of fun, but a regular practical joker.
      And having a day off
      He thought he would play off
A trick on young Algy, old grudges to pay off.

Himself superstitious, it made him almost
Boil over with rage to hear Algernon's boast,
  And he thought he would see
  Where his bragging would be
When "the beggar should really set eyes on a
  ghost."
So first to his enemy's bedroom he crept,
Took the pistol that under his pillow was kept,
Adroitly extracted the bullet, and then
Put it carefully under the pillow again.
  Then at dead of the night
  He arrayed him in white,
And in Algernon's room, with the moon shining
  bright,
He planted himself, with his back to the light,
And prepared to give Algy a terrible fright.

The young man was lying in slumber's embrace,
And the moonbeams shone full on his innocent face.
A smile had just parted his lips in a fashion
That ought to have roused his tormentor's compassion;
  But Percival Chubb,
  Being rather a scrub,
Merely chuckled to think how his eyes he would rub
  When he saw at the post
  Of his bed a real ghost—
"My young friend," muttered Percy, "I've got you on
  toast."
  Then, striking a pose,
  To his full height he rose,
And broke in on unfortunate Algy's repose
With an awful "Aha!" which he brought from his
  toes—
The correct ghostly greeting, as every one knows.

Algernon Hugh
Alexander Carew
Woke up in a most unmistakable stew,
And turned to a hue
You might fairly call blue,
When the dread apparition encountered his view.
Its face wore a smile that was gruesome and grim,
And—O horror of horrors! that chilled every limb—
The ghastly thing's finger was pointing at *him*.
Lieutenant Carew
Didn't know what to do,
And he stared at the ghost for a minute or two,
As he lay there in bed,
While the hair on his head
Grew as stiff as a poker with horror and dread.
Then keeping his eye on the gaunt apparition,
He slowly adopted a sitting position,
And stealthily felt for his pistol, the while
The spectre looked on with the same mocking smile.
Then raising it quickly the trigger he prest
And fired at his visitor full in the chest.

When the smoke cleared away,
To poor Algy's dismay,
The ghost was still smiling, as one who should say:
" I'm here, and I've every intention to stay "—
Which he might have expressed
By "*j'y suis et j'y reste*,"
But his French conversation was none of the best,
But see, what is that in his finger and thumb?
A sight that made Algy's extremities numb.
Great Pepper! it can't be—it is—it's the bullet!—
If he'd been awake, he'd have seen the ghost pull it
Five minutes before from his pocket, in view

Of what French people call a "theatrical *coup*."
With another "Aha!" that he brought as before
From a part of his person adjoining the floor,

The bullet he nipped
With his thumbnail, and flipped—

Like a schoolboy propelling the swift "alley-taw,"
As Algernon noticed in spite of his awe—
Right up to the ceiling: it fell with a thud,
That froze up his marrow and curdled his blood.

Algernon's brains—
That's to say, the remains

That were left by a season or two in the plains—
Were unequal to any unusual strains.
He was always considered a little bit mad
In the social resorts of Mofussilabad;
And now he was seized with a frenzy—poor fellow!—
That, coupled with fear, turned him perfectly yellow,
And made him appear like a washed-out Othello.
By the side of his bed was his cavalry-sword,
Which Chubb in his hurry had somehow ignored—
A fact that he afterwards deeply deplored.
So he jumped out of bed with the rage of despair,
And brandished his cavalry-sword in the air;

Then with fury he fell
On the spectre pell-mell:

" Take that with you back, cursed vision,—" a yell
At this moment arose, so I really can't tell
How he ended the phrase—and perhaps it's as well.

The grim apparition
Soon grasped the position,

And rushed from the chamber with great expedition.

A horrible gash in his shoulders declared
How Chubb with his practical joking had fared.
Away to his rooms fled the terrified subaltern,
And gave to the lock of his bedroom a double turn ;
Then, spent with excitement and faint from his wound,
Poor Percival staggered a moment and swooned.

When after six weeks of monotonous pain
Percy Chubb was restored to the mess-room again,
 His life he began
 On a new sort of plan,
And people said Chubb was a different man.
The awful events of that terrible morning
In Algernon's room had imparted a warning
That Percival wasn't the man to be scorning.

 Henceforth I am glad
 To record that he had
No grudge or ill-will towards that innocent lad—
There were no closer friends in Mofussilabad.
 And instead of the Chubb
 Who was rather a scrub,
Too fond of his pipe and his glass and his "rub,"
 He became an exemplary
 Staid and Good Templary
Model of all you could wish in a "sub."
He abjured Baccarat, gave up Whist, Nap, and Poker,
Became an abstainer and eke a non-smoker,
And never again was a practical joker.

MORAL.

Take warning from Algernon H. A. Carew,
And sternly henceforth and for ever eschew
The practice of reading ghost-stories in bed,

Which are apt, like strong liquor, to go to your head.
If you *must* read in bed, as a mild soporific
A three-volume novel is quite a specific.
Some say that this species of literature
For insomnia's really too ghastly a cure.
If so, I'd allow the nocturnal bookworm an
Abstruse philosophical treatise in German—
One *might* even go to a tract or a sermon.

And, secondly, never forget that before
Retiring to rest you should fasten your door.

And last, but not least, never try to provoke
A laugh at a man by a practical joke.
   In the first place, you see,
   The unhappy *jokee*
Is frightened clean out of his wits, it may be;
And secondly no oné will pity the joker
If he should encounter a sword or a poker.
'Twas owing to practical joking that Chubb
Had to give up his pipe, and his glass, and his "rub."
So lest such delights you should have to disown,
Leave practical joking severely alone.
   Then the pleasures of virtue
   Will never desert you:
A rubber of three-penny whist will not hurt you;
The moderate glass you may still put away;
Still relish the sweetness of meerschaum and clay.

The Christian World Magazine, JUNE, 1887.

THE ALMIGHTY DOLLAR.

*P*OETA *nascitur non fit :*
    " 'Tis Nature " (so I render it)
" That makes the poet."
But Nature, fashioning my clay,
Did not (alas !) build me that way—
    What's more, I know it.

Yet if the Muse, from out a score
Of babes, had chosen me to pour
    Poetic fire on,
E'en so I would not tune my lays
To nondescript young women's praise,
    Like Keats or Byron.

And I would spend poetic hours,
Without apostrophising flowers,
    Like Edmund Waller ;
One theme alone would fire my song :
I'd sing of thee the whole day long,
    Almighty Dollar !

What " Hamlet " *sans* the Prince would be,
Or grand old W. E. G.
    Without his collar—
Such and so poor our England is,
And has been all these centuries,
    Without her dollar.

How in the world have we survived
So many ages, and contrived
    To do without it?
It really almost strikes me dumb
With sheer amazement when I come
    To think about it.

The Yankee and the Mexican,
And even poor John Chinaman
    In all his squalor,
Has long possessed this piece of pelf
(With much advantage to himself),
    The mighty Dollar.

But hitherto Chinese and "Japs"
Have been before us, and, perhaps,
    This nonchalant age
Its business would have gone about,
And still been satisfied without
    This coin of 'vantage.

But happily a fact, that I
Need not more closely specify,
    Has roused the nation;
And now the dollar takes its place
Among us in this year of grace
    And jubilation.

And yet herein 'tis plain to see
Our insular antipathy
    To all things foreign;
To call it "dollar" we're ashamed,
So it's unconscionably named
    The "double florin."

That such a term will not go down,
" Bob," " tanner," " tizzy," " quid," and " brown,"
   Are ample warning.
Imagine this : " Just lend me, Jack,
A double florin—pay you back
   To-morrow morning."

Or, " Pray, what might this card-case be ? "
" A double florin, Sir—you see
   It's Russian leather."
Or, " Now, then, cabby, what's your fare ? "
" It's wuth a double florin—there !—
   In thisher weather."

But designate it, if you will,
A " double florin," I can still
   Restrain my choler ;
For, after all, what's in a name ?
In any case the coin's the same,
   And it's a dollar.

And what a work of art and grace !
Though, to be sure, the royal face
   It does not flatter.
And though the crown appears inclined
To slip and tumble off behind,
   What *does* it matter ?

And it has use as well as show ;
Worn round the neck 'twould make, you know,
   A pretty locket.
Then its capacity's unique
For wearing holes within a week
   In any pocket.

Some say for getting change it's not
Adapted to the coins we've got.
    What nonsense! Why, Sir,
Just think of its convenience :
It's half-a-crown and eighteenpence !
    What could be nicer ?

So now the lounger in Pall Mall,
The Park and Piccadilly swell,
    The Bond Street loller,
In making wagers in his set,
Without absurdity can bet
    His " bottom dollar."

A fig for him who prates of " mils,"
And vaunts, as balm for all our ills,
    The system decimal;
The irritating bore who splits
A pound into a thousand bits
    Infinitesimal.

Let faddist deputations wait
On weary Ministers of State
    To urge their notion ;
And let them still be sent about
Their business, snuffed politely out,
    By Mr. Goschen.

But with our dollar we'll be glad ;
There's plenty of them to be had,
    Where England's Bank is.
Our satisfaction's now complete,
For we no more need take a seat
    Behind the Yankees.

And as for me, whate'er my lot,
Whether the mansion or the cot,
   In wealth or squalor,
To my abode, where'er it be,
I'll always warmly welcome thee,
   Almighty Dollar!

The Christian World Magazine, JULY, 1887.

MY FIRST LOVE.

L AST summer, feeling rather low,
   I thought I might as well as not
Enjoy a quiet month or so
   At some unfashionable spot—

Some seaside place unknown to fame,
   For Fashion is my pet abhorrence;
Bob Sparke, my chum, thought just the same,
   And in the end we chose St. Lawrence.

So Bob and I went down one day,
   And put up at the George Hotel;
And so a fortnight passed away,
   And we enjoyed it very well.

And then one evening in the cool,
   As from my window I protruded,
There passed a certain Ladies' School,
   In which an angel was included.

Words fail me to describe her face,
　　Which I would back against all comers—
A dream of loveliness and grace,
　　Of, roughly speaking, sixteen summers.

And from that hour, by night and day,
　　That vision smiled upon me sweetly;
I could not think of work or play,
　　For I was broken up completely.

I tried to read; but oh, that face!
　　Upon the head it seemed to knock work;
And every evening at my place
　　I sat as regular as clock-work.

I ascertained the school was one
　　Of high repute beyond compare,
Kept by the Misses Simpkinson,
　　At No. 30, Worcester Square.

My angel's name, unknown to me,
　　I would not e'en presume to guess;
She figured in my thoughts as " She,"
　　With capital initial S.

I never spoke a word to her,
　　Because I never had the chance,
Nor can I truthfully aver
　　She gave me e'er a tender glance.

The darling hardly looked at me,
　　But all the same I loved her madly;
First love was my complaint, you see,
　　And I had got it pretty badly.

Bob's counsel and advice I sought;
  In him, of course, I had confided,
And it was fortunate, I thought,
  He didn't worship her as I did.

But Bob's suggestions were absurd;
  He wanted me to bribe the maid
At Worcester Square, and "like a bird,"
  He said I'd get a note conveyed.

I thought it far too boldly planned,
  The course that Robert recommended;
My angel would not understand;
  She might be mortally offended.

So time went on, till with a growl
  Bob voted it uncommon slow,
Said I was stupid as an owl,
  And "Fit for nothing, don't you know."

One day, a little after three,
  In passing by the letter stand,
I found a note addressed to me,
  In what appeared a female hand.

I felt a kind of odd sensation
  In opening the note, and there—
Great heavens! I found an invitation
  To No. 30, Worcester Square.

In phantasy I seemed to roam
  In near proximity to Heaven—
"The Misses Simpkinson at home;
  Lawn tennis half-past four to seven."

The date ?   This very afternoon ;
  I must prepare to go at once ;
But stay !   I won't arrive too soon,
  Or She'll consider me a dunce.

P'raps I may walk with her alone
  To where a seat beneath the shade is.
How kind to me the fates have grown !
  And how I bless those maiden ladies !

If ever She should pity take
  Upon my love, and answer " Yes,"
I'll send a piece of wedding-cake—
  A large piece—to the Misses S.

It looks like rain, and flannels shrink,
  So I must take a mackintosh—
Good gracious ! now I come think,
  My flannels all are at the wash.

Well, beggars, so they say, can't choose—
  At least, the lawn I must not cut up ;
I'll buy a pair of tennis shoes—
  Bank Holiday ! the shops are shut up.

Well, there, I don't much care to play ;
  But all the same I'll take my racket—
Well, really, now—oh, come, I say—
  The careless maid forgot to pack it.

Well, I must go in what I've on ;
  And, after all, what does it matter
What sort of clothes a man may don,
  Who makes his boots, or who's his hatter ?

My coat I thought looked worse for wear,
    My trousers seemed a trifle dirty,
When I arrived in Worcester Square,
    And rang the bell of No. 30.

My heart beat loud; the deed was done;
    And soon the door was opened wide,
And, murmuring "Miss Simpkinson,"
    In muffled tones, I stepped inside.

I waited in a darkened room,
    Where everything was quite "genteel,"
And I was thankful that the gloom
    My agitation would conceal.

A neighb'ring door creaked noisily;
    I heard a momentary hum
Of conversation broken by—
    "A young man called to see you, mum."

Miss S. arrives; she's tall and thin,
    And from her neck an eyeglass dangles;
Her nose is long and aquiline,
    Her figure mainly lines and angles.

Miss S.'s eyes are weak and blear,
    And that is why the room's so shady;
Her mien is stately and severe.
    But still I love that maiden lady.

What though her form is gaunt and thin?
    Her heart, I'm sure, is full of charity;
And if the heart is fair within,
    What matters outward angularity?

7

I soon found out Miss Simpkinson
  Was most abominably deaf;
Her voice was shrill, and pitched upon
  The G above the treble clef.

" I hope you understand, young man,
  About a lawn, and grass, and so on ? "
" Why, yes—I think so," I began,
  And didn't quite know how to go on.

" We have it mown three times a week;
  It's quite the chief thing in the garden."
" Indeed ! " I said,   " Eh ! did you speak ? "
  " Oh, nothing, ma'am—I beg your pardon."

" Of course, I shall expect of you
  To see the lawn is kept in order ;
And you must be most careful, too,
  About the tulips round the border."

" Oh, I'll be careful not to tread
  Upon the tulips—heaven forbid ! "
" Eh ! did you speak ? "   " Oh, no," I said.
  " Oh !—beg your pardon—thought you did."

What *is* Miss Simpkinson about ?
  Thought I; it's rather poorish sport;
She knows I'm dying to go out ;
  I wish she'd try and cut it short.

" The orchard," she resumed, " you'll find
  Well stocked with apples, pears, and such."
" Oh, thank you, ma'am, you're very kind ;
  But fruit's a thing I never touch."

I spoke so loud the lady heard;
 " I'm glad to hear it," answered she;
"I hope, young man, you'll keep your word,
 And never touch a single tree."

Well, now, thought I, this *is* a go;
 She talks as if I were the gardener.
I'm sure she doesn't mean it, though.
 For rudeness! so, of course, I pardon her.

" What wages do you ask? Of course,
 I can't engage you till I've seen——"
" What!" shouted I, in accents hoarse,
 " My wages! What does all this mean ?"

Was this an insult coolly planned?
 The blood came rushing to my face.
" Your wages—yes; I understand,
 You've come about the gardener's place."

" Excuse me," I replied, severe
 And calm, despite my indignation;
" To play at tennis I am here,
 At your especial invitation."

She gazed at me with scorn, and then:
 " The man's a madman or a fool!
What! do you think we ask young men
 To tennis at a ladies' school ? "

Across my fevered brain there came
 A dark suspicion, burning, blighting.
" The card!" I cried. " In heaven's name,
 Read that, and say if it's your writing!"

The lady calmly read it through;
　　I watched her face in dire suspense.
"Young man, they've made a fool of you!
　　I *should* have thought you'd have more sense."

I rushed in fury to the door;
　　My heart was filled with passions dark;
Yes, now I saw it all, and swore
　　To have the blood of Robert Sparke.

And when at last I was alone,
　　In No. 20, George Hotel.
"Pistols for two, and tea for one!"
　　I muttered, as I rang the bell.

"Is Mr. Sparke within?" I cried—
　　The waiter quailed before my mien—
"He's gone to town, sir," he replied;
　　"He left, sir, by the three-fifteen."

Wild schemes at first inflamed my breast;
　　"I'll follow him, as I'm a sinner!"
On second thoughts, I deemed it best
　　To stop at home and order dinner.

Rest and reflection braced me up;
　　Next morning, feeling slightly better,
I found beside my breakfast cup,
　　The following audacious letter:

"DEAR JACK,—I hope you understood
　　The object that I had in view;
I knew you'd never do much good,
　　If everything were left to you.

" And so I introduced you there—
  My plan, I think, was rather cunning—
And, once in 30, Worcester Square,
  Of course, old chap, you made the running.

" Just write and tell me what you did—
  And, by-the-way, you want a cob;
I've got a stunner—fifty quid—
  As cheap as dirt.—Yours truly, Bob."

The Christian World Magazine, SEPTEMBER, 1887.

⁓⁓⁓⁓⁓⁓⁓⁓

A FANCY BAZAAR.

O MASTERLY mind! O bewildering brain!
  O cunning of counsel and greedy of gain!
I sing in your honour, whoever you are,
Who evolved the idea of a Fancy Bazaar.
For endowing a hospital, founding a school,
For dressing up niggers in cotton and wool,
For supplying old women with sugar and tea,
For reforming the victims of " Soda and B,"
For buying an organ, restoring a church,
Leave sermons and meetings away in the lurch:
Of all the devices—search near or search far—
There's nothing on earth like a Fancy Bazaar!

The women are all in their element there;
For the due subjugation of man they prepare.
Professional beauties and stars operatic,

And ladies plebeian and aristocratic,
All mix for the nonce without any compunction,
And all volunteer to take part in the function.
For Fancy Bazaars afford plenty of room
For striking departures in fancy costume;
And each is convinced that the whole thing's success
Depends on her own individual dress.
Sometimes Early English attire is the fashion,
Sometimes for Shakespearean *rôles* there's a passion;
Sometimes they astonish their friends and relations
By boldly adopting costumes of all nations;
Then a motley assemblage encounters the view,
Fair daughters of France in the red, white and blue,
Bright-eyed Irish beauties, the loveliest types,
The tartan of Scotland, the stars and the stripes;
The loose flowing robes of the Heathen Chinee,
From the trammels of fashion so glad to be free;
The graceful " kimmono " of old-world Japan,
One garment, one fashion, for woman and man;
The Turk's jealous veil that sets off the dark eyes
And enhances the charms that it cannot disguise;
The Indian nautch-girl with trinkets o'erladen,
The laughing Italian, the dark Spanish maiden;
Egyptians, Armenians, and Persians galore,
Swiss, Germans, and goodness knows how many more.

Yes, such is the army that's banded to vex
And pillage and plunder the opposite sex.
As soon as he enters, they straightway assail
Their unfortunate victim, the innocent male;
And before he's had time their intention to note,
Deft fingers have fastened a flower in his coat.
So he pays his five shillings, is told he looks nice,
And thinks it uncommonly dear at the price.

See, there is a lady well known on the stage,
Whose talent and beauty have made her the rage.
Her photo in every shop-window is seen
By the side of the Princess of Wales and the Queen,
And a crowd stops to gaze at her charms photographic
Entirely obstructing pedestrian traffic.
Yet here in the flesh she presides at a stall,
As if—so to speak—she were no one at all,
Selling rather expensive tea, coffee, and ices—
At Fancy Bazaars you must pay fancy prices.
With such a tea-maker, who wouldn't be willing
To reckon a cup of tea cheap at a shilling?
But when she just touches the cup with her lips,
And, taking the least of diminutive sips,
Says, "Now it's a sovereign"—you *feel*, as a rule,
And in all probability *look*, like a fool.
But you can't well refuse, so you pay like a man,
And try to extract from the tea, if you can,
By sipping as if 'twere the choicest of wine,
All the sweetness imparted by lips so divine.
Or perhaps you might follow the plan of campaign
Of a certain old bachelor, cross in the grain,
Who calmly and coldly his sovereign paid up,
And then asked if she'd kindly supply a clean cup!

Then you're lured to your fate in the form of a
    raffle,
And no strength of mind their persistence can baffle.
" Just look at this cushion—now isn't it nice?
" And notice the wholly inadequate price;
" If you'll only just help me to make a beginning,
" I'm sure you are perfectly certain of winning."
Or they bring you a "cosy"—a thing that, no doubt,
A well-ordered household is never without;

It is placed, I believe, on the top of the pot,
And—a thing I detest—keeps the tea boiling hot.
You remark that you like not the cosy in question;
They scout as bad taste the outrageous suggestion.
You say you're a bachelor, try to look sulky,
And hint that a cosy's both useless and bulky;
It's all to no purpose: they only look pleasant,
And say it will do for a nice little present.

" Now do take a chance in this sandalwood box,
" It's beautiful Indian work—and it locks!
" It will do to keep gloves in, or collars, or ties,
" Or anything else of a moderate size:
" It would do for the things that you use when you
        shave,
" Or if not—well, it's always a nice thing to have."
And so they extract, with their blandishments killing,
The reluctant half-crown and the lingering shilling.
They show you some slippers in yellow and green,
Whose size. roughly speaking, 's an easy sixteen;
Or a smoking-cap, gaily embroidered in red,
Three sizes too big for a rational head.
And about as much use to a man as a bonnet,
For who ever knew a true smoker to don it?

So you put in for all the most useless affairs,
For antimacassars and footstools and chairs,
For tea-caddies, paper-knives, travelling-lamps,
And flimsy concerns to hold paper and stamps,
For a crewel-work screen, or a hand-painted tray,
While change for a sovereign melts swiftly away.
But you mustn't object of your coin to be eased,
You must pay up serenely and try to look pleased.

And oh ! the proud joy, on the list as you glance,
To find that you've won by the favour of chance
A flower-pot thing, with a fern or two in it,
That's cost you a couple of sovereigns to win it!

'Tis strange a Bazaar should become an occasion
For plunder by friends of the female persuasion;
And strange that a meeting so churchy and parsony
Develops a system of legalised larceny.
But every one knows that the object is good,
So no one would ever object if he could.
It's all very well for some people to say,
" I like to subscribe in the usual way;
" And I hate at a Fancy Bazaar to be hoaxed
" And bothered and pulled about, wheedled and
      coaxed."
If charity only depended on " lists,"
Would these people so readily open their fists ?
I strongly suspect that the sovereigns and crowns,
The florins and shillings and diffident " browns,"
Would lurk undisturbed in their own fluffy lair,
If not lured by the smiles and the charms of the fair.
Then come to the show in your thousands, and mind
That your pockets with current coin amply are lined.
Be sure you'll have lots of amusement and laughter,
And also be sure that you'll pay for it after.
So gather, good people, from near and from far,
To be swindled and fleeced at the Fancy Bazaar.

The Christian World Magazine, OCTOBER, 1887.

"POOR GREEN!"

JOSIAH GREEN was short and lean—
   He couldn't well be shorter—
In boots complete, he stood five feet
   Two inches and a quarter!

His wife was tall, and stout withal,
   No high-heeled shoes she needed;
And the people said the lady weighed
   As much again as he did.

A month had sped since they were wed—
   Perhaps a trifle longer—
When Mrs. G. resolved to see
   If he or she were stronger.

And when a "scene" showed Mrs. Green
   Her lord was not high-mettled,
Their proper shares in home affairs
   Were very promptly settled.

Thenceforth without dispute or doubt,
   Or difference of opinion,
She exercised an undisguised
   And absolute dominion.

To free his life from rows and strife
   And peaceably enjoy it, he
Let it be seen that Mrs. Green
   Was his superior moiety.

But still howe'er uneasy were
　　His conjugal relations,
Josiah's lot in life was not
　　Without its compensations.

Though Fate, no doubt, had marked him out
　　A pathway somewhat hilly,
Yet he possessed one place of rest—
　　A club in Piccadilly.

A club and friends will make amends
　　For all the woes of mortals;
And Green began to feel a man
　　When once within its portals.

"Poor Green!" they dub him at the club,
　　And wonder "how he bore it";
In fact, his name but rarely came
　　Without a "poor" before it.

Now, though we've seen that Mrs. Green
　　A despot's sceptre wielded,
Her exercise of power was wise,
　　And here and there she yielded.

For e'en the worm, as folks affirm,
　　Will turn in pure distraction.
(Though should it turn, I can't discern
　　Its further course of action.)

So it had been arranged that Green,
　　With Mrs. G.'s permission,
Three nights a week was free to seek
　　His club without suspicion.

A time of bliss to Green was this,
  A kind of earthly heaven;
But dread his lot, if he were not
  At home before eleven.

And therefore when 'twas half-past ten,
  Like wretched Cinderella,
His way he'd make downstairs and take
  His hat and his umbrella.

No power could stay him on his way;
  His friends would oft entreat him;
But only too, too well he knew
  How Mrs. G. would greet him.

One evening at the club he sat
  With friends in near proximity—
We'll put them down as Jones and Brown,
  Avoiding anonymity.

Now, Brown and Jones in undertones
  Were all the time conspiring
To try and make poor Green mistake
  The hour for his retiring.

To sleight-of-hand, as they had planned,
  The conversation drifted;
Brown said he knew a trick or two,
  Though not exactly gifted.

And soon he got by this dark plot
  Green's watch within his power.
And all unseen by Mr. Green
  He set it back an hour.

Then Jones whose mind to cards inclined,
  Being an adept at euchre.
I grieve to say, proposed to play
  That sinful game for lucre.

For mischief's sake he meant to make
  Poor Green get home belated ;
Meantime to win his victim's " tin "
  He basely contemplated.

His wickedness I can't suppress
  In this veracious history ;
For, to his shame, he thought the game
  To Green was quite a mystery.

So Green sat down with Jones and Brown
  To this unseemly pastime.
Although, I'm proud to say, he vowed
  That it should be the last time.

But strange to say that, as the play
  Went on, the mere beginner,
The guileless Green, was quickly seen
  To be the only winner.

Still undismayed, they played and played,
  For they were quite delighted
To see, meanwhile, that Fortune's smile
  Was making Green excited.

The time went fast : his hour was past,
  But he continued playing ;
And serious grew the other two.
  As they continued paying.

But though the play went all one way—
  Nought e'er was seen to match it—
They felt consoled for loss of gold
  To think how Green would catch it.

Midnight had struck, and Green's good luck
  Was getting quite offensive,
And they began to think their plan
  Decidedly expensive.

At 12.15 they vowed that Green
  Had had sufficient innings :
" It's time," they said, " to go to bed ;
  So, Green, collect your winnings."

All eager were the guilty pair,
  With keen impatience burning,
Resolved to see how Mrs. G.
  Would greet her lord returning.

So with a smile of crafty guile
  Their sentiments concealing,
Said they, " We'll come and see you home,
  To show there's no ill-feeling."

They'd lost, it's true, but still they knew
  That it was worth the money ;
So forth they fared, full well prepared
  For something really funny.

They pictured to themselves the view
  Of Mrs. G.'s excitement :
Poor Green would learn what his return
  At such a time of night meant.

In vain they tried their mirth to hide,
  Their wicked smiles to smother;
They chuckled oft, and choked and coughed,
  And winked at one another.

The luckless Green was quite serene:
  With jauntiness he bore him,
And seemed, poor wight! unconscious quite
  Of doom impending o'er him.

And when before Josiah's door
  They reach their destination,
The guilty twain could not contain
  Their ill-suppressed elation.

For now the fun was just begun,
  The fruit of all their labours;
There'd be a " scene " with Mrs. Green
  Enough to wake the neighbours.

So Jones began : " Well, Green, old man,
  You look uncommon happy;
But "—with a wink to Brown—" I think
  It's rather late, old chappie.

"There goes the chime! You know the time?
  It's one o'clock that's striking.
It seems to me that Mrs. G.
  Won't find it to her liking.

"This sad delay, I need not say,
  Most bitterly we both rue,
We can't express our great distress
  At what you'll have to go through.

" We feel for you—we really do ;
    Our hearts are soft as butter—
I speak for Brown, whose feelings drown
    The words he fain would utter."

Then answered Green, while tears between
    His eyelids were collecting :
" Your sympathy, my friends, to me
    Is really quite affecting.

" Friendship is still for every ill
    The one all-healing potion ;
And what I feel, I can't conceal—
    Pray, pardon my emotion !

" Ah ! Jones, my friend till life shall end !
    And Brown, you dear old pal, you !
The sympathy you feel for me,
    Full well I know its value.

" But, I am glad to say, your sad
    Forebodings I can lighten :
Be not cast down, dear Jones and Brown—
    My wife's away at Brighton ! "

The Christian World Magazine, DECEMBER, 1887.

THE STRANGER AT MACVITTEY'S.

THERE stands not far from Temple Bar
    The Restaurant MacVittey,
A house whose fame is on a par
    With any in the City.

Indeed, it's quite beyond compare
    In one respect, worth knowing,
For men declare they give you there
    The finest oysters going.

So toothsome, whether plain or dressed,
    So full of luscious juices;
In fact they are the very best
    That Whitstable produces.

You know your oyster's freshly caught,
    Without the slightest question,
A *native*—not a *settler*, fraught
    With danger to digestion.

An oyster supper there is quite
    What Yankees call *exquisite*—
Though that, I think, is not the right
    Pronunciation—is it?

And there's no place for many a mile
    Where guests get more attention,
Or things are served in better style,
    Than at the house I mention.

8

And then there's William! Who more bland?
   Who brisker, brighter, cheerier ?
No other waiter in the land
   Is William Grubb's superior.

The place is crowded every day,
   The hansoms often block it ;
And many a shilling finds its way
   To William's trouser-pocket.

Though guests may try his temper, ne'er
   A word by him is muttered,
For William Grubb is quite aware
   Which side his bread is buttered.

One evening at MacVittey's door
   A well-dressed stranger entered,
And William's whole attention more
   And more upon him centred.

If any man knew how to dress,
   The stranger clearly knew it ;
He seemed moreover to possess
   The wherewithal to do it.

The fashionable hat he wore
   Was glossy and untarnished ;
His gaiters fitted neatly o'er
   His boots superbly varnished.

His clothes were exquisitely made,
   And of the latest fashion ;
In fact, his whole get-up betrayed
   That dress must be his passion.

He seemed some thirty-three or four,
  But ghastly pale his visage,
And on his brow were wrinkles more
  Than you'd expect at his age.

He'd raven locks, that emphasize
  The depth of pale complexions;
A curious look was in his eyes,
  Which roved in all directions.

With haughty pride the stranger cried,
  " A private room, please, waiter ! "
And William Grubb remarked aside,
  " Well, he's a reel fust-rater."

For William thought he knew a " gent "
  From those whose sort is baser ;
So pompously in front he went,
  With, " Please to step this way, sir."

For in this stranger William saw
  A something that impressed him ;
He listened in a state of awe
  When thus the gent addressed him :

Just bring me up a score or two
  Of native oysters, waiter ;
But first I want a talk with you :
  I hope you're not a prater.

It's this way—oysters don't like me,
  Though I like nothing better ;
To me an oyster's apt to be
  A terrible upsetter.

"They tell me that, as oysters go,
   The best are at MacVittey's ;
But still there's danger—do you know
   What a *bivalvic* fit is ?

"That's my complaint—it's very rife—
   And I've a grave misgiving
That oysters are the cause, though life
   Without them's not worth living.

"I had to give them up last year—
   It's awful self-denial—
But now, you understand, I'm here
   To make another trial.

"They *may* not make me ill at all :
   My health is now much stronger ;
But any how, whate'er befall,
   I can't resist them longer.

"Well, if I'm taken ill that way,
   Though lately I've been better,
Just carry out—you'll find it pay—
   My orders to the letter.

"If I begin to writhe like *this*,
   About my second plateful,
Let no one know that aught's amiss :
   A fuss to me is hateful.

"But help me out, and there's no ground
   For serious apprehension,
For in the air I'll soon come round ;
   But don't attract attention.

" Just take me to some quiet lane :
  There's one at no great distance ;
Then quickly run back here again—
  I'll stand without assistance—

" And bring a glass of water neat
  With nothing stronger in it,
And that will set me on my feet
  In less than half a minute.

" Of course, my friend, I sha'n't forget
  To pay you well—don't doubt it ;
Look here ! a sovereign you shall get
  If you're discreet about it.

" Well, bring me up two score at first,
  And have another ready ;
And then—I've got an awful thirst,
  But stout is rather heady.

" Just show me what you've got in wine.
  Ah ! Pommery and Greno
Of '74—a drink divine,
  To which I never say ' No.'

" Of course you'll have to be at hand :
  Your help I may be needing ;
You'll take a chair—you needn't stand—
  And closely watch me feeding."

And soon the oysters glibly slipped
  Adown the stranger's throttle ;
While tranquilly his wine he sipped
  At one-pound-four the bottle.

And William sat with anxious face;
  His heart beat quick and quicker,
To see them go at such a pace—
  The oysters and the liquor.

And now the gentleman's third score
  Was sensibly diminished;
The Pommery of '74
  Was actually finished.

His face with satisfaction beamed.
  Thought William, "That's the ticket!"
And certainly the stranger seemed
  As merry as a cricket.

When something suddenly occurred
  That made poor William start up;
And, as he afterwards averred,
  It nearly brought his heart up.

An awful change swept o'er that face,
  But now so bright and cheerful;
The eyes seemed starting from their place;
  Their look was something fearful.

He clutched the air, and gasped for breath,
  His features were contorted;
He seemed upon the point of death,
  With agony transported.

His tortured body writhed and squirmed
  Without the least cessation;
As William said, the fit confirmed
  His worst anticipation.

Then William Grubb, though not without
  A feeling of compunction,
At once began to carry out
  The stranger's strict injunction.

He took him down a quiet street,
  And left him there a minute ;
Then fetched a glass of water neat
  With nothing stronger in it.

But though the stranger could not stand
  Without the wall behind him,
When William came back, glass in hand,
  He somehow could not find him.

Thrice up and down the street he ran,
  Of every one inquiring;
But nobody had seen the man,
  And William found it tiring.

So finally he ceased his quest ;
  His energy had dwindled ;
And William to himself confessed
  That he'd been nicely swindled.

" There'd not be much to wonder at
  With such a youngster, may be ;
But *me* to be took in like that,
  As easy as a baby !

" And by a chap of that 'ere trim
  For all 'is 'ighth o' fashion,
As soon as I set eyes on 'im
  I knew 'e was a flash 'un.

" Why there, I saw 'e was a scrub,
  And quite infer'or looking :
O William Grubb, O William Grubb,
  To think that *you* was took in ! "

That Pommery, and such a lot
  Of oysters all unpaid for !
He stood awhile, and wondered what
  Such rogues and thieves were made for.

Then, in a state of sheer collapse,
  Just like a punctured bladder,
Went back, a wiser man, perhaps,
  But certainly a sadder.

The Christian World Magazine, JANUARY, 1898.

LORD TOMNODDY.

A UGUSTUS S. B. O. de V.,
    The 15th Lord Tomnoddy,
Was very long in pedigree,
  But very short in body.

Dame Nature had not favoured him—
  His parents even said it—
In face and feature, form and limb,
  He did them little credit.

And this, perhaps, was why the Fates,
  By way of some requital,
Had made him heir to large estates
  And given him a title.

And when his peerage he had got
  And an enormous rental,
What mattered it that he was not
  Exactly ornamental?

His character was rather bad,
  His habits dissipated;
What little breeding he had had
  Was quite obliterated.

His manners, too, were hardly those
  Of the refined patrician;
In fact, a stranger would suppose
  He was of low condition.

Yet every mother who possessed
  A marriageable daughter,
Invariably did her best
  To lead her to the slaughter.

For mothers can't afford, you see,
  To criticise severely
A lord of ancient pedigree
  With eighty thousand yearly.

Great wealth can whitewash any peer
  Whose character is shady,
And every mother likes to hear
  Her daughter called " My lady."

So, with his ancient origin,
   His lands and halls baronial,
He had a high quotation in
   The market matrimonial.

Among the women-folk my lord
   Gave rise to keen discussions,
But he was obviously bored
   By feminine attentions.

Far other things—here was the rub—
   Attracted Lord Tomnoddy—
His boon-companions at the club,
   His cards and whiskey-toddy.

Though sprung from the Tomnoddy race.
   Whose fame was European,
His lordship's tastes were, like his face,
   Decidedly plebeian.

And so the daughters sighed in vain,
   In vain the mothers plotted,
And all agreed that it was plain
   Tomnoddy was besotted.

One day he rode in Rotten Row
   By shady friends surrounded,
When suddenly a cry of woe
   In female tones resounded.

A lady's horse came rushing past :
   All powerless its rider;
But Lord Tomnoddy's steed was fast,
   And soon he was beside her.

The horse was stopped: a lovely maid
  Was thanking her preserver
In winning accents, that betrayed
  Her gratitude and fervour.

Tomnoddy gazed upon that face:
  He ne'er had seen its equal;
It seemed instinct with every grace—
  You can divine the sequel.

For all at once his hardened heart,
  Which ne'er before had quivered,
Gave such an unexpected start,
  Tomnoddy fairly shivered.

The beauteous maiden he had saved
  Had wrought a transformation,
And he was hopelessly enslaved—
  A wholly new sensation.

This lovely girl should be his wife,
  However poor or birthless;
Without her he perceived that life
  Was absolutely worthless.

Her home might be in villadom,
  Her people might be " shoddy ";
'Twould make a difference to some,
  But not to Lord Tomnoddy.

He longed to know the maiden's name,
  Yet hardly durst demand it.
He gave his card: she did the same;
  And eagerly he scanned it.

"*Miss Mabel Gray.*" With reverent touch
 He held the dainty label ;
He never knew till then how much
 He liked the name of Mabel.

He called as early as he deemed
 Consistent with propriety :
To his delight, the Grays, it seemed.
 Were people " in Society."

He found they knew his brother Jack
 (Most excellent of topics) ;
They asked when he was coming back
 From cruising in the tropics.

For Jack was with his ship just then—
 A smart and handsome sailor ;
A veritable prince of men,
 The idol of his tailor.

A finer form of human mould
 No sculptor could embody ;
And more than this, a heart of gold
 Had handsome Jack Tomnoddy.

And though my lord was, as you see,
 A despicable creature,
His love for Jack was said to be
 His one redeeming feature.

Henceforth, his lordship, wet or fair,
 Found some excuse or other
To fly to Mabel's side, and there
 Be bored by Mabel's mother.

And Mrs. Gray saw very clear
   Advantages marital
In eighty thousand pounds a year
   Attaching to a title.

At length my lord declared himself,
   As well as he was able,
And laid his title, lands, and pelf
   Before the lovely Mabel.

The answer of Miss Mabel Gray
   Was rather unexpected :
For in the sweetest, kindest way
   His lordship was rejected.

She ne'er had seen him show before
   Such signs of deep emotion ;
A dignity his features wore,
   Of which she had no notion.

He gravely bowed without a word,
   And mournfully departed ;
In truth the wretched little lord
   Was fairly broken-hearted.

For months he travelled far and wide
   In all the haunts of fashion ;
And, plunged in dissipation, tried
   To cure his hopeless passion.

He went to theatre, ball, and race ;
   He tried the gaming-table ;
But everywhere he saw the face
   And heard the voice of Mabel.

He occupied six months or so
  In never-ceasing movement,
But after all detected no
  Perceptible improvement.

For, whether climbing Alpine heights,
  Or on the ocean sailing,
He found his struggles and his flights
  Completely unavailing.

He travelled far, he travelled fast,
  Through every part of Europe—
In vain ! So he resolved at last
  To give the travel-cure up.

Then home he came, with grizzled hair.
  And health and vigour waning,
And found his brother Jack was there—
  His only joy remaining.

And soon he learnt, to his surprise.
  Jack knew his love's brief history ;
And, gazing in his brother's eyes,
  He understood the mystery.

My Lord Tomnoddy now began
  To see the why and wherefore :
His brother was the only man
  That she could ever care for.

He read the truth he had not heard :
  He knew their troth was plighted ;
He tried in vain to speak a word,
  To say he was delighted.

He wrung Jack's hand, and went away,
    With nothing more explicit—
The valet at his door next day
    No answer could elicit.

They broke the door and on the ground,
    A cold and lifeless body,
Shot by his own rash hand, they found
    The fifteenth Lord Tomnoddy.

A note was crumpled in his hand,
    His dying words expressing:
" Dear Jack, I'm sure you'll understand.
    I wish you every blessing.

" I've found the surest of all cures—
    I felt I could not face it—
I'm glad to think the title's yours;
    And Mabel—she will grace it.

" Good bye! My brain is overwrought—
    You'll break it to my mother:
And sometimes give a kindly thought
    To your unhappy brother."

The Christian World Magazine, FEBRUARY, 1888.

THE PASSENGER FOR CREWE.

A T half-past six on a winter's eve,
 The Irish Mail was about to leave
  The Terminus. Euston Square;
When an elderly gentleman. hot and flushed,
Through the lingering crowd on the platform brushed,
And straight to the door of a first class rushed
  In a state of wild despair.

Himself and his luggage inside were crammed
With the aid of a porter; the door was slammed,
  As the train had almost started.
The engine snorted, as who should say.
"If you want to be left behind. you may."
Then a "Right behind!" and a "Right away!"
And into the darkness without delay
  The Irish Mail departed.

The elderly gentleman breathed again
When he found himself safely inside the train
  That had nearly gone off without him.
Asleep in a very short time he dropped.
But awoke when the train at Willesden stopped,
And out of the window his head he popped.
  And anxiously looked about him.

"Guard! guard!" he exclaimed, as in direst need;
And the kindly official came up with speed.
  "Guard, have we arrived at Crewe?"

"No, sir," said the man, as he turned aside,
A very perceptible grin to hide.
"Oh, thank you," the elderly gent replied,
    "I am much obliged to you."

Then the engine whistled and moved ahead,
And rapidly out of the station sped
    The Irish Boat Express;
And the elderly gentleman, as before,
Curled up in his corner, and soon once more
Fell sweetly asleep and began to snore
    In dreamy forgetfulness.

And after a time he awoke again,
As the brake was applied and the groaning train
    Rolled into the Rugby station.
He pulled down the window, and peering out,
For the name of the station he looked about,
And finding none, he began to shout
    For the guard in desperation.

"Guard! guard!" in agonised tones he cried
And the guard came hurrying to his side.
    "Guard, have we arrived at Crewe?"
"No, sir; it's a long ways from this yer.
I'll tell you what, sir; you needn't stir,
But when we get there, why, I'll call you, sir."
"Oh, thank you, guard," said the passenger,
    "I am greatly obliged to you."

The guard, as he shut himself in his van,
Thought, "Ain't he a fussy old gentleman?
    But he's good for a tip," he said.

They stopped at Nuneaton and Stafford, too,
And when, about ten minutes overdue.
The train rattled noisily into Crewe,
He had such a number of things to do,
That the thought of the gent in the first-class flew
　　Clean out of the poor guard's head.

And the innocent passenger took his rest,
And never (poor man!) for an instant guessed
　　That Crewe had been left behind;
And possibly, if he had been aware
Of the terrible truth, he'd have torn his hair,
Or in some other manner portrayed despair;
But he sat as he might in his own arm-chair.
And peacefully slumbered without a care,
And trusting the guard to awake him there,
　　Reposed with easy mind.

On, on the train through the darkness flew,
And now it had run to the north of Crewe
　　Some mile and-a-half or more,
When all of a sudden a something brought
To the mind of the guard the appalling thought
Of the elderly first-class gent he ought
　　To have called some time before.

With trembling hand and bewildered brain
He clutched at the cord, and along the train
　　To the driver the signal ran.
For here was a gent, and a first-class, too,
Perhaps a director, for all he knew,
Who'd told him he wanted to stop at Crewe,
And was now being carried away right through
　　To Chester, at least, poor man!

And quickly the driver applied the brake,
Though he couldn't make out why the guard should take
    Such a sudden and grave decision ;
And the passengers put out their heads to see
What the reason for stopping the train could be.
And some were affrighted, and some were free
In their language regarding the company,
And somebody shouted " It's all UP ;
    We're in for a big collision."

And then as the train moved slowly back,
Their faces grew blacker and yet more black,
    And their wonderment still increased.
And after a time they arrived at Crewe,
And the guard was in a decided stew,
For the risk he was running full well he knew.
But he thought, " The old gent didn't seem a screw ;
If he does as a first-class ought to do,
    He's good for a bob, at least."

So he put a good face on a baddish job,
Looking smart and cheerful to earn his " bob "—
    No guard on the line was sprucer —
And so without losing a moment's space,
He ran to the door at his nimblest pace,
And opened it wide with a smiling face,
    Saying, " Here we are at Crewe, sir.

" We're just a bit late, sir—I hope you've slept."
And into the carriage he lightly stepped ;
    And then without more ado,
To take out the gentleman's things began,
Saying, " Please look as lively, sir, as you can.

Have you got any other things in the van ? "
" Stay, stay," said the elderly gentleman ;
    " I'm not getting out at Crewe.

" I wanted to know when the train got there,
But the reason, of course, is my own affair ;
    Still, I don't mind telling *you*.
The fact is, I've lately been rather ill—
I think I must somewhere have caught a chill—
And of course I'm obliged to be careful still,
On pain of another long doctor's bill ;
So, on leaving my home at Camden Hill,
I promised my daughter I'd take a pill
    When the train arrived at Crewe."

The Christian World Magazine, MARCH, 1888.

"A FOOL AND HIS MONEY."

SOME years ago, on a certain door
   In Bishopsgate Street Without,
Was an old brassplate, but the words it bore
   You wouldn't perhaps make out.

The plate was decidedly worse for wear,
   But you possibly might decipher it ;
And the name of a well-known firm was there,
   If you looked with a careful eye for it.

Messrs. Swindell and Rooke were a wealthy house,
  Though their name was obscure and dim ;
And Benjamin Rooke was a man of *nous :*
  There was no getting over him.

When a " good thing " was going, this wily firm
  Was sure to be there, I've heard ;
And they always got hold of the fattest worm,
  For the Rooke was an early bird.

His rivals were easily left behind
  By the smartness of Mr. Rooke ;
And though sailing uncommonly near the wind,
  He had never been brought to book.

So none of the mercantile houses bore
  An older repute or higher,
And very few men were respected more
  Than Benjamin Rooke, Esquire.

One day, when his morning's work was done
  And he felt it was time to eat,
As the bells of St. Paul's chimed half-past one
  He stepped into Bishopsgate Street.

He walked along with a lordly air
  (He was rich, and he let you know it)
To his mutton chop "rare," his usual fare,
  Washed down with a pint of Moët.

And as Benjamin Rooke to his luncheon hied,
  A man from behind him passed,
Looked earnestly into his face, and cried,
  In a tone of relief, " At last "

His Lincoln and Bennett was smart and bright,
  And elegant his attire,
And he took off his hat with an air polite
  To Benjamin Rooke, Esquire.

" Ah, many a long, long day I've sought
  For you, Sir," the stranger said ;
And Benjamin Rooke, as he heard him, thought
  He seemed by his tone well-bred.

" I fear that you hardly remember me,
  And I couldn't, of course, expect it ;
But if I may tell you my history
  Perhaps you will recollect it.

" On a winter's morning in '72—
  It's nearly ten years ago—
A half-starved beggar accosted you,
  And the ground was white with snow.

" His face was pallid and gaunt and wan,
  His teeth in the cold wind chattered ;
And what little clothes the poor wretch had on
  Were shabby and worn and tattered.

" Five hungry children, an ailing wife,
  Had driven him almost mad ;
He wondered if aught could be worse than life—
  If death could be half as bad.

" His piteous tale of want he told,
  And suffice it, Sir, to say,
You listened—you pitied—you gave him gold—
  You saved seven lives that day !

" And an oath that shivering beggar swore,
   While his eyes with tears were wet,
That if Fate ever smiled upon him once more
   He would pay that sacred debt.

"It was little, perhaps, to a man like you,
   Whose coffers are full to the brim ;
But oh, my good Sir, if you only knew
   What that sovereign meant to *him !*

" It gave him the power of winning back
   His place among decent men ;
It gave him a start on the upward track—
   He has prospered much since then.

" Though your name was unknown to him, yet, I trow,
   Your face he could ne'er forget ;
That beggar is standing before you now—
   I have come, Sir, to pay my debt ! "

Now, Benjamin made it a rule to " pass "
   When a beggar held out his hat,
And he knew he had never been " such an ass "
   As to part with a pound like that.

The stranger had made a mistake, he knew,
   And he thought, " Well, it's really funny
That *I* should resemble a booby who
   Goes chucking away his money."

" You haven't made any mistake by chance ? "
   Said he ; " for I'm bound to mention
That I don't remember the circumstance
   To which you have called attention."

" Oh, no," said the stranger; " I ne'er mistook
  A face in my life; don't doubt it."
" Well, I won't contradict you," said Mr. Rooke,
  " If you're perfectly sure about it.

"But you've done the right thing, and I sha'n't forget
  Among all my friends to spread it;
You have come to discharge what you call a debt
  In a manner that does you credit."

The stranger produced a well-filled book
  From a pocket inside his coat,
And out of a pretty thick bundle took
  A brand-new five-pound note.

" I haven't, I find to my great regret,
  Any smaller amount," said he;
" But perhaps you will add to my previous debt
  By changing this note for me."

So Benjamin Rooke the fiver took,
  And gave him the change in gold;
And he thought, as his hand the stranger shook,
  He never would loose his hold.

" It's a good day's work that I've done," he said.
  " I couldn't have done a better;
And, believe me, although the amount I've paid,
  Yet still I remain your debtor."

" Well, ' fools and their money,'" thought Mr. Rooke,
  As the stranger walked away;
" Yet I shouldn't have thought, by the fellow's look,
  He was such a confounded ' jay.'"

So he went to his lunch, where a cosy place
  Was reserved for him near the fire ;
And the head-waiter bowed when he saw the face
  Of Benjamin Rooke, Esquire.

" No, I'd never have thought he was such an ass ;
  For he looked like a man of sense,"
Said Benjamin Rooke, as he sipped his glass
  At his unknown friend's expense.

The stranger had paid for his lunch that day,
  So he made up his mind to " go it,"
And he ordered up, in a lordly way,
  An additional pint of Moët.

He smiled when they handed to him the score,
  For somebody else defrayed it,
And, by way of enjoying the joke still more,
  With the stranger's note he paid it.

But the satisfied smile forsook his brow
  In a very decided fashion,
When the waiter came back to report "as how
  This 'ere fi'-pun' note's a flash 'un ! "

The Christian World Magazine, APRIL, 1888.

ODE TO A MASHER.

CHOICE product of a cultured age!
   Fit theme to grace a poet's page
    With ode or lyric!
O Masher, may I make so free
As humbly to indite to thee
    A panegyric?

What joy and pride thou dost impart
To all who have an eye for art,
    O matchless Masher!
What happiness thou dost confer
On tailor, hatter, shoemaker,
    And haberdasher!

Yet some there are whose sluggish sense
Can e'en resist the effluence
    Of thy perfection;
Yea, some who unto all thy kind
Can entertain a well-defined
    And strong objection.

Such deadened souls—I know them well—
Whene'er they meet thee in Pall Mall
    Or Piccadilly,
Are wont to curl the scornful lip,
And crack the senseless gibe and quip,
    And call thee silly.

And urchins greet thee passing by
With, " Ain't 'e got 'em on ?   Oh, my ! "
    Or " Oo's yer 'atter ? "
Not that the comments or the jokes
Of ignorant and vulgar folks
    Can greatly matter.

The Yankees designate thee " dude,"
A term that sounds extremely rude,
    Although its history,
And sense seem likely to remain,
As far as I can ascertain,
    Involved in mystery.

Oh ! I could gaze till crack of doom
Upon thine exquisite costume
    In wonder ceaseless :
Thy pantaloons so superfine
That bag not at the knees like mine,
    Thy coat so creaseless.

When'er I meet thee in the street
I almost grovel at thy feet,
    Thy splendour seeing ;
Yet there are things I fain would know,
Could I presume to question so
    Superb a being.

And first, O Masher, I am fain
To ask thee where thou dost obtain
    Thy faultless raiment.
Thy tailor's name confide to me,
And, further, tell me what may be
    His terms of payment.

And pray expound the reason why
A collar so extremely high
 Thy neck's encased in.
Its cut severe recalls the jar
That Mr. Keiller's Dundee mar-
 malade is placed in.

So white and bright, and round and tight,
I do not doubt that it is quite
 Of style the acme;
But how thy throat endures the strain
I can't conceive; with frightful pain
 The thing would rack me.

Good heavens! to be trussed up like that
The whole day long! I shudder at
 The bare idea.
Yet thou cans't smile and look at ease.
Though there must be an awful squeeze
 On thy trachea.

And why those spats of spotless hue,
That half conceal thy pointed shoe
 Of patent leather?
It cannot be to warm thy feet,
For thou dost wear them through the heat
 Of July weather.

Perhaps to amateurs of dress
Like thee, O Masher, they possess
 Their fascination;
But to the inexperienced eye
They seem to spoil the set of thy
 Continuations.

Why does thine eye that glass retain,
Though not without apparent pain,
    From hour to hour?
To aid thy sight 'tis not employed,
For it is absolutely void
    Of optic power.

Yet, though its merits are but few,
That glass can never make thy view
    Of objects hazier;
For very closely 'tis allied
To that for window panes supplied
    By any glazier.

Thy spacious, spotless, twelve-inch cuff
Is worth exhibiting to puff
    Some patent mangle;
But why beneath its ample fold
Do my astonished eyes behold
    A golden bangle?

And is my confidence misplaced,
That nature made that slender waist,
    That figure blameless?
Or dost thou don, as some declare,
An article of female wear
    That shall be nameless?

How splendid is thy haughty air!
How dignified thy changeless stare!
    How supercilious!
Tho' some, to see thine arching brow
And languid eye, might think that thou
    Wert simply bilious.

Intelligence, so prized by some,
Is justly deemed by masherdom
　　A superfluity;
And so we know that days and days
Are spent in practising that gaze
　　Of mere vacuity.

For that inordinate respect
That once was paid to intellect
　　Is fast receding.
A fatuous and haughty stare
Is now considered everywhere
　　The height of breeding.

O Masher, some in thee have found
An argument on which to ground
　　The faith Darwinian;
For clothe th' ancestral ape like thee,
Thy very likeness it would be
　　In their opinion.

Oh! let some famous sculptor strike
From deathless stone thine image, like
　　In form and feature;
Thy clothes, thy collar, cuffs, and hat,
Thine eye-glass (oh, forget not that!),
　　Thou precious creature!

That so the Antipodean* eye
'Mid London's wreck thy form may spy
　　With wonder smitten;
And to a future age declare
What sort of looking creatures were
　　The sons of Britain.

　　　　* Macaulay's New Zealander,

And if to doubt he should begin
What place thou occupiest in
   Creation's plan,
Dame Nature, should she pass that way,
Might usefully stand up and say,
   "This was a *man*."

The Christian World Magazine, MAY, 1888.

THE TALE OF A TIN BOX.

A NOBLE house was Bantam Hall;
   A wealthy dame lived in it,
Of temper short, of figure tall—
   Miss Anastasia Spinnett.

Her youth was somewhat in arrears;
   In fact, this maiden lady
Was on the side of fifty years
   Denominated "shady."

The love of men she long had proved
   To be a vain delusion;
And now, from social life removed,
   She lived in strict seclusion.

Her maiden heart no more inclined
   In masculine directions:
On bipeds of another kind
   She lavished her affections.

The chicken-house at Bantam Hall
  Was elegant and spacious.
Constructed with a view to all
  Requirements gallinaceous.

Her fowls were as a priceless gem
  To good Miss Anastasia ;
She would have scorned to part with them
  For all the wealth of Asia.

For they were of the finest breeds,
  And fit for king or caliph ;
And well looked after were their needs
  By William Stubbs the bailiff.

Now on a February morn
  The day was slowly breaking,
When Stubbs the customary corn
  Was to the chickens taking.

But when he came, he looked about.
  And muttered, " What the dickens "—
A phrase he used when much put out—
  " Has got the Missus' chickens ? "

Alas ! the finest fowls were gone.
  As Stubbs at once detected ;
" Oh. how the Missus *will* take on ! "
  He ruefully reflected.

Then wrapt in thought with insight rare
  He quickly reached the bottom
Of this mysterious affair :
  Says he, " It's thieves has got 'em ! "

He went within and told the tale :
Miss Spinnett was distracted.
But it were best to draw a veil
Upon the scene enacted.

And when her wrath had softened down
She reached the stage reflective :
" Quick, William, ride into the town,
And summon a detective."

And soon Inspector Payne was there,
A silent man and serious ;
No word he uttered, and his air
To Stubbs appeared mysterious.

He poked about the fowl-house locks,
Explored the nests and perches—
At last a tin tobacco-box
Rewarded his researches.

For o'er the most expert of thieves
There hangs a kind of nemesis,
By which he generally leaves
A something on the premises.

Inspector Payne had found a clue,
And though 'twas what he needed,
Yet clues deceive, as no one knew
More thoroughly than he did.

The box was one that you might take
And with a thousand mate it,
For there was nought about its make
To differentiate it.

But one important point was clear :
    The theft had been enacted
By one whose criminal career
    Must needs have been protracted.

So Payne, without delaying aught,
    Or taking time to think, went
In search of one who was, he thought,
    The probable delinquent.

Elias Stokes, I'm bound to own,
    Was one among the many
Whose characters are called " well-known,"
    And yet they haven't any.

The man was healthy, young, and strong,
    But dissolute and lazy,
And his ideas of right and wrong
    Were lamentably hazy.

The property of other folks
    To him was most attractive ;
In its pursuit Elias Stokes
    Was very smart and active.

He never tried to earn his bread
    By honest work and labour,
And most of all he coveted
    The chickens of his neighbour.

When Payne arrived, Elias knew
    The object of his visit—
A thing he was accustomed to—
    But still he asked, " What is it ? "

And when he heard the charge preferred,
    His mien was limp and flabby,
Although he swore he " knew no more
    About it than a babby."

Before the Bench he had to go,
    But spite his best endeavour,
Against Elias Payne could show
    No evidence whatever.

Elias solemnly averred
    That stealing wasn't in him,
And, though as guiltless as a bird,
    "The p'lice 'ad took agin 'im."

But many times before that day
    The bench had seen Elias,
And so against him, truth to say,
    They had a certain bias.

So by his previous history
    The wretched man was stranded,
And for a week in custody
    Elias was remanded.

Now Payne had got a crafty plan—
    In dodges none could match him—
He knew Elias was the man,
    And he resolved to catch him.

Six more that day upon the scene
    Had made their forced appearance,
And of their pockets there had been
    The customary clearance.

So Payne took all the things within,
  And on the table flung them,
And artfully he placed the tin
  Tobacco-box among them.

With manner unconcerned enough
  Inspector Payne inspected,
While each from out the heap of stuff
  His property selected.

Poor Stokes was taken unaware—
  Without the least suspicion
He picked the box up with an air
  Of sudden recognition.

" Hullo, now ! none of that ! " said Payne,
  In brutal accents speaking ;
" Now just you put it back again ;
  That box I saw you sneaking."

" Why, Mr. Payne, it's mine, I swear ;
  I lost it somewheres, lately ;
I bought it for a bob, sir—there !—
  Last month, of Mr. Whateley."

" Oh, yes ! " said Payne.   " That's very fine !
  You *do* know how to go it."
Said Stokes, " Why, I can prove it's mine :
  I'll tell you how I know it.

" Just underneath the lid there'll be
  A kind of S, just faint-like ;
The knife it slipped, and so, you see,
  It's like, and yet it ain't like."

" Yes, there's the mark," said Payne, " 1 see;
Well, then you're sure about it ? "
" I'll take my Bible oath," said he,
" It's mine—you needn't doubt it."

" Well, I can tell you something more,"
Said Payne, his victim eyeing ;
" That box inside the fowl-house door
At Bantam Hall was lying ! "

Elias looked like one distraught,
And blank was his expression ;
Then, feeling he was fairly caught,
He made a full confession.

And when he'd served upon the mill
His fifteen months' hard labour,
He did not cease to covet still
The chickens of his neighbour.

But now, whene'er at dewy eve
He prowls around, you'll find him
Extremely careful not to leave
His property behind him.

The Christian World Magazine, JULY, 1888.

THE WAIL OF A WEARY M.P.

O YOU, whose short-sighted ambition
   Aspires to political fame,
Give ear to an old politician
   Who knows all the moves of the game.
There are no more detestable fetters,
   For one who's supposed to be free,
Than the bondage implied in the letters—
   The coveted letters, " M.P."

It's all very well for officials
   Who pocket five thousand a year,
But for others the magic initials
   Are purchased uncommonly dear.
Not to mention the cost of elections
   And endless subscriptions—ah, me !—
There are other more weighty objections
   To being a British M.P.

Till they started the earlier closing
   We often till morning were kept;
And small were our chances of dozing,
   For, if for an instant we slept,
We heard the division-bell tinkling
   To hinder us taking our ease—
Oh! believe me, you haven't an inkling
   Of the woes of unhappy M.P.s.

Now it's certainly very much better;
   But still it's annoying, you know,
When you're just in the midst of a letter,
   To hear the division-bell go.

Whene'er you sit down to your victuals,
　　Interrupted you're certain to be;
So you see it's not *all* "beer and skittles,"
　　The life of a British M.P.

Then you probably come in collision
　　With a Whip, when you're sneaking away;
" We're expecting a tightish division;
　　I really must beg you to stay."
So you can't get away when you want to,
　　However fatigued you may be,
And frequently not till it's gone two
　　His home sees the weary M.P.

When first you are sent to St. Stephen's
　　You think you're a very big man;
You intend to redress ev'ry grievance
　　And do all the good that you can.
Where'er there are wrongs, you will right 'em.
　　Make ev'ry one happy and free—
But you quickly become a mere item,
　　A commonplace party M.P.

You ask any number of questions,
　　And badger the party in power;
You make the most useful suggestions,
　　And often declaim by the hour.
But it rather disturbs your composure,
　　In your finest oration, to see
The Leader proposing the closure,
　　That bane of the zealous M.P.

You mean to obey your convictions,
　　With conscience alone as your guide;

But you find there are certain restrictions—
　You never can tell till you've tried.
It is useless to raise an objection :
　With your party you've got to agree;
Or you'll find at another election
　Your name will be minus " M.P."

You must stick to your party allegiance
　Without hesitation or doubt,
Though your mind be as blank as a Fijian's
　On what you are voting about.
Though possessed of convictions undying,
　You rarely can vote as you please :
It is often excessively trying
　For scrupulous-minded M.P.s.

And then in the month of September,
　Although it's the Autumn Recess,
Little shooting you get, if a Member,
　For meetings you're bound to address.
Away with your gun and your cartridges !
　A hundred miles off you must be.
You must give up your days with the partridges
　If you're an unhappy M.P.

Then the chances are far more than " evens "
　That after the " Autumn Campaign "
You have to be back at St. Stephen's,
　And go into harness again.
Why, I've not had a chance at a pheasant,
　And now there's no hunting for me.
Oh ! existence is not very pleasant
　For one who's a British M.P.

Yes, the worst are these Sessions in autumn;
  They're really a crying abuse.
And lately they seem to have brought 'em
  As regular things into use.
To St. Stephen's the Government drags you—
  It's useless attempting to flee—
And there the majority gags you,
  And makes you a silent M.P.

Autumn Sessions I call an iniquity,
  At Government's door to be laid;
A symptom of moral obliquity
  In those who resort to their aid.
They encourage a wasting of time, Sir,
  In ever increasing degrees.
They're a high constitutional crime, Sir!
  An outrage on Britain's M.P.s.

It's useless repining, however;
  We must go, whether willing or not;
But for Ministers I shall endeavour
  To make it uncommonly hot.
We shall be at Supply in Committee,
  With most of us wholly at sea:
If you knew what it was, you would pity
  The weary and jaded M.P.

It often has struck me with wonder
  To think how we ever survive;
How few of us seem to knock under,
  How many of us are alive.
One would think, if we got through the rigour
  Of the work, we should die of *ennui;*
But it shows what exceptional vigour
  Must dwell in a British M.P.

Then be warned by my pitiful story—
　　Though I very much fear that you won't—
You, who seek for political glory,
　　Take *Punch's* wise counsel, and " Don't ! "
Abandon your fond aspiration ;
　　My friends, you may take it from me,
That there's no greater fraud in creation
　　Than the magical letters, " M.P."

The Christian World Magazine, DECEMBER, 1888.

~~~~~~~~~~~~~~~~~~~~~

THE AMATEUR DETECTIVE.

WHEN I was quite a little lad
　　Of seven and a fraction,
Detective stories always had
　　For me a strange attraction.
I used to bite my finger nails
　　(Which met with sharp correction)
While poring over thrilling tales
　　Of crime and its detection.

My small ambitious heart was fired
　　With dreams of future glories ;
I read and read and never tired
　　Of those delightful stories ;
And even then my infant mind
　　Was made up, irrespective
Of what my parents had designed,
　　To be a great detective.

I used to scare the parlour-maid
  And give the "dad" surprises
By knocking at the door, arrayed
  In various disguises.
And as my early years unfold
  In vision retrospective,
I see myself at eight years old
  An embryo detective.

At school I had a valued friend,
  A certain local "bobby,"
And many a stolen hour I'd spend
  In talking of my hobby.
In class my mind I could not fix
  On surd or conic section,
Evolving artful schemes and tricks
  Of criminal detection.

And as I grew to man's estate
  I used to haunt the places
Where rogues and thieves do congregate—
  I even went to races.
But soon parental tyranny
  Applied a stern corrective
To visions fond, that pictured me
  A world-renowned detective.

My father sent for me one day—
  The interview was stormy—
He told me once for all that they
  Had other prospects for me.
My threats his stubbornness increased,
  My prayers were ineffective,
But I resolved to be, at least,
  An *amateur* detective.

To yield to such decided views
   I deemed it only prudent;
And so at St. Bartholomew's
   I entered as a student.
Soon came the chance that I had dreamed
   In days of deep dejection;
Great crimes occurred, and helpless seemed
   Professional detection.

Crime stalked abroad unchecked; I saw
   A golden opportunity.
I swore I'd vindicate the law,
   And save the whole community.
Policemen were at sea, because
   Their training was defective;
The thing distinctly wanted was
   An amateur detective.

And now at last I found the good
   Of all my childish reading;
For thanks to that I understood
   The method of proceeding.
Of course you must be well disguised,
   To compass your objective;
Or else you might be recognised
   As being a detective.

So, first, you black your face with care—
   Burnt cork's the best material—
A false moustache of course you wear,
   And eke a false imperial.
To don a coat would never do:
   Shirt-sleeves are more effective;
And none can then discern in you
   The vigilant detective.

'Twas thus equipped I wandered where
   A crime had been committed;
With stealthy and mysterious air
   About the place I flitted.
I questioned men, and women too,
   In this and that direction—
For, if there's one thing I can do,
   It's amateur detection.

I skipped among them, staring hard
   Right into people's faces,
And, just to take them off their guard,
   I made absurd grimaces.
I meant to scare the guilty man
   And catch him unsuspecting—
But people did not like my plan
   Of amateur-detecting.

They crowded round with aspect grim:
   I stood my ground unflinching.
Then some one shouted out, "That's him!"
   And recommended lynching.
They seized me, swore I'd done the crime,
   With loud and coarse invective.
In vain I cried, "Good people, I'm
   An amateur detective."

Though I endeavoured all I knew
   To show the mob their blunder,
They came within an inch or two
   Of tearing me asunder.
A horrible and ghastly scene
   Was clearly in prospective:
In two more minutes there'd have been
   A stiff and stark detective.

But two policemen chanced that way,
    And dragged me from their clutches.
(For some time after, I may say,
    I went about on crutches.)
Then to the station, one each side,
    They marched me for inspection.
I told them I was occupied
    In amateur detection.

A brusque inspector put me through
    A searching inquisition;
Then in the cells without ado
    They locked me on suspicion.
Next day my freedom I regained—
    Since then, upon reflection,
I rather think my zeal has waned
    For amateur detection.

The Christian World Magazine, JANUARY, 1889.

THE BRITISH JUROR.

WHEN first I took a house in town,
    To make me sad and gloomy
My friend and neighbour, Thomas Brown,
    Explained my duties to me.
He ended thus :—"The worst of woes
    That householders endure is
The duty, which the laws impose,
    To serve on British juries."

" Nay, then," said I, " if that's the worst,
 'Tis not what I was fearing ;
It may be rather strange at first,
 But I am persevering.
And what idea could be more grand,
 What aspiration purer,
Than thus to serve one's native land
 And be a British juror ? "

I'd never been inside the Courts,
 But I enjoyed perusing
The daily papers' law reports,
 And found them most amusing.
I'd read of " scenes," of desperate men,
 And women wild with fury,
Who struggled in the dock, and then
 Abused the judge and jury.

I thought with glee that I should see
 Most interesting cases,
And vowed the jury-box must be
 The pleasantest of places.
But soon I knew the sober truth,
 And saw how premature is
The notion of one's early youth
 Regarding British juries.

I'd read how once a judge's wit
 Convulsed the Court with laughter.
How counsel nearly had a fit
 For twenty minutes after ;
But by the most complete of tests
 I've found there's nothing poorer
Than such of these forensic jests
 As reach the British juror.

I'll ne'er forget the case that first
 Came under my decision;
A ship (of vessels most accursed)
 Was sunk by a collision;
And some one sued a firm, who'd been
 So weak as to insure her—
But what on earth they meant was clean
 Beyond the British juror.

A host of strange sea terms they used,
 And no suspicion harboured
That most of us were quite confused,
 Not knowing "port" from "starboard."
And when they read a dreary log,
 The case grew still obscurer,
Till they contrived to fairly fog
 The wretched British juror.

And then, when we could not agree,
 The judge, a monster cruel,
Just clapped us under lock and key,
 With neither food nor fuel.
And after six long hours were past
 (How frail and insecure is
A suitor's chance!), we tossed at last—
 A way with British juries.

But infinitely worse than that,
 Much harsher, far absurder
My treatment was, when once I sat
 Upon a charge of murder.
The progress of the case was slow:
 Perhaps 'twas all the surer:
But it was nearly death, I know,
 To one unhappy juror.

At four p.m., I grieve to tell,
  A bailiff came and took us,
And at the Cannon Street Hotel
  Proceeded straight to book us.
A man would surely have to be
  Of ills a rare endurer,
To realise the misery
  Of an imprisoned juror.

Eleven strangers! and to be
  A week in their society!
Such imbeciles they seemed to me,
  I longed for some variety.
I chafed and fumed, I raved and swore;
  It put me in a fury;
The days dragged on, and more and more
  I loathed that British jury.

The bailiff would not let me speak
  To any other creature;
In durance vile I passed the week
  With no redeeming feature.
And every night he locked us up;
  No felons were securer.
Oh, passing bitter is the cup
  Of an imprisoned juror.

How I abhorred that gaoler grim!
  Like convicts we were treated.
And now, as I look back on him
  (I don't want this repeated),
It would not grieve my soul at all,
  Nor should I weep or wail if
Some dire disaster should befall
  That loathsome jury bailiff.

11

Yes, Thomas Brown was right to quiz
  My foolish aspiration;
For serving on a jury is
  My pet abomination.
My fond illusions all are o'er;
  My judgment's now maturer;
If I can help it, never more
  I'll be a British juror.

I'm now as crafty as a fox,
  And oft, without suspicion,
I have escaped the jury-box
  By feigned indisposition.
A doctor in my room's installed,
  And I am swathed in flannel,
Whene'er I hear that I've been called
  Upon a jury-panel.

It isn't quite the thing, I know;
  The fraud is undeniable;
But when they treat a jury so,
  I think it justifiable.
It's all the system that's at fault:
  I don't know what the cure is,
But statesmen, if they're worth their salt,
  Should think of British juries.

The Christian World Magazine, MARCH, 1889.

BRIBERY AND CORRUPTION!

OR,

THE COMIC COMPANION TO THE CORRUPT PRACTICES ACT.

———

[*Published with Six Engravings.*]

———

" No payment or contract for payment shall . . . be made on
account of bands of music, torches, flags, banners,
cockades, *ribbons*, or other marks of distinction."—16 and
47 Vict. cap. 51, section 16.

*Penalty, on summary conviction, a fine not exceeding one
hundred pounds.—Ibid. section 21.*

THE DRAPER'S DILEMMA.

" TWO dozen blue rosettes at nine and half is nineteen
shillings.

What else, mum, can I show you?—I've a novelty in
frillings—

Ten yards of satin ribbon? Thank you—yes, mum,
charming weather—

Nineteen and seven—one pound six and six, mum,
altogether.

Is there nothing else this morning?" Quoth the lady,
" Nothing more,"

As she picked the parcel up and moved serenely to the
door.

"Stay, madam!" cried the shopman. "You'll excuse
me if I say

Our terms are strictly cash, mum, and you've quite
forgot to pay."

"Not at all, I never meant to pay," the lady said
demurely,

"It's against the law to do so—you're aware of *that*
sir, surely."

"You never meant to pay," the shopman cried, "for
what you bought?"

"Of course not," answered she; "I never harboured
such a thought.

I think," she added, sweetly, "that the law is rather
hard on

An enterprising tradesman, and I really beg your
pardon;

If it weren't for the Election, I would pay you in a
minute,

But, as it is, of course, I can't—you see, there's danger
in it."

"And you call yourself a lady?" cried the shopman,
in a passion,

"To go and swindle honest folks in this here sort of
fashion!

But it won't succeed with *me*—I'm up to these shop-
lifting tricks,

And I tell you straight I mean to have my one pound
six and six.

So you'd better pay up quickly, or I'll fetch a bobby——"
"Stop, man!"

The lady cried. "Remember, I'm a lady, you a
shopman!

And ere you stigmatise me as a shifty or 'shoplifty'
one,

Read Forty-six and Forty-seven Victoria, Chapter
    Fifty-one.

I've got a copy with me, and if you have no
    objection,

I'll read the words—let's see, oh! here it is—the 16th
    section—

'No payment shall be made for bands of music, torches,
    flags,

Banners, ribbons, or cockades'—or other emblematic
    rags.

So you see that if I paid the sum for which you are a
    claimant,

I should incur the penalty for an 'Illegal Payment.'

And you, my friend, would share the crime, and run
    the risk that I did;

You, too, would get the punishment the statute has
    provided.

I need not say that it would be to me a real affliction

To see you fined a hundred pounds on summary
    conviction.

I trust that this will lead your mind to serious
    reflections;

It's well that you should know the law relating to
    elections;

And when folks come for ribbons—let this be a timely
    warning—

Don't let them *pay* for what they buy: it isn't safe.
    Good morning!"

" No payment or contract for payment shall . . . be made on account of the conveyance of electors to or from the poll."
—46 and 47 Vict. cap. 51, section 7.

Penalty, on summary conviction, a fine not exceeding one hundred pounds,—Ibid. section 10.

A CAUTION TO CABMEN.

"THANK you, cabman," said the gentleman;
    " we've had, upon the whole,
A pleasant ride enough, and now we're all in time to
    poll.
It's better far than walking in the slush; although, of
    course,
I can't commend your taste in the selection of a horse.
I don't like ostentation, for a man's a fool who swaggers,
But I *do* prefer a horse that isn't suffering from staggers,
It's an interesting question whether, ere that horse
    deceases,
The wheezy vehicle you call a cab will fall to pieces.
And then, you know, your harness is unutterably
    shabby;
Still, on the whole——" "My fare is 'arf a crown,"
    remarked the cabby.
" Still, on the whole, I won't complain, for rare indeed
    my fate is
To get a lift of any sort for such a distance *gratis.*
And, cabman, you've a vote—I hope you'll poll for Mr.
    Brown."
The cabman answered nothing but " My fare is 'arf a
    crown."

" You made the same remark before," severely said the
gent,

As from his pocket he produced an Act of Parliament.

"Why, man, you surely are aware that this is polling
day,

And consequently, it's against the law for us to pay.

Consid'ring its importance to a person of your calling,

Your ignorance of statute-law is really quite appalling.

You ought to read and ascertain what Parliament has
done

By Forty-six and seven Victoria, Chapter Fifty-one.

You don't appear to know at all how very strict the Act
is—

What punishment it has assigned for each Illegal
Practice.

You've never heard about it, I suppose, but I (thank
Heaven !)

Have got a copy with me, and I'll read you section seven.

' *No payment shall be made for the conveyance of electors
Either to or from the poll '—*you see how much those
words affect us.

We're both of us electors—so I fear you're in a hole ;

For it's clear you can't be paid for *our* conveyance to
the poll.

I sympathise sincerely with a man in your position,

And as a friend I'll give you just one parting admonition.

When gentlemen engage your cab on polling day, much
safer it

Will be to see beforehand that they're qualified to pay
for it.

Such payment by electors, mind, a criminal offence is :

Both you and they are liable to awkward consequences.

The fine's a hundred pounds, you know, if you should
be convicted—

I say, that horse appears to me most seriously afflicted;
The shafts are pretty solid, and it's just as well,
      perhaps;
For if it weren't for their support, I'll wager he'd
      collapse.
And, by the bye, perhaps you want another job, my
      man;
So, if you'd like to drive us back this afternoon, you can.
Don't fear that I shall pay your fare and get you into
      trouble;
I wouldn't think of doing so—not if the fare was double!
No thanks, I beg; believe me that I feel a real enjoy-
      ment
In doing what I can to give the unemployed employ-
      ment.
Let's see, what time? The roads are so abominably
      dirty,
That it will be a stiffish pull—suppose we say 5.30?
We'll meet you at the Crown Hotel; perhaps we may
      be late—
We've got so many things to do—if so, of course you'll
      wait.
You'll see us—what? Ah yes, of course, you'll see us
      at the Crown
At half-past five. Ta-ta, my friend; I hope you'll vote
      for Brown."

THE WORKING MAN'S WOES.

" YOU'VE come to get your wages ? Well, I much
        regret to say,
You really can't be paid, my men, because its Polling-day.
I'll show you in a minute, if you'll give me your attention,
That you are clearly victims of a grave misapprehension.
In asking for your wages, my deluded friends, you make
What, in the circumstances, is a natural mistake.
In former days the law was lax, and so at most elections
The money used, as you're aware, to fly in all directions ;
The longest purse was pretty sure of winning in a canter,
But times are changed—as some one puts it, *tempora*
        mutantur.
(Excuse my inadvertent use of classic phrase: I know it's
A shocking habit that I have of quoting Latin poets.)
Now, at elections, if a man distributes money *liberè*,
Or *liberally,* as we say, they run him in for bribery.
The good old times are gone, and we may well say
        Transit gloria !
Since Chapter Fifty-one of Forty-six and seven Victoria,
That Act was passed expressly for the purpose of
        defeating
All Practices Corrupt, and chiefly bribery and treating.
And, though it's not so clearly wrong as giving beer or
        whisky,
It seems that paying wages to a voter's rather risky.
It's not expressly stated in the Statute's various sections,
But you'll see the matter well discussed in ' Rogers on
        Elections.'
I find, upon referring to that learned writer's pages,
That it's dangerous on Polling-day to pay your men
        their wages.

That is, if they're electors; for, of course, if you were
    not,
I hardly need observe that I would pay you like a shot.
It's true, the point is doubtful, but one cannot be too
    wary;
We're all so apt to make mistakes—*humanum est errare.*
At any rate, whatever the intention of the Act is,
I don't propose to run the risk of an Illegal Practice.
And if you don't believe *my* word, but go and ask the
    boss, you must
Expect, I tell you plainly, to be once for all '*non
    possumus'd* '—
You don't quite understand that phrase historic and
    oracular:
'*It simply can't be done*' conveys its force in the
    vernacular.
I'm rather glad to have the chance of bringing to your
    notice,
How doubtful an advantage the possession of a vote is.
And now, my friends, vamose the ranch—*cundum est*, in
    Latin :
This room is hardly big enough, you see, to swing a
    cat in;
And though, of course, your company is singularly
    pleasant,
Your room would be, if possible, more welcome just at
    present.
I very much regret I can't accede to your entreaty,
And so I wish you both Good-day—as Terence says,
    ' *Valete.*' "

" A person shall not let, lend, or employ for the purpose of the conveyance of electors to or from the poll . . . any carriage, horse, or other animal which he keeps or uses for the purpose of letting out for hire."—46 and 47 Vict. cap. 51, section 14.

Penalty, a fine not exceeding one hundred pounds.—Ibid. section 10.

WANTED—A LIFT.

" HI, Guv'nor! half a moment: will you take me in
your trap,
And drive me into town? You see I've had a slight
mishap.
I can't imagine how it was, but something broke the
girth,
And in a trice I found myself saluting mother earth.
It's clear that I can never catch the mare without
assistance :
She's galloping away like mad—you see her in the
distance.
It's just a bit disheartening to see your horse skedaddle,
While you are landed in the road with nothing but the
saddle.
Your passing at the moment was most lucky, on the
whole,
For otherwise I never should have been in time to poll.
I've come an awful distance, and to register my vote I'm
Most anxious, and that nag of yours will run us up in
no time.
I'll put the saddle in behind, and jump up in a
second——"
" Hold hard!" remarked the publican. " Without
your host you've reckoned.

It's very well for you to say you're quite prepared to
    nip in,
And ride with me to town, but I've a voice in that, my
    pippin.
Of course, if it was lawful, I would take you like a
    bird,
But there's a difficulty which to you has not occurred.
You see you've got to know the law, when you're in my
    profession ;
They're always passing Acts for us—a new 'un every
    Session.
I always keep 'em by me, and the number of 'em's
    awful ;
Why, bless your heart ! I've got at home, I do believe,
    a draw'full.
Of course you haven't learnt the law, and you can do
    without it ;
But if you care to listen, I can tell you all about it.
You see, it's all along of them teetotal chaps, that
    made,
In '83—I think it was—a dead set on the trade.
They hated seeing voters at elections taking beer,
And Parliament was somehow got to come and
    interfere ;
And so they passed a statute, by Her Majesty's
    directions,
To put a stop to bribery and treating at elections ;
And into it they put a lot of idiotic clauses,
Which show you what the ignorance of those who
    make the laws is.
Now one of these refers to traps, I think it's Section
    fourteen,
I'd like to know the fool who put a clause of such a
    sort in :

' *No horse or trap that's kept for hire shall be employed*
   to take
A voter to or from the poll '—and if the law you break,
The magistrates will quickly on your wheel apply the
   skid :
On summary conviction you'll be fined a hundred quid.
And so not only mayn't you stand a glass to e'er a soul,
But you mustn't give a friend a lift to take him to the
   poll,
Although the horse and cart's your own : this law you
   must admit is an
Outrageous interference with the freedom of a citizen.
Still, I'm a law-abiding man, as any one on earth,
And so I always try to give the ' beaks ' a widish berth :
They're kittle cattle, no mistake—I don't know any
   kittler ;
And if they're down on any man, it's on a licensed
   victualler.
And so, you see, I musn't do the service you require
Because I keep this horse and trap for letting out on
   hire.
You'll have to foot it, and, you know, you're young and
   in your prime—
I shouldn't be at all surprised if you got there in time.
It's quite a tidy distance, and I mustn't stop and talk,
And so I'll say ' Good afternoon '—I hope you'll like
   your walk."

"No refreshment of any kind must be allowed in the Committee Room."—Edge and Hardy's Practice of Elections, p. 73.

THE COMMITTEEMAN'S COMPLAINT.

"NOW just a little wee bit more," the fond wife kept
 entreating,
"Remember you'll be twelve long hours without a
 chance of eating.
I do declare, I'm quite afraid you'll die of inanition
Before the day is done—Jemima, put that other dish on,
And take away the empty ones. Now do, my dearest
 Tom, let
Me give you just a tiny bit of this delicious omelette."
"No, no, my dear," the victim cried; "I simply cannot
 do it;
Too much I've eaten, as it is—I fear that I shall rue it.
You mustn't think me wanting in politeness or in
 bonhomie,
But it's beyond the limits of my physical economy.
You don't appear to realise what I've already taken—
A mutton chop, two sausages, and twice of eggs and
 bacon,
Besides the haddock and the ham, and last, not least,
 the marmalade,
Which, I've been solemnly assured, digestion like a
 charm'll aid.
And then, you know, there's nothing like the oft
 replenished tea-cup
For filling each unoccupied recess of one's physique up.
It's possible that if I were a generation younger,
I still might feel, or think I felt, a lingering spark of
 hunger.

I remember, I remember—ah! I never shall forget it—
When I was young and greedy—if I liked a thing I
ate it.
Ah! then I was unconscious of the process of digestion,
And whether things agreed with me I never used to
question.
Whenever any dish was brought, to which I chanced to
cotton,
The things I'd previously consumed were instantly
forgotten;
The feeling of repletion vanished when I saw my
favourite,
No matter what I'd had before, I managed to make
way for it.
Alas! those days are gone, and though I think I'm
just as greedy,
I cannot eat as once I did, because it makes me seedy.
Already at my waist I feel a check upon my appetite,
My waistcoat seems too small for me—why ever did I
strap it tight?
So take away that omelette. As I said before, my lass,
it is
A thing that's quite beyond my alimentary capacities."
"Do make an effort," urged his wife, "for I should be
so cut up
If hungry you should feel before the polling booth is
shut up.
You're not allowed a morsel of refreshment—that's the
mandate—
Till eight o'clock to-night, my dear—I'm sure you'll
never stand it.
Of course, I'm very anxious for our candidate to get in,
But all the same I think that you've decidedly been
let in;

I wouldn't work for such a man—I'd very quickly quit
him, an

Ungrateful wretch, forbidding food and drink to his
Committee-man!

To keep you starving there from 8 a.m. to ditto p.m.!

They wouldn't play such tricks on *me*, I *should* just
like to see 'em—

Trust me, I'd teach them pretty sharp to mind their
stops and commas.

Now *do* just make an effort: try and eat for *my* sake,
Thomas!"

"No, no, my dear, I simply couldn't take another scrap;

Remember, I've already, as the Yankees say, 'gone
Nap.'

I think you really ought to let me off that omelette,
when you

Consider calmly what it means to go through such a
menu;

You've noticed that I haven't missed a solitary dish,

And on the top of all I've put the final layer of
'squish,'

In point of fact, you've stuffed me so that I can hardly
speak—

I do believe I've had enough to last me for a week!

And as to no refreshments in Committee-rooms, you
see,

They passed a law about such things in 1883.

The Act might well upon this point be clearer and
expliciter,

But still in the opinion of our candidate's solicitor,

Refreshments in Committee-rooms are dangerous; in
fact, he says

That it would probably be classed among Illegal
Practices.

Good gracious! why, it's nearly eight—I haven't got a
   minute ;

Here, quick, my coat! I doubt if I shall get my body
   in it.

I say, just look, dear, at **my nose**—I think I've got a
   smut on it.

No ? Very well—oh! look at this ; I knew I couldn't
   button it,

And only yesterday I thought how loose the coat had
   got.

I must be there before it strikes. We have to poll
   a lot

The moment that the polling booth is open ; they're to
   bring 'em

At eight o'clock precisely—where the dickens is my
   gingham ?

Oh, thanks. Now I must say 'Good bye'; I'm in an
   awful hurry—

Oh, I shall get along all right, my dear—you needn't
   worry.

And, by the bye, I sha'n't want any supper, love, to-
   night—

Why did I strap this waistcoat so abominably tight ? "

" Every elector who . . . accepts or takes any meat, drink,
entertainment, or provision shall be guilty of treating."—
46 and 47 Vict. cap. 51, section 1.

*Penalty, imprisonment, with or without hard labour, for a term
not exceeding one year, or a fine not exceeding two hundred
pounds.—Ibid, section 6.*

SONG OF THE STARVING ELECTORS.

WE'RE a body of starving electors—
    Though it isn't much *body* we own ;
You might easily take us for spectres,
    Except that we show every bone.

We're simply exhausted by famine,
    And as lean as a mummy Egyptian ;
If we had but the chance, we could cram in
    A meal of the squarest description.

It's all on account of a measure,
    That in '83 Parliament passed—
I suppose it was Heaven's displeasure
    At people neglecting to fast.

Or perhaps it was done by the Caucus,
    At any rate this is a fact—
When we want to get victuals they baulk us
    With this new Corrupt Practices Act.

It comes down with the swoop of an eagle
    On all who commit any kind
Of Practice Corrupt or Illegal—
    They're promptly imprison'd or fined.

I don't want to do what's unlawful,
  Such a thing never entered my head ;
But the hardship is something too awful,
  For the Act says we're not to be fed.

Its meaning in places is hidden,
  But one thing is clear on the whole—
Feeding voters is strictly forbidden
  Before, at, or after the poll.

" *No person shall give entertainment*
  To voters "—most plainly it speaks—
Under pain of a speedy arraignment
  Before Quarter Sessional " beaks."

This Statute prevents all collisions
  And conflicts of law and of fact !
For it gives us, by way of *provisions*,
  No others but those of the Act.

So, simply because I'm a voter,
  My weight is reduced to a feather ;
I can't get so much as a bloater
  To keep soul and body together.

And my body's so wasted with pining,
  I scarcely can crawl to the poll ;
If it goes on at this rate declining,
  I shall shortly be nothing but soul !

The law's so severe against treating,
  I sha'n't be surprised if in time
A Statute is passed to make eating
  Of any description a crime.

Perhaps what I'm saying is treason,
  And maybe I ought to be shot;
But I *should* like to know what's the reason
  Why pigs may eat, voters may not.

To *plump* for McPhamish they ask us,
  But its famishing makes us so *slim*,
And McPhamish I'll see at Damascus
  Before I go voting for *him*.

If this is the good of the franchise,
  To attenuate one at this rate;
You can't be surprised if a man shies
  At such a deplorable fate.

A vote isn't all beer and skittles,
  Though folks talk so grandly about it;
And if it's to cut off our victuals,
  I think we are better without it.

It's possible I may survive it,
  With the good constitution I've got;
But if you should ask me my private
  Opinion, I rather think not.

If I ever get through this election—
  A thing that remains to be proved—
I've resolved, after careful reflection,
  From the register I'll be removed.

I've no wish, at St. Stephen's a hero,
  The country's affairs to arrange,
And although a political zero,
  My *figure* will gain by the change.

My pathway in life will be brightened
    When this horrible franchise I lose;
I shall no more be free and enlightened,
    But at least I shall eat when I choose.

I shall merrily sit at my dinner,
    When future elections take place;
And notice the voters grow thinner
    In body, and paler in face.

With a sigh of relief I shall look back,
    In comfort possessing my soul,
At the time when, with limp knee and crook back,
    I wearily crawled to the poll.

~~~~~~~~~~~~~~~~~~~~~

PADDY'S REFLECTIONS ON THE FOURTH
OF JULY.

HURROO, my brave boys, for the glorious Fourth,
    When the bloodthirsty Britisher fled from oui
    shore—
Or was it the South that was bate by the North—
    It's meself that don't know—but I'll shout all the
    more.

It's the day that relased us from tyranny's bond,
    That made ivery one aiqual, a man and a brother;
For Freedom dwells only on this side the "pond,"
    And divil a bit have they got on the other.

If a gintleman *here* uses pistol or rifle—
  As gintlemen should, when it comes to a pinch—
They make no commotion about such a trifle—
  That's barrin' that murtherin' blackguard, Judge
  Lynch.

But out *there* if we'd taken such harmless divarsion,
  As some of us have, they would surely have hung us,
An' if we had stayed there—I'll make the assartion—
  Bedad, there'd be divil a whole neck among us.

There ye can't shoot the land-thief that lives by your
  labours;
  An' shure an' it's ivery thrue Irishman's right;
But *here* if we suffered the same wrongs, bejabers,
  We'd pepper the thievin' ould haythen on sight.

Here we're all of us free an' enlightened electors:
  Our votes have their price, tho', begorrah, it's small;
But the tyrants out *there* at the polls would reject us,
  An' divil a vote would they give us at all.

Then, hurroo, my brave boys, for the land of the free,
  Where we all have a fair chance our dollars to win,
So long as we shut out the Haythen Chinee,
  And sind back the immigrant paupers agin.

An' it's pleasant to-night, boys, whin business is done,
  We'll empty our glasses and fill up our pipes,
An' cursin' the Saxon, thank God, ivery one,
  That we live in the land of the Stars and the Sthripes.

The Wasp, SAN FRANCISCO,
  SATURDAY, JULY 7TH, 1883.

MY CONFESSION.

OH, shade of Great Edward, yclept the Confessor!—
I trow you're the party to whom to address a
Request for assistance—look downward with ruth
On a very ill-used and unfortunate youth,
On the point of inscribing—a gross indiscretion—
In a young lady's album his so-called Confession.
Are Confessions supposed with our secrets to deal,
Or merely, like language, our thoughts to conceal?
The safer result to achieve is the latter;
At any rate, that is *my* view of the matter:
Experience teaches that one may be landed
In great complications by being too candid.
And my character, too! I must try to maintain it,
For "*littera scripta*"—the poet says—"*manet.*"
Some Confessions attempt to be witty, some serious:
In either event they may easily weary us,
For when a man tries, and yet fails to be witty,
There's not a more suitable object for pity.
I suppose I must write, so as not to seem dense,
Lots of nonsense and just a suspicion of sense,
But the questions I'm asked! a most awkward selection,
That amounts to a species of moral dissection;
Though fortunately for ingenuous youth,
The *last* thing one needs to consider is *truth*.
My ideal of womanwood? Heavens!—what a question!
"The book's owner" is rather a hackneyed suggestion;
Yet how in one line to describe, as I ought to,
A theme that would fill up a volume in quarto!
Then who in the world is my favourite hero?
Is it Wellington, Hannibal, Turpin, or Nero?—

My modesty tells me to put on the shelf
The natural impulse to answer, "Myself"!
Am I a believer in love at first sight ?
And do I think girls to propose have a right ?
Has love had the power my bosom to soften ?
And if that's the case, will I please state how often ?
As if I were such a quintessence of meekness
As to publish the record of every weakness !
My favourite study ? My pet occupation ?
My favourite animal ? proverb ? quotation ?
My favourite novelist ? orator ? poet ?
Pet flower ? Pet colour ? Pet everything ? Blow it !
Till I throw down the pen, with my brain in a whirl,
And say, in my heart of hearts, "Deuce take the girl!"
My mind is distracted, my senses opprest,
I'm wringing my hands, and I'm beating my breast ;
I'm pacing my room in the wildest despair,
And the carpet is covered with handfuls of hair ;
I write down all manner of drivelling inanity,
And feel in a state of incipient insanity.
Yes, such is, fair tyrant, the plight of your victim,
And such are the tortures with which you afflict him.
In fact, all who ever have gone through the ordeal
Will say, with conviction most lively and cordial,
Of all artful methods of female oppression
There's nothing to equal the Book of Confession.

Life, JANUARY 21, 1886.

THE BRIEFLESS BRIGADE.

IN the days of my first juvenility,
 I was under the foolish impression
That, given hard work and ability,
 The Bar was a splendid profession;
But from New Year's Day to December,
 For years not a penny I made,
And now I'm a permanent member
 Of the Barristers' Briefless Brigade.

  For nobody gave me a brief —
   'Twas in vain that I waited and prayed
  For a chance to examine a witness in chief—
   I was one of the Briefless Brigade!

Six guineas I paid for my wig,
 And the rest of my outfit proportionate;
The prices appeared to me big,
 Some people would call them extortionate.
Then my Call-fee, some ninety-five guineas—
 In these times of commercial depression!
Oh, the way to get rid of your " tin " is
 To start in the legal profession!

  Each morning expecting a brief,
   In my chambers I patiently stayed,
  And cherished a wholly delusive belief
   Of escaping the Briefless Brigade.

I looked so surpassingly learned
 When my legal apparel I set up,
I fancied that any attorney'd
 Be struck with my general get-up.

My wig was so gracefully curled,
  As I gazed in the glass I decided,
That no Bar-at-law in the world
  Ever looked so bewitching as I did.

    So, fearful of missing a brief,
      Over luncheon I never delayed,
    And none would have thought, as I bolted my beef,
      I was one of the Briefless Brigade.

I thought I'd get plenty of practice,
  But I've come to another conclusion,
For the plain, undeniable fact is
  The Bar is a snare and delusion.
No matter how well you may know law,
  The necessity seldom arises;
The right thing to know is a " solor "
  Who'll give you a chance at Assizes.

    But nobody gives me a brief;
      My learning I've never displayed;
    'Pon my honour, it fairly surpasses belief
      How I stick to the Briefless Brigade.

To Sessions, a quarterly visitor,
  I journey with steady persistence;
But ah! not a single solicitor
  Seems cognisant of my existence.
I travel to all the Assizes,
  The wearisome round of the circuit,
But the other men get all the prizes—
  I *should* like to know how they work it.

    For nobody gives *me* a brief,
      Though I feel I simply was *made*
    For conducting the crafty defence of a thief,
      And not for the Briefless Brigade.

I'm not wanting, I know, in audacity,
　I flatter myself, too, that few men
Surpass me in easy loquacity,
　Or legal research and acumen.
I passed my exams. in a canter;
　Of law I'm a walking miscellany;
I can draw the distinction *instanter*
　Between misdemeanour and felony.

　　If for once they would give me a brief,
　　　Of its stiffness I'd not be afraid:
　　What matters the prospect of coming to grief?
　　　Better *that* than the Briefless Brigade.

But the prisoners now are so few;
　As I see the decrease I'm perplexed;
Whatever are Counsel to do?
　And what are we coming to next?
We shall soon be an unknown variety—
　It's merely a question of time,
Unless somebody starts a society
　For the better promotion of crime.

　　I wish I could just get a brief,
　　　Ere into oblivion we fade;
　　And then I would drift to the sere, yellow leaf
　　　But not of the Briefless Brigade.

What with Exeter Hall and Good Templars,
　Blue Ribbons and Total Abstaining,
And such like perfidious examplars,
　The crime of the country is waning.

It's awful to see men and women all
  Ever more and more widely the drink shun;
The class we denominate " criminal "
  Is in danger of speedy extinction.

> There won't *be* such a thing as a brief,
>   There won't be any fees to be paid,
> And when matters have reached such a pass,
>   I'd as lief
>   Belong to the Briefless Brigade.

So now I've resolved upon tossing
  The law and its works to perdition;
A good metropolitan crossing
  Is the aim of my present ambition:
Or I'll take off my wig and my gown,
  The garb emblematic of Counsel,
And walk through the streets of the town,
  An itinerant vendor of groundsel.

> For nobody gives me a brief,
>   And the Bar is a ruinous trade;
> I shall shortly be asking for parish relief
>   For I'm one of the Briefless Brigade!

Life, APRIL 8, 1886.

"VICS" ET PRÆTEREA NIHIL.

"*VICS*" *et Præterea Nihil!* According to one of
my correspondents, the new Servian Cabinet is
composed as follows :—

AGAIN at Servia's helm is Garashanin,
And faith, she couldn't put a better man in.
"Old hand in Parliament," and full of tricks,
In choosing colleagues, to one rule he sticks,
And asks from each one of his trusted six
The shibboleth of entrance, namely " vics ";
So concord in his Cabinet he fixes,
By having none but homogeneous " vicses."

When quarrels with her neighbours Servia picks,
She look to General Horvatovics;
To guard the halfpence and to get the kicks,
Devolves upon Monsieur Mijatovics.
And you, good Colonel, public works must fix,
They mus'n't topple over, Topalovics.
To guard the Church, and punish heretics,
Refuse you couldn't, could you, Kujndvics ?
While in the field of foreign politics
None takes you for an ass, Franassovics !
To deal with justice one should be prolix—
Learn, then, to sling more ink, Marinkovics

Great Garashanin shepherds up the six,
And sees that none shall kick against the pricks;
Discordant elements he shuns to mix,
All have one end in common—namely, " vics."
A Cabinet of six harmonious " vicses "
Can surely never be at sevens and sixes !

Life, APRIL 15, 1886.

GOOSE AND GANDER.

MR. A. A. POLLARD, a Tipperary clothier, has written to Mr. Gladstone to say that, as an ardent admirer of his transcendent genius, he has placed a bust of the right hon. gentlemen in front of his establishment. It is, he adds, a small indication of the esteem in which Mr. Gladstone is held by the matchless sons of gallant Tipperary.

Mr. Gladstone replied as follows :—

DEAR SIR,—I am truly sensible of the honour you have done me, and I beg you to accept my acknow-ledgment.—Your very faithful servant,

W. E. GLADSTONE.

OH, now may I contented die,
　And say my *Nunc Dimittis;*
So long I've pined true joy to find,
　And now I know what it is.
A bust of me, for all to see,
　In situation airy,
Is set before a tailor's door
　In dear old Tipperary.

My rival, who was made an earl,
　Stands opposite the Abbey,
And with " goatee " and foppish curl,
　Looks underbred and shabby,
But there he's one among a score
　Of statesmen, soldiers, sailors ;
I hold the field, alone, before
　That Tipperary tailor's.

How nice the tailor's letter, too !
　How free and independent !
How true his view of what is due
　To " genius transcendent " !
False modesty he proudly shuns,
　　In praises never chary,
" The matchless sons," his letter runs,
　" Of gallant Tipperary."

Sneer, dukes and earls ! But common folks
　Will laugh not with, but at you ;
And all your gibes and vapid jokes
　Will never budge my statue.
The lordly scoffer I defy,
　　And spurn the ducal railer,
As long as I am honoured by
　My Tipperary tailor.

The classes in their jealous pride
　Give me the shoulder chilly ;
But well I know, whate'er betide,
　The masses love their Willie.
And spite of dukes, and earls, and lords,
　　Whose star is growing paler,
The People's heart goes out towards
　That Tipperary tailor.

I fain would raise a hymn of praise,
　A rhapsody Homeric ;
But Erin's sons (the artless ones !)
　Would deem the thing hysteric.
They care not for Homeric lore,
　　And I must really drop " shop "
Now that my image stands before
　A Tipperary slop-shop.

How sweet the zeal of partisans,
　When one is feeling "collared"!
An old man's heart—a grand old man's—
　Is grateful, Mr. Pollard.
Oh, may thy shadow ne'er grow less,
　Thy body never frailer!
My dying words thy name shall bless,
　Thou Tipperary tailor!

The Globe, JANUARY 25, 1887.

LABBY IN OUR ABBEY.

OF all the Rads that are so smart,
　There's none like witty Labby;
He's played of late a leading part,
　So he'll be at the Abbey;
No institution in the land
　Escapes the sneers of Labby,
But all the same, I understand,
　He's going to the Abbey.

Of all the days within the week,
　There's one that will be *the* day,
And that's the day that's quite unique,
　Victoria's Jubilee Day.
Then he'll be dressed all in his best
　With nothing old or shabby:
He may be snarling in his heart,
　But he'll be at the Abbey.

He tried to dock the vote, you know,
  For fitting up the Abbey;
Perhaps he'd like the Queen to go
  And hail the nearest cabby;
All sentiment for England's Queen
  He designates as "flabby;"
But *Truth* must needs describe the scene,
  So he'll be at the Abbey.

The Globe, JUNE 20, 1887.

THE NEW OBADIAHS.

The Grand Old Man and His Faithful Follower.

SAID the old William Ewart to the young Halley
  Stewart,
"Do you fancy, Halley Stewart, you'll get in?"
Said the young Halley Stewart to the old William
  Ewart,
"My Committee, William Ewart, say I'll win.
But there's one unlucky circumstance I deeply deplore,
I was beaten last election rather worse than before;
Home Rule don't seem to prosper, and I feel more and
  more
That our platform, William Ewart, 's rather thin."

Said the young Halley Stewart to the old William
    Ewart,
"Things are looking pretty bad for us, you know."
Said the old William Ewart to the young Halley
    Stewart,
"I'm afraid, Halley Stewart, that is so.
The time is getting on, and though I'm grand, yet I'm
    old,
And the men I used to count upon have all left the
    fold:
I manage in the country to appear pretty bold,
    But I'm feeling, Halley Stewart, rather low."

Said the old William Ewart to the young Halley
    Stewart,
"Tell me what you think of Tryon, I entreat."
Said the young Halley Stewart to the old William
    Ewart,
"He's like the British lion, bad to beat.
The voters seem to like him, and though straight from
    his ship,
When he takes a thing in hand he quickly gets a
    thorough grip."
Said the old William Ewart, "Many thanks for the tip,
    I sha'n't back you. Halley Stewart, for the seat."

Said the young Halley Stewart to the old William
    Ewart,
"Old England doesn't cotton to Home Rule."
Said the old William Ewart to the young Halley
    Stewart,
"These English I'm determined I will school."

Said the young Halley Stewart, "Don't you think it
  would be well,
If against the Irish faction we were all to rebel ? "
Said the old William Ewart, " Give offence to Parnell !
  You are talking, Halley Stewart, like a fool."

Said the old William Ewart to the young Halley
  Stewart,
" I'll telegraph to you on polling-day."
Said the young Halley Stewart to the old William
  Ewart,
" Do nothing of the sort, I beg and pray.
For wherever you sent telegrams and post-cards, it
  was queer,
How our candidates were always beaten hopelessly last
  year."
Said the old William Ewart, " Well, from all I can hear,
  You'll be beaten, Halley Stewart, any way."
                              [*But he wasn't !*]

Boston Independent, JUNE 25, 1887.

A HAIR-BREADTH 'SCAPE.

MR. HEALY excitedly complained to the Court
that he had been twice pointed at with a
bayonet, and had narrowly escaped with his life.—
Daily Paper.

> O DEED of infamy untold !
>   The times must be disjointed,
> When at a form of patriot mould
>   A bayonet twice is pointed.

'Tis true, the bayonet did no more
    Than point at him, but nathless,
We ask, remembering Gweedore,
    How did he come off scatheless?

He pointed *once*, did Colonel D.,
    A rifle all unloaded,
And straightway (*teste* Mr. G.)
    He nearly shot his foe dead.

And yet this murderous device,
    This dread unloaded rifle,
Beside a bayonet pointed *twice*
    Was surely but a trifle.

Well may we, dumb with horror, gape,
    Not knowing what to say on it,
Astounded at the hairbreadth 'scape
    From that insidious bayonet.

The Globe, JANUARY 29, 1889.

THE BUSY B.

HOW doth the little busy B,
    Improve the writer's power
Of setting forth the infamy
    Of Arthur J. Balfour!

The big, big D, of course, is good
  And useful in a manner ;
But it's considered coarse and rude—
  Except by Dr. Tanner.

But oh ! the fierce, explosive B
  Is quite without a rival
In piling up the agony
  By insults adjectival.

Thus : Brutal Brigand, Bathed in Blood,
  Bombastic, Blatant Braggart,
Base Buntling, Born of Bomba's Brood,
  Blood-boltered, Brazen Blaggart !

The amplest wealth of attribute
  Could ne'er describe thee fully,
Thou Bare-faced Butcher, Barb'rous Brute,
  Big, Blustering, Bungling Bully !

Ah, yes, the B's sharp sting is best
  For an initial letter,
And nought can stir the Irish breast,
  Or loose the purse-strings better.

And thus the little busy B,
  Improves the patriot's powers,
To gather money all the day
  For " This Great Cause of Ours."

The Globe, FEBRUARY 1, 1889.

A PATRIOT'S PLAINT.

IV'RY bone in my body is achin',
    I'm kapin' my bed, and, bedad!
It's myself that can hardly be spakin',
    I've got the bronchitus so bad.

An' there's sorra a dog in creation,
    But my cough would be drownin' his bark;
An' it's all through the great dimonsthration
    The pathriots held in the Park.

I'm a pathriot, too, like my neighbours,
    An' whin the boys axed me to go,
I took my blackthorn, and, be jabers!
    I wint like a man to the show.

But the Londoners, shure they're faint-hearted,
    The matin' it seemed mighty small;
And divil a row could be started
    To kape up our spirits at all.

Mighty little it was that was spoken,
    But fine risolutions was passed;
An' we quickly dispersed—more by token,
    The snow it was drownin' us fast.

By the powers! I was bad on the morrow—
    How bad, it's myself that can't tell;
An' I'm achin' all over, begorrah!
    There's divil a part of me well.

An' it's Balfour the blackguard has done it,
Divil take him! it's no fault of mine.
Shure an' faith, it was him that begun it,
By stalin' the clothes of O'Brine.

Av coorse, av he hadn't been tratin'
O'Brine like a felon, ye know,
We would niver have been dimonsthratin',
An' I'd have kept out of the snow.

Faith, he does all he can for to spite us;
From him all our troubles are sprung;
An' bedad! av I die of bronchitus,
It's Balfour that ought to be hung.

The Globe, FEBRUARY 12, 1889.

A VOICE FROM DELPHI.

PROFESSOR NORTON, of Harvard University, is trying to persuade the Americans to purchase the complete site of Delphi, which, he avers, can be bought for 80,000 dollars.

Φεῦ φεῦ. Ah me! That I should see
My home beneath the hammer!
There was a time when all sublime
O'er Greece I shed a glamour.
All Hellas loved my praise to tell
Through every hill and hollow;
In Homer, too, I figured well,
The " silver-bowed Apollo."

A first-class god—it does seem odd
    That now upon the shelf I
Am laid so low, that they can go
    And sell my place at Delphi—
My shrine, where I was wont to sit,
    My fountain of Castalia,
My oracle—which I'll admit
    Was on the whole a failure.

Eternal shame upon the name
    Of that Professor Norton,
Who to my sacred Delphi came
    Its value to report on!
And now the place will soon belong
    To those detested Yankees,
As he expressed it, " for a song "—
    A hymn, perhaps, of Sankey's.

A paltry sum ! In years to come
    My head I ne'er can hold up.
Oh, Ichabod! That I, a god,
    By men should thus be sold up!
The price, I vow, would hardly keep
    A god in shirts and collars.
Alas, that I should go so cheap
    As eighty thousand dollars !

The Globe, FEBRUARY 15, 1889.

"EXCRESCENCES."

" I DEPLORE the excesses which have occurred in
Ireland, but I believe they are only the excre-
scences which accompany all popular movements for
reform."—*Mr. Childers at Perth.*

O PREJUDICED coercionist,
    Give ear to Mr. Childers,
A statesman high upon the list
    Of Constitution-builders.
If you would read Home Rule aright,
    Look only at its essence,
For outrages and dynamite
    Are merely an excrescence.

The things a few young men may do
    Are wholly unimportant;
They put "pitch-caps" on girls, perhaps,
    Who talk to men they oughtn't;
But these are tricks, when all is said,
    Of thoughtless adolescence,
And tar upon the female head
    Is surely an excrescence.

Perhaps you're shocked when tails are docked
    From cows and other creatures?
It is not well too much to dwell
    On these external features;
For it's a fact that cannot fail
    To meet with acquiescence,
That, logically viewed, a tail
    Is merely an excrescence.

This point of view enables you
   To disregard moonlighters,
And you can quite put out of sight
   Those awkward dynamiters.
Then read, mark, learn, and ponder this
   Most comforting of lessons,
That outrages you can dismiss
   As merely an excrescence.

The Globe, FEBRUARY 19, 1889.

"ONE GOOD TURN DESERVES ANOTHER."

M. ZANKOFF confides to the *Standard* correspondent that Mr. Gladstone once, at the conclusion of an interview, accompanied him to the hall and held his overcoat for him to put on. On M. Zankoff begging him not to do so, Mr. Gladstone said, "It is our custom in England." "So," added M. Zankoff, smiling, "I always help an Englishman on with his coat in memory of Mr. Gladstone."

To help a man on with his coat, I may say,
   Is always my regular custom ;
Nay, more, when I get a fair chance anyway
   At my enemies' jackets, I dust 'em.
I always said Zankoff was far from a fool,
   And it's nice my politeness to quote ;
I am glad that I always have made it a rule
   To help a man on with his coat.

Parnell took his coat off to cut the " last link,"
  And matters became so unpleasant,
'Twas prudent to help him resume it, I think,
  And that's what I'm doing at present.
It wasn't, of course, that I yielded to fright,
  Still less that I wanted his vote ;
But seeing him coatless, I thought it polite
  To help the man on with his coat.

And there's Harcourt, whose changes of coat,
    you're aware,
  Are really so quick and so recent ;
I'm weary of helping him on, I declare,
  And I never can make him look decent.
Poor Harcourt ! I fear, when my days end in night
  (Though I trust that that hour is remote),
Not one of the lot will be large enough quite
  To put on the G. O. M.'s coat.

The Globe, MARCH 30, 1889.

OFF !

A HOUSE OF COMMONS Steeplechase !
    How thankful we should be !
For now, what England needs, *a race*
  Of Statesmen we shall see.

I've often thought how much akin
  St. Stephen's to a race is,
For parties struggle hard to win,
  And always hope for *places*.

And very natural withal
  This quaint resemblance seemed;
For in all *commons*, great and small,
  The *turf* is much esteemed.

Pitt ruled the land at twenty-three,
  We read in history's page;
But now to reach the Treasury
  A man must *wait for age.*

To keep a seat for big debates
  They leave their hats, you see;
How useful, then, to hairless pates
  A *handy cap* must be!

And some with hatred, fierce and keen,
  Pursue the Church apace;
And so, 'tis easy to be seen,
  They love a *steeple-chase.*

The skilled debater parries well
  His foeman's thrusts, and hence
He must, as any one can tell,
  Be " clever at a *fence.*"

The working-class some represent,
  And some paternal acres;
While some, of literary bent,
  Have always been *bookmakers.*

With *hacks* one party's well supplied;
  It keeps for these affairs
A *Hunter*, and a *Cobb* beside,
  And several *Irish mayors.*

The Tories, too, have got a *Mount*,
  Although of *Hope* bereft;
But none on victory can count,
  To *Chance* it must be left.

So many *whips* each member gets
  That they will quite suffice;
And those who wish can make their bets,
  If there's a *starting Price*.

Let others back the chestnut horse,
  The brown, and eke the grey;
But every statesman's hopes, of course,
  Are fixed upon the *bay*.

A mighty throng of members gay
  Towards the racecourse fares;
There'll be no *cab in it* to-day,
  But there'll be lots of *pairs*.

The rider's colours now are seen,
  Of every varied hue,
For our M.P.'s have always been
  A *party-coloured* crew.

On Courtney some will surely dare
  Their faith and pelf to pin;
The Chairman of Committee's there,
  He *weighs and means* to win.

And Smith will smartly take a fence
  ('Tis plainest of deductions).
For great is his experience
  In coping with *obstructions*.

Some horses, though, will fail to clear
   That ditch's further border;
Some at that hedge will stop, I fear,
   And will not *rise to order*.

And he who all the course would run
   Must do some valiant feats;
And—absit omen!—ere it's done,
   There'll be some *vacant seats*.

The Globe, APRIL 6, 1889.

~~~~~~~~~~~~~~~

HOME RULE HAS WON.

MR. GLADSTONE received, by telegram, from Mr. Cyril Flower, the gratifying intelligence that Home Rule had won.—*Daily News.*

THE Grand Magician worked the spell,
   And straightway Homer's ghost arose,
"O Master, I would have thee tell
   The fate that none of mortals knows.
Those sightless orbs of thine can see
   The future doom revealed to none;
This legend read aright to me:
   ' *Home Rule has won!* ' "

And thus the ancient bard replied:
   "The urn of fate doth swiftly turn;
The lot that shall Home Rule decide
   Will leap ere long from out the urn.

And thus the legend I declare:
As round and round the lots are spun,
Of all the hundred chances there
Home Rule has one ! ''

The Globe, APRIL 9, 1889.

THE LAW AND THE LADIES.

OUR fair politicians may well be concerned,
For the law simply treats them as drudges:
" You may *stand,* if you like, but (although you're
    returned)
We won't let you *sit,*" say the judges.

But to take all the feminine wisdom and wit
From the Council were surely a pity.
We have it ! The ladies, forbidden to *sit,*
Can be put on a *Standing Committee.*

Judy, JUNE 12, 1889.

𝕌𝔫𝔭𝔲𝔟𝔩𝔦𝔰𝔥𝔢𝔡 𝔙𝔢𝔯𝔰𝔢𝔰 𝔬𝔫 𝔙𝔞𝔯𝔦𝔬𝔲𝔰 𝔖𝔲𝔟𝔧𝔢𝔠𝔱𝔰.

NEW YEAR'S THOUGHTS. 1888.

By an Old Bachelor.

THE Old Year lies a-dying, like
   Too many others I remember;
In half a minute it will strike
   The last sad moments of December.

How time *does* fly! *Ehew! fugaces—*
   As Horace says—*labuntur anni.*
But what's the use of wry grimaces?
   I can't prevent it flying, can I?

I wonder if my watch is right?
   I should have set it at eleven—
Ah! there's the chime! And so, Good night!
   Good night, Old Eighteen Eighty-seven.

The King is dead! Long live the King!
   So they begin to make night hideous.
With such indecent haste to ring
   His rival in, is most invidious.

The heartless New Year's bells peal out,
    And all men seem so glad and merry;
Though what they've got to crow about
    To me is problematic—very.

In every coffin one more nail,
    Another load on every shoulder,
And every cheek's a shade more pale,
    And every one's a twelvemonth older.

We're nearer to the last long night;
    But why they call to our attention
That painful fact with such delight,
    Is past my humble comprehension.

What grain of pleasure can be brought?
    What satisfaction under Heaven
Can be imparted by the thought,
    " This year I shall be fifty-seven "?

To me, this imbecile parade
    Of joy is simply irritating;
I think of Christmas bills unpaid,
    And tradesmen getting tired of waiting;

Of snow and slush, and cold wet feet,
    Of pavements slippery as butter,
Of snowballs flying down the street
    That knock one's hat into the gutter:

Of slides that threaten dangers grave
    To men, like me, of portly habit,
Who have to walk the treach'rous pave
    Because they can't afford to cab it.

Oh! drat those bells! They quite confuse
　My New Year's Thoughts and spoil my verses.
How truly awful if my Muse
　Should launch out into oaths and curses!

It almost makes me feel unwell
　To hear those idiotic tinkles;
To me, at least, they only tell
　Of thinner hair and deeper wrinkles.

Alas! I once was quite hirsute,
　But now—'tis idle to conceal it—
I'm getting bald as any coot,
　And no one knows how much I feel it.

Ah yes! It's getting sparse and grey,
　The hair that once was thick and flaxen—
I've got that paper, by the way,—
　That article by Dr. Jackson.

I wonder if it's really true;
　He says it's all because we're careless
That scalps become exposed to view,
　And men grow gradually hairless.

The hat peculiar to my sex
　I've doffed, obeying his instruction;
For " want of ventilation checks
　" And starves capillary production."

I've noticed, when the barber's fingers
　Find nought upon the crown to cut,
A fringe, unblighted, always lingers
　Around the baldest occiput.

The woman, too, who's used to wear
  A flimsy fashionable bonnet—
Her head has always lots of air,
  And so there's lots of hair upon it.

The amply ventilating savage
  Of Zululand or Polynesia
With hatless head escapes the ravage
  Of what the wise call, " Alopecia."

" Too frequent washing kills the hope
  Of vigorous hair," says Dr. Jackson,
" But once a fortnight wash with soap,
  Or put some water with borax on.

" The head should shun the morning tub :
  Above the water keep it high up,
And never with a towel rub
  The hair when wet, but let it dry up.

" And don't indulge in mental strains ;
  Don't pore o'er problems algebraic ;
For men who overwork their brains
  Are apt to be alopecaic.

" Observe professors scientific,
  The F.S.A.'s and F.R.S.'s
With what rapidity terrific
  They lose their once luxuriant tresses.

" Go to their meetings and survey—
  A thing of common notoriety—
The shining pates in long array
  Of Fellows of the Royal Society."

But doctors always disagree,
    And we are warned by Dr. Hammond
By Dr. Jackson not to be—
    To use a low expression—gammoned.

Says Dr. H., " The hairless pate
    Should be a source of pride and vanity,
Because it indicates a state
    Of highly civilised humanity.

" The balder we become the more
    We grow distinct "—in his opinion—
" From that pithecoid ancestor,
    Whose form is sketched in books Darwinian.

" Let savages delight in hair,
    For thus the laws of nature shaped 'em ;
But well-developed heads are bare
    Of this degrading badge of apedom.

" A time will come when women all
    Will scorn the man of ample tresses ;
The head that's like a billiard ball
    Will win their tenderest caresses."

Perhaps this tilt at flowing locks
    Is all a piece of quaint facetia ;
Or is he, like the tailless fox,
    Himself a prey to alopecia ?

Well, I am over fifty-six ;
    But, if I can, I'll keep my hair on
Until I reach the banks of Styx
    And doff my ghostly hat to Charon.

The bells ! the bells ! that hideous row
  To me is really quite unnerving ;
I understand the horror now
  Portrayed by Mr. Henry Irving.

Against a murderer, as such,
  I always felt a certain bias ;
But oh ! his punishment's too much :
  I sympathise with poor Mathias.

Those bells with their distracting chime
  Poetic inspiration ruin ;
They've rung the Old Year out some time—
  They must, by now, have rung the New in.

This New Year's fuss is so absurd—
  But I'm morose and misanthropic ;
I wish it had to me occurred
  To take the *Old* Year as my topic.

I loved it well, and for its sake
  I look with coldness on the New Year.
Things old are best. Who would not take
  Old Stilton as compared with Gruyère ?

Well, well ! the Old Year's fairly dead :
  The bells have ceased that roused my ire.
I think it's time to go to bed—
  My pipe is out, and so's the fire.

THE INVENTIONS COMMITTEE.

THE hour of ten
　　Is striking when
A committee of elderly gentlemen,
　Whose names I decline to mention,
May be seen well-armed with paper and pen
　And every good intention.
　　　They sit in a room
　　　Pronouncing doom,
In a general atmosphere of gloom;
And consign to the peace of an early tomb
　Full many a bold invention.
　　　And all to the end
　　　Of their names append
A number of proud initials,
Which to astonishing lengths extend.
And dignity and importance lend
　To the names of high officials.
There are K.C.M.G.'s and K.C.B.'s,
K.P.'s, K.T.'s, P.C.'s and M.P.'s ;
There are K.C.S.I.'s and C.I.E.'s,
And F.R.S.'s and LL.D.'s.
　　　And if you please
　　　You can add to these
As many again with the greatest ease.
　　　But of one thing you
　　　May be sure, that few
Are content with the commonplace E.s.q.
For they are persons of high degree,

The Committee
Of the I.I.E.,
Resolved to defend
To the bitter end
The little remaining space that's free
From the ruthless greed of the Patentee :
And so they politely but firmly sit upon
Men whose inventive brains have hit upon
Wonderful schemes that would surely set
The Thames on fire if it were not wet.
With a hardened heart and a stubborn will
The invidious duty they fulfil.
And on vain aspirations cold water douse,
Like the Hanging Committee of Burlington House.
And, sweetly unconscious of their doom,
The inventors throng in the ante-room.

In a terrible state
Of mind they wait,
And eagerly rush to their hapless fate.
One by one,
Till the tale is done,
They go to the fearful ordeal ;
And the heavy oak door is closed behind
The victim of confidence all too blind.
Who's made up his mind
That he's designed
To confer a benefit on mankind.
But when he gets in he's surprised to find
The Committee is far from cordial.
And the man who's got
The next turn by lot
Is eager and hopeful and flushed and hot :
And to and fro,
As the animals do,

When they know it's feeding-time at the Zoo,
He paces the corridor
Mopping his forehead, or
Cursing, with soft pedal down, that horrid door
Which, with its ponderous oaken frame,
Is shutting him out from wealth and fame ;
For he feels that his scheme he has but to name
To meet on all sides with a loud acclaim.
And he wonders how the Committee can
Waste even a single minute
On the rubbishy plan
Of the previous man—
A notion that's antediluvian—
Picked up by a rascally charlatan,
For, of course, there's nothing in it.

The difference quickly can be detected
'Twixt those selected
And those rejected ;
A thing that was only to be expected.
For some look glum,
As they slowly come
From the presence of the Committee.
Some mutter, and some
With despair are dumb,
As if life henceforth were a vacuum ;
While others with playful fingers strum
An imaginary harmonium
Or an airy imperceptible drum,
And under their rivals' noses hum
A row-de-iddity rum-ti-tum ;
With a toss of the contumelious thumb
In mingled scorn and pity.

The Anti-Lucifer Match.

The first Inventor was ushered in,
    His face was thin,
    With a parchment skin,
And he constantly rubbed an obtrusive chin,
And greeted with a familiar grin
    The Committee of the Inventions.
And first having carefully shut the door,
His hat he deposited on the floor,
And produced from his pocket about a score
(There might be less and there might be more)
    Tin boxes of small dimensions ;
        And passing them round,
        With a look profound,
    To the members of the Committee,
In a voice that was neither subdued nor weak,
But a fitful resonant kind of creak,
        With plenty of cheek
        He began to speak,
" I think you'll agree that the thing's unique,
    Its useful and cheap and pretty.
        P'raps, gentlemen,
        You remember when
    With a flint and steel and tinder
    They used to beguile the tedious hours
    And waste their tissue and vital powers
(Their time was less valuable then than ours)
While the fire descended in reckless showers,
    With nothing on earth to hinder
The sparks from setting the house a-blaze
        (For such were the ways
        Of the good old days)
    And reducing the place to a cinder.

And many deplored the woful waste
Of time and energy so misplaced ;
Till the difficulty was boldly faced
By a man with a scientific taste,
Who the old-fashioned flint and steel replaced
 By a thing that was less uncertain.
   To wit : a lucifer,
   Made from the juicy fir.
Still, it was likely to play the deuce if a
   Head should detach
   Itself from the match,
And, frolicking off at a tangent, catch
 A neighbouring dress or curtain.
So one of a well-known firm one day,
   I can't quite say
   Whether Bryant or May,
From fire to afford protection,
Invented a match that would only ignite
On the box—and not always on that, despite
The frequent injunction to rub them light.
But anyhow this, you'll agree, was quite
 A step in the right direction.
But as Cicero says, ' It ain't "*quantum suff*"'—
I mean that they didn't go far enough,
 And that's why I reprobate 'em ;
Their principle's good without a doubt,
As far as it goes, but to work it out
With a will that's firm and a heart that's stout
 Is the great desideratum.
Now I've brought the principle to maturity,
   More security
   For futurity ;
That is my plan in its naked purity—
 Thither my heart aspires.

And he who would compass this end must pause,
And make a study of nature's laws,
He'll see what catastrophes matches cause :
If he'll only refer to Captain Shaw's
    Reports on our London fires.

" So now I must crave your condescension
    And kind attention,
    While I just mention
The principal points of my new invention
    With diffidence and humility.
    You see, I begin
    By packing them in
A non-inflammable box of tin,
Which renders an accident akin
    To a moral impossibility.
I think my invention will simply floor
Both Bryant and May, and the "Tandstickor,"
Though they're ' *utan svafvel och fosfor,*'
Which, I take it, is Scandinavian for
  ' Without either sulphur or phosphorus.'
I must say, by the way, when foreigners send
Their wares over here, they might condescend
To a tongue that their customers comprehend ;
    At least at the end
    They might append
A something by way of a gloss for us.
Now lucifer heads are apt to fly ;
But with these your efforts I can defy.
All day and all night you might freely try—
It can't be done, and I'll tell you why :
    No head to the match attaches.
They simply consist, as all matches should,

Of nothing but good
Substantial wood.
So their name will be readily understood,
　The 'ANTI-LUCIFER MATCHES!'
　　Messrs. Bryant and May
　　Have had their day ;
For though their notion, I'm bound to say,
Was highly commendable in its way,
　Mine's happier, simpler, newer.
For with these it's immaterial, quite,
How hard you rub 'em, they won't ignite
On the box or anything else—you might
As well endeavour to coax a light
　From the end of a wooden skewer.
　　So I beg of your grace
　　To grant me space ;
I should like a good conspicuous place,
　For it's my belief sincerely,
That if it is prominently displayed
My match will do an enormous trade.
The danger from fire will be so allayed,
And soon it will hardly be gainsaid,
For the Metropolitan Fire Brigade
　Will be ornamental merely."
He ceased, and the Chairman answered thus :—
" Your idea most excellent seems to us,
　The matter you ably handle ;
But what I have hitherto failed to catch
Is how you propose, with a headless match,
　To light your bedroom candle."
　　　The confident look
　　　Of pride forsook
The inventor's face ; with a hand that shook
　He picked up his battered hat.

He simply ejaculated " Eh ? "
And made for the door without delay
In a limp condition; he did not stay
To collect his boxes, or say, " Good-day ";
But was heard to remark as he crept away,
  " Why didn't I think of that ? "

THE CHIN-MOWER.

The next to pass the ordeal's rigour
  Entered the chamber stepping lightly;
He was tall and thin, and his bony figure
  Was wrapped in a frock-coat buttoned tightly.
The lone goatee, demurely flowing
  Beneath his chin, excites suspicion
That its escape is solely owing
  To some fortuitous omission.
His hair behind curls stiffly out,
  His nose is long, his figure lanky;
In fact he is, beyond a doubt,
  A genuine true full-blooded Yankee.
His accent's anything but pure,
  His voice monotonous and twangy,
His diction's frequently obscure,
  And his vocabulary slangy.
He strokes his chin, expectorates,
  And thus addresses the Committee :
" My name is Phineas T. Bates,
  And I was raised in New York City;
Into a white-goods store I went—
  A line of life I thought degrading.
I couldn't do it worth a cent,
  I didn't have a taste for trading ;

So when in eighteen months about.
　In manner rather firm than gentle,
The boss one morning fired me out,
　I didn't care a continental.
The inventing business seemed to me
　A bang-up sort of line to enter.
To tell the square-toed truth, you see,
　I felt I was a born inventor.
But in the States we're crowded so,
　The business don't remunerate us.
So I've come over here to show
　My patent shaving apparatus.

" Now, if from prejudice you're free,
　And not to present fashion wedded;
If you have any claim to be
　Considered cute and level-headed,
I guess you will at once allow,
　Without the slightest hesitation,
That this machine I show you now—
　To put it mildly—licks creation.
I like to call a spade a spade,
　I hate your high-falutin phrases,
I say that nature never made
　Such blamed all-fired machines as razors.

" You all must know some silly youth
　Who tries to hurry nature's working;
Who thinks that even now, in truth,
　Beneath the skin the hair is lurking.
On his expectant upper lip,
　With thoughtful tug he'll fondly linger,
And o'er his lower features trip
　With gently meditative finger.

Each morning to the glass he'll rush
   To see if he has grown more hairy,
And deftly ply the rasping brush
   On whiskers quite imaginary;
He sees no beauty in the face
   Of beardless Belvedere Apollo,
And thinks for manliness and grace
   The hairy Esau beats him hollow.
And so, to foster on his chin
   The beard that yet is embryonic,
He spends his pocket money in
   The latest hair-producing tonic.
He'll hopefully procure Latreilles'
   Hair-unguent, and with steady *pursuit*
Smear lips with this that never fails
   The smoothest face to render hirsute.
Upon his sparsely dotted chin
   The hair as yet is not gregarious,
But still to shave he must begin—
   An operation most precarious.
His unresisting face he'll slash,
   Like some blood-thirsty ancient Druid,
With an expenditure most rash
   Of precious time and vital fluid.
And when he's through, with anxious care
   The soapy mass he'll fondly gather,
And proudly note the infrequent hair
   That lurks amid the gory lather.
Now, if you'd total up the blood
   That's daily shed by people shaving,
You'd think the razor'd be tabooed
   Except by madmen, stark and raving.
Then there's the great inducement lent
   To persons reckless and besotted;

It's such a handy instrument
    For use on arteries carotid.
Reflect how dangerous it is,
    To what atrocious deeds it may lure—
For all innocuous purposes
    The razor is a dismal failure.
In this department, strange to find
    There's still a terrible hiatus;
And someone's got to give mankind
    A safety shaving apparatus.
It's true, as everybody knows,
    That recently a man invented
An instrument that clearly shows
    Its author to have been demented.
I don't propose to entertain
    The company with such a topic;
The thing was just a kind of plane
    Of awkward shape and microscopic.
The prospects of the hopeful plan
    In this unique advantage centred,
That if it slipped, no deeper than
    A sixteenth of an inch it entered.
The fool thought this would make it pay;
    But other people, somewhat warier,
Perceived that it could scoop away
    A slab of flesh of any area.
It was the meanest implement,
    And didn't have a show to speak of;
It couldn't shave you worth a cent,
    But yanked great pieces of your cheek off.
I wish to speak of it, you see,
    In terms of friendly moderation.
I'll only say, it seemed to me,
    The sickest thing in all creation.

And now, as you're aware no doubt,
  Its head it can no longer hold up,
The blamed concern has petered out,
  The patentee was lately sold up.

" But time I guess is on the wing—
  To my invention, gents, we'll get on,
Its just a bang-up kind of thing,—
  That statement you may freely bet on.
Its pretty smart, and that's a fact,—
  I don't desire to overrate it,—
But if on my advice you'll act,
  Right in the front you will locate it.
You know the elegant machine
  That overgrowth on lawns reduces ;
I reckoned it, as will be seen,
  Might be applied to other uses.
So, with a stroke of genius, I
  Made it my fundamental basis,
And boldly ventured to apply
  The principle to human faces.
And so, without a minute's lapse,
  I put in hand my new CHIN MOWER :
'Tain't very much to look at p'raps,
  You bet your lives, though, it's a goer.
It's one advantage, which, I guess,
  Will take the British Public rather,
It don't require a dirty mess
  Of soap, or any sort of lather.
So you may get your dollars out,
  And on this notion freely stake 'em
For, take my tip, its just about
  As smart and handy as they make 'em.

Around your chin 'twill gently roll;
   (Its operation is so simple),
It lightly skims the obtrusive mole,
   And rides serenely o'er the pimple.

" It doesn't have a slicking blade,
   Or ought that's dangerous or frightening;
It's more like scissors that's it's made;
   And it'll shave you quicker 'n lightning.
'Twill shave you old 'uns without pain,
   Whose hand uncertain and infirm is,
And when you're through, you'll still retain
   Your full amount of epidermis,
One application renders you
   As hairless as a paper collar;
On that, my friends, I'm ready to
   Plank down my fundamental dollar.
It leaves you smoother than a clam,
   With no more bristles than a baby.
You see the sort of man I am,
   And you'll believe my statement, maybe.
If not, and I may be allowed
   A moment to take off my coat, I'm
Prepared right here to shave the crowd,
   Free, gratis, gents, in less than no time.
And there's a point which I opine
   Is liable to take your fancies;
You'll find that this machine of mine
   Adapts itself to circumstances.

" To suit the crop upon your cheeks
   The knives you elevate or lower
And, like the coon, the growth of weeks
   Will just ' come down ' to my Chin Mower.

A thousand dollars I'll divide
 If anywhere around you scare up
A thing like this, that once applied,
 Won't leave a solitary hair up.
For shaving you will not discover
 Its equal, you may bet your hat;
All other schemes it just lays over,—
 There ain't no discount, boss, on that.
And now it's my opinion, gents,
 That every British son of Shem
Will chuck all other implements,
 And just freeze on to my C. M.
If I can only find the takers,
 I'll seize an early opportunity
Of betting that the razor makers
 Will be a busted-up community.
There'll be a rough time, anyway,
 For Taylor, and for Mappin Brothers;
And it'll be a coldish day
 For Rodgers, Elliott, and others."

With this, the ghastly instrument
 He brandished with an air satanic;
And through the whole Committee went
 A helpless universal panic.
At last the Chairman, pale as death,
 His vital organs in a flutter,
And gasping nervously for breath,
 A few brief words contrived to utter:
" Your offer upon *us* to practise
 We've no intention, sir, of scorning;
It would be charming, but the fact is
 We all of us were shaved this morning.

Your Mower charmed us on the spot—
So novel and ingenious is it—
If I may say so, it is what
Your countrymen would call ' exquisite.'
We can't, at present, promise you
A place—I mention it with sorrow—
But we will try what we can do
If you will kindly call to-morrow."

The Yankee turned upon his heel,
And promised to return quite early;
Which only made the Chairman feel
Particularly riled and surly.
He gave his orders in this strain :
" Just see that ruffian off the premises,
And if you let him in again
You'll undergo a frightful nemesis."

These verses were never revised by the author, who intended to add to them various other "inventions," such as
"A Talking Machine for M.P.'s," "A Dressing Machine,"
"Foot-boats to walk on the water with," "Bellows to fill sails
in a calm," " Non-effervescent soda-water," &c.

AFTER THE JUBILEE.

OH ! what shall we do with our flags,
  That on Jubilee-Day looked so nice ?
Must they go with the bones and the rags
  To be sold at a nominal price ?
The Union Jack, Royal Standard,
  And others of nondescript hues,
Upon which our resources we squandered—
  Must they go to itinerant Jews ?

Oh ! what shall we do with our flags ?
  Must we sternly all sentiment squash,
And cut them to make into bags
  For sending our clothes to the wash ?
And our banners, too—what are they worth ?
  Our " Welcomes," " V.R.'s," Crowns Imperial,
And " God save the Queens "—what on earth
  Can we do with the surplus material ?

Oh ! what shall we do with our lamps,
  The Jubilee lamps that we bought,
For which the unprincipled scamps
  Charged us three times as much as they ought?
Which we hung in such pretty devices,
  Our windows and balconies round—
I'll inquire, by the way, what the price is
  Of old coloured glass by the pound.

Nothing could have looked smarter or spicker,
  When we managed to light them at last ;
Though after a weak little flicker
  They mostly succumbed to the blast.

As night-lights they'd do in the nursery,
    And—if they're not broken by then—
On the Jubilee-Day anniversary,
    Perhaps we might use them again.

For representations dramatic
    The bunting may haply come in;
To put it away in the attic
    Would seem to be almost a sin
Perhaps a Zenana Society
    Could use it for clothing the blacks—
It would make a delightful variety
    To dress them in Union Jacks.

But stay! I've a bright inspiration.
    Our remnants, you'll surely agree,
Would find their correct destination
    Adorning a Primrose League Tea!
For each village, and borough, and city,
    Where the League has its teas, there's enough;
So we'll look to the Primrose Committee
    To buy up our Jubilee stuff.

June 25, 1887.

ON LEFROY, THE MURDERER OF MR. GOLD.

P ERCY LEFROY
   Was a good little boy,
Though it seems his good angel forgot him.
   To his praise be it told
   That he didn't love *Gold*—
If he had, he would never have shot him.

   And you, whose stern mind
   For his fate cannot find
A tear that his innocence hallows;
   Though your heart be as board,
   He will sure touch a *cord*
When he takes his last drop on the gallows.

   For *my* part, I must say,
   That if *I* had my way,
With such folks as Lefroy or as Guiteau,
   I'd lynch the whole lot,
   Right away on the spot,
As I'd squash an obnoxious mosquito.

NOVEMBER 27, 1881.

~~~~~~~~~~~~~~

THE CAT.

S OME hate the beetle, some the mouse,
   Some shudder at the harmless spider;
Some like poor puss about the house,
   But there are some who can't abide her.

All have their likes and eke their hates,
   And there is nought to wonder at
If William Sykes abominates
   " The harmless, necessary cat."
'Tis odd this prejudice should hold
   O'er William's class such wide dominion ;
But burglars are, as I am told,
   Unanimous in this opinion.
And is it right, then, that the State,
   In spite of their repugnance flat,
Should force these men to cultivate
   A close acquaintance with the cat ?
'Tis true the modern Sykes is not
   Renowned for probity and meekness :
Indeed, for lethal arms he's got,
   Of late, a most decided weakness.

" ORANGE."

THERE once was a fellow spent quite a long time.
   In ranging through Webster to hit on a rhyme
     To the almost unrhymable " orange ";
But, finding at length that his search was no good,
He finally made up his mind that he would
     Through Webster's dry pages no more range.

August 20, 1883.

A NURSERY RHYME REVISED.

A Canon objects to Dancing in his parish.

HEY diddle, diddle! The Dance and the Fiddle!
    I can't understand it at all ;
The Church has come down on the heads of the town,
And the *Canon* finds fault with the *Ball*.

DECEMBER 28, 1884.

THE COMMERCIAL TRAVELLER.

"WILL you buy my patent burner?" said the
    bland commercial gent.;
" In a fortnight it will save you all the money you have
    spent;
There's been such a rush upon them that I've only left
    a few,
And I thought before they'd all been sold, I'd offer
    them to you.
    Will you, won't you, will you, won't you, will you
      take the lot?
    Will you, won't you, will you, won't you, will you
      take the lot?

" You can really have no notion how delightful they
    will be,
How much you'll save in gas, and how distinctly you
    will see."

But the Dr. had been sold before, and knew it was a
    chouse,
And wrathfully he answered, " Will you walk out of
    my house ?
  Will you, won't you, will you, won't you, will you
    leave the house ?
  Will you, won't you, will you, won't you, will you
    leave the house ? "

~~~~~~~~~~~~~~~~~~~~~~~~~~

PARLIAMENTARY ALPHABET.

A 'S the Address they present to the Queen,
    B's Mr. Bradlaugh, who made such a scene.
C is the Censure so helplessly parried,
D's the Division which discipline carried.
E stands for Egypt, 'tis plain to the tyro—
F is the Fainéant ruler at Cairo.
G is the Government, scarcely at ease,
H the Home-Rulers it's anxious to please.
I is the Irishman known as their captain,
J is the Jail that he ought to be clapt in.
K is Kilmainham to suit his convenience;
L is the Loss he would be to the Fenians.
M is the Member, as half-and-half cast,
N is Northampton which " sticks to its *lust.*"
O is the Oath he unlawfully took,
P is the Party which brought him to book.
Q is the Question that's so indiscreet.
R the Reply so evasively neat.
S is the Speaker, who rules the debate,
T is the Trials he's gone through of late.

U is the Unparliamentary phrase,
V the Vulgarity which it displays.
W's Westminster just before four;
X the policeman who stands at the door.
Y is the Youth who at meetings can prate,
Z is the Zero he forms in debate.

MARCH 6, 1884.

BOARD OF WORKS—OBITUARY.

POOR Board! 'tis the fated morning,
  The hated "appointed day";
Thy masters have given the warning,
  And now thou must pass away.
Yes, thy members have had their pickings—
  Commissions, and jobs, and "perks";
Thy record, I fear, is not quite so clear
  As it might be, O Board of Works.

Oh! put not your trust in Ritchies—
  Once more is this truth impressed—
For into thee Ritchie pitches
  As fiercely as all the rest.
The Firths get their armour ready,
  The Roseberys draw their dirks,
And I hear them say, "The appointed day
  Has come for thee, Board of Works."

Our Councillors now watch o'er us,
  But haply as years shall wane,
And their record is laid before us,
  We may wish for thee back again.

Thou hast done good work in thy season,
And a touch of regret still lurks
Right down in my heart, as I see thee part,
Unfortunate Board of Works!

March, 1889.

~~~~~~~~~~~~~~~~~~~

GORDON TO THE RESCUE.

THERE once was a Cabinet sorely perplexed.
They didn't know what in the world to do next,
They couldn't do less
Than ignobly confess
That they'd got themselves into a deuce of a mess.

They'd brought up their navy, and knocked, so to speak,
Alexandria into the midst of next week.
And Arabi bold
Into space had been hurled,
And his army expunged from the face of the world.

Then the Mahdi arose, most determined of foes.
And put his prophetic thumb up to his nose;
He was down upon Hicks
Like a hundred of bricks,
And he put the Khedive in a terrible fix.

So the Cabinet met and took counsel together,
And talked of more serious things than the weather
And the Grand Old Man
To his chums began,
" I think, my dear boys, that I've hit on a plan
To pacify Egypt and cut the Soudan.

" You've all heard of Gordon—I mean the Chinese—
Who scatters his foes like as chaff to the breeze.
With the confident ease of a man shelling peas :
       Now he is the man
      To set right the Soudan,
And settle the Mahdi, if any one can.

" You've heard, I presume, of a place called Khartoum.
It's a fort, I believe, where there's plenty of room.
Now if Gordon could once at Khartoum show his face,
The Mahdi would be in a pretty tight place,
And we should be saved from defeat and disgrace."

So to Gordon they wired, twenty words for a shilling,
And quickly the answer came, " Barkis is willing."
      He's a rum'un is Gordon
      When he buckles his sword on.
He'll be back in a month from the banks of the Jordan
      (I should say the Nile—
      I see some of you smile),
With the Mahdi disgraced and this troublesome war
   done.

      Without further delay,
      On the very same day,
The General packed up and started away.
And all of the luggage he took from his home
Was a sponge-bag, containing sponge, toothbrush,
   and comb.

And when in due course he arrived at Khartoum
He wrote manifestoes proclaiming the doom
Of the Mahdi and Osman and Heaven knows whom,
But somehow they didn't produce the effect
That the General thought he'd a right to expect.
      Unfinished.

THE CHAIR! THE CHAIR! THE CHAIR.

MY grand old age is crushed of late
By one unending care,
Which thus succinctly I may state :
The Chair, the Chair, the Chair !

The interviewer now I prize,
Whom once I could not bear ;
And this the sum of my replies :
" The Chair, the Chair, the Chair ! "

The *Peel* unto the *Orange* sticks
Till all is *blue*, I swear ;
And we're in such an awkward fix.
We must re-Peel the Chair !

Whene'er I fall two stools between—
A thing which is not rare—
I mutter, " This would not have been
Had I been in the Chair."

When at my desk I sit all day,
I'm most uneasy there,
And if I'm asked the cause, I say
" The Chair, the Chair, the Chair ! "

With " Chairs to mend " I hear folks wend
Along the thoroughfare ;
But in our case no power can mend
The Chair, the Chair, the Chair.

MR. GLADSTONE AND THE EISTEDDFOD.

THE Druids all to Albert Hall
　　Gathered from far and wide;
The Grand Old Man—so rumour ran—
　　Had promised to preside.

" A Welsh address!　He can't do less
　　For ' gallant little Wales ';
Though Welsh is tough, he'll learn enough :
　　He's one who never fails."

The reverend *Hwfa Môn* arrives,
　　And *Clwydfardd*, too, Arch-Druid,
Their hands no longer armed with knives,
　　Nor stained with vital fluid.

Assembled is the Eisteddfod,
　　And people—to be honest—
Begin to think it rather odd
　　That Mr. G. is " *non est.*"

A note is read : " Have kept my bed
　　Since Friday—most unpleasant—
Engagement off—a tightish cough—
　　Regret I can't be present."

His Welsh address he must suppress :
　　The cough applies the closure ;
But is it true that that is due,
　　As he says, to exposure ?

It's plain to see that Mr. G.
　　Unjustly blames the weather :
He's got his cough by reeling off
　　Twelve consonants together !

August 10, 1887.

THE EISTEDDFOD OF WALES.

Note.

*C*LWYDFARDD, the Chief Druid, having attained the great age of 85 years, *Hwfa Môn* (the Rev. R. Williams), acting as Chief Druid, delivered an address in Welsh. . . . Considerable disappointment was felt at the absence of Mr. Gladstone, as president. The right hon. gentleman, however, sent the following letter of apology, which was read by Mr. Richard, M.P. :

"21, Carlton House Terrace,

"*August* 4.

"Dear Mr. Richard,—After addressing the representative London meeting last Friday, I caught *from exposure* a sore throat, which passed into a *tight cough*, and I was *confined to bed until yesterday*. It has given way, but I could not undertake so soon after the attack to address a public meeting on the 9th. It is true that I had intended, and still intend, to go to Hawarden this week; but even if in London I should not have been able to undertake the office of President of the Eisteddfod.

"Accept, therefore, my cordial good wishes for the celebrations of next week, and believe me, dear Mr. Richard,

"Most faithfully yours,

"W. E. GLADSTONE."

Standard, August 10, 1887.

MR. GLADSTONE AND THE WASP.

MR. GLADSTONE, while felling a tree on
Saturday, was stung by an insect, which produced a swelling of the eyelid, but no serious results
are anticipated.—*Times*, Monday, October 25, 1886.

You say 'twas a wasp or a fly,
 That went for the master of Hawarden,
And stung the old man in the eye—
 Well, you're out of it, begging your pardon.
I happen to know as a fact,
 And I'll stake my existence upon it.
That William E. G. was attacked
 By the bee that he's got in his bonnet.

October 28, 1886.

TREVELYAN THE TRIMMER.

OH, who has not heard of George Otto Trevelyan,
 The rising young star in the Liberal skies?
For all used to say he was one in a million,
 So statesmanlike, steady, courageous, and wise!
 But George O.
 Trevelyan, you know,
As a statesman has shown himself rather so-so.

Trevelyan and Chamberlain both left the Cabinet,
  When Gladstone caved in to Pat Ford and Parnell;
The Bill was brought in, and when Joe put a stab in it,
  George had a hand in the slaughter as well;
            For George O.
            Trevelyan, you know,
Thought he couldn't be wrong if he stuck to his Joe.

His support of the Union was loyal and hearty;
  He spoke like a man without favour or fear:
" When the country's in danger, what care I for party ?
  A fig for ambition and future career ! "
            And George O.
            Trevelyan, you know,
Said the nastiest things about Parnell and Co.

In so noble a cause he cared nought for the schism
  That split up his party and crippled its might;
He talked very big about patriotism,
  And fought his election for justice and right.
            But George O.
            Trevelyan, you know,
At Hawick received a disheartening blow.

Oh, then was the winter of *his* discontent!
  To be out of the House didn't quite suit his book;
And he very soon let it be seen that he meant
  To get back to St. Stephen's by hook or by crook.
            For George O.
            Trevelyan, you know,
Said, " To be an outsider's uncommonly slow."

He was asked to go in for the contest at Brighton,
    But George at the time hadn't made up his mind.
Poor fellow! he didn't know which side to fight on,
    And so he politely but firmly declined.
            And George O.
            Trevelyan, you know,
Was aware that he wouldn't have much of a show.

So he " sat on the fence " in the dolefullest dumps,
    And he couldn't determine which side to descend.
Said he, " I must notice which way the cat jumps—
    Meantime to both parties I'll pose as a friend."
            For George O.
            Trevelyan, you know,
Was a little uncertain how matters would go.

But at Glasgow when asked " Under which King,
        Bezonian ? "
    By the Liberal party of Bridgeton, to wit,
He saw a safe seat, and said, " I'm a Gladstonian,
    Although I've not changed my opinions a bit."
            For George O.
            Trevelyan, you know,
Professes to think that he's got *quid pro quo.*

So George has gone over to Parnell and Davitt,
    Though once he was sternly opposed to Home Rule,
And declared that the man who'd allow them to have it
    Must be, in two words, either traitor or fool.
            But George O.
            Trevelyan, you know,
Says that's what he said more than twelve months ago,

" Law and order ! " he cried, and " The loyal minority ! "
    " My public life haply may come to a close ;
But I'll never consent to give power and authority
    To subsidised agents of alien foes."
                But George O.
                Trevelyan, you know,
Says he made those remarks fully six months ago.

So Glasgow has sent him once more to St. Stephen's
    To back up the Grand Old Magician's pet hobby ;
But if Home Rule comes forward, it's just about evens
    That George will be found in the opposite lobby.
                For George O.
                Trevelyan, you know,
May possibly kick at Ford, Egan and Co.

What then ?   Is the star of the Unionists dimmer
    Because such a man has deserted the flag ?
No ; let them rejoice to be rid of a trimmer,
    Whose backbone's as limp as a piece of wet rag.
                For George O.
                Trevelyan, you know,
Did more harm as a friend that he can as a foe.

1887.

PAIRS AND THE ALL-NIGHT SITTING OF MARCH 21, 1887.

By our Special Reporter.

OH, they had such a rollicking time at St. Stephen's !
All night they determined to keep up the fun ;
And the betting appeared to be just about evens
That a couple of sittings they'd roll into one.

I discovered O'Grady, M.P., with a Hansard,
At 7 a.m. fast asleep in a chair :
" They're dividing," I cried ; " go and vote." But he
answered :
" Bedad ! I can't vote, Sorr, because I'm a pair."

" You a *peer !* " I exclaimed, the expression mistaking ;
For the brogue of O'Grady is second to none.
" Whoever a peer out of you has been making ? "
" Be aisy," he answered, " wid pokin' yer fun."

Then another came in, looking pale and dejected,
And said, " I am anxious to vote, but I mayn't."
Till a crowd of impatient M.P.'s had collected,
And this was the burden of each one's complaint :

" I'm a pair, in the lobby forbidden to mingle :
The whip says I mustn't at present go there.
At 9, I am told, I shall once more be single,
But up to that moment, alas ! I'm a pair "

MARCH 30, 1887.

Mr. Akers Douglas: In answer to the question just put to me by the hon. member for the Scotland Division of Liverpool, I beg to say that, as far as I know, no member who was paired for the night voted in the closure division. In answer to my hon. friend the member for Nottingham, I believe that some twenty-five members of this House, supporters of the Government, paired for the night on Monday, the 21st inst., but I cannot admit that they voted "during the continuance of such pairs." Of these members, twenty-two voted after 9.30 in the morning of Tuesday with my sanction, and in so voting I contend that they were acting in concert with and not "in opposition to the recognised rules which govern the practice of pairs between members of this House." *I have always understood that a pair entered into for "the night" is only intended to hold good until the morning, and that if two members wish to pair for the whole sitting, such an arrangement is specified in the pair list by the words "For sitting." On the occasion alluded to, several hon. members came down to the House desiring to vote in the closure division, but acting upon my advice refrained from voting until after 9 o'clock in the morning, at which time I considered there could be no question but that "pairs" for the night had lapsed.—Times.*

March 30, 1887.

FIRST CLASS.

MR. O'BRIEN, being removed from Clonmel to Killarney, refused to go into a third or second class carriage. He said, "If you attempt to make me go by any other than first class you will have to use force."

Oh, shameful outrageous indignity;
  The like of it never was heard :
Vile offspring of Balfour's malignity,
  To make an O'Brien go "third."

In petty devices and small ways
  Of plaguing his foes he is versed.
So he sends a man "third" who is always
  Accustomed to travelling "first."

By my ancestors' bones! the O'Briens
  Would vastly prefer to be cast,
Like the Christians of old, to the lions,
  Than thus with the "thirds" to be classed.

We say to the mob, very truly,
  We're fighting with them side by side ;
But to press such a theory unduly
  Is foolish—I know, for I've tried.

Regarded as just an abstraction,
  I grant that we're all on a level ;
But the theory when put into action
  Infallibly goes to the d——.

Mr. Balfour is apt to mistake me ;
  He thinks with the vulgar I'll herd ;
But it's only by force he can make me
  Wear prison costume, or go " third."

Yes, I flatter myself I'm more knowing ;
  I've always as yet had the sense
To travel first-class—when I'm going
  At somebody else's expense.

~~~~~~~~~~~~~~~~~~~~~

THE MISSING LINK.

THE shade of Darwin crossed the Styx
  And landed on Elysium's brink ;
One thought alone his mind could fix—
  The problem of the Missing Link.

Then in the regions of the blest
  He met a priestess of Apollo ;
And she, when asked to aid his quest,
  Responded in the lines that follow :

" When mingled genius and fool
  For England's sins shall mount to power,
And yield to traitors' threats Home Rule
    In evil hour ;

" In that ' last link,' that's left to bind
  Two lands, as dreamers fondly think,
Thy countrymen too late shall find
    The Missing Link ! "

APRIL, 1887.

PARNELL ON HIS "LAST LINK" SPEECH.

THESE Englishmen are so absurd,
    So wanting in imagination,
They always give one's every word
    Its literal interpretation.
Rebellious phrases may be quite
    Innocuous when used in my sense ;
Regarded in the proper light
    It's mere electioneering licence.
I praised the hand of fellowship
    Stretched out by Nolan's shady party.
I must confess I made a slip,
    But they expected something hearty.
And "à la Gladstone," I'll explain—
    If not entirely metaphorical,
Yet, on the whole, and in the main,
    'Twas just a flourish oratorical.
And when I spoke of that "last link"—
    Although I don't admit I said it,
For such reporters none can think
    Deserving of the slightest credit—
But, anyhow, the phrase 'tis clear
    Admits of easy explanation,
For, obviously, it was mere
    Rhetorical exaggeration.

THE RAPE OF THE MOUSTACHE.

THE wife of Mr. E. Harrington, M.P., writing from Tralee to a correspondent respecting her husband's imprisonment, says :—"Nothing could equal the indignation of the people here at Balfour's cowardly act in cutting off my husband's moustache. Numbers of Conservatives have expressed their disgust to me in regard to the mean act. But even Balfour could not remove the roots of it, so that one as good will grow again. And I am sure that a moustache never had so many kind friends sympathetically watching its growth as that one will have."—*Standard*, February 1, 1888.

When they took off my Edward to prison,
   I felt just as wild as a bear.
But my anger has sensibly risen
   At what they have done to him there.

'Tis not that he's forced willy-nilly
   To put on the prison costume ;
'Tis not on account of the skilly
   My Edward's obliged to consume.

'Tis not that he misses his toddy ;
   'Tis not that he's mighty ill-fed ;
'Tis not that his fine handsome body
   Is laid on an ugly plank-bed.

His hands of such elegant whiteness
   Are spoilt with the oakum he picks ;
And him, that's the pink of politeness,
   They force him with felons to mix.

But it isn't these hardships so cruel,
  For which Bloody Balfour I curse ;
They have put upon Edward, my jewel,
  An outrage a thousand times worse.

Oh ! worse than all other atrocities !
  Ay, worse than the torturer's lash !
Most foul of inhuman monstrosities—
  They've cut off my Edward's moustache !

But yet, spite of Balfour the craven,
  And all of the cowardly brutes—
Though my Edward's moustache is clean-shaven,
  They couldn't get rid of the roots !

And when his captivity's ended,
  And Balfour at last lets him out,
Another moustache just as splendid
  Will soon be beginning to sprout.

Sure, never moustache in creation
  Excited folks' interest so ;
For every one's chief occupation
  Will just be observing it grow.

In the finest of Irish society
  It's we will be cutting the dash,
While they're watching with tender anxiety
  The state of my Edward's moustache.

"NOT TO-DAY, BAKER!"

THE gallant Boulanger,
   Had just got his *congé*,
And felt in a quarrelsome mood ;
   When Citizen Ferry
   Thought well to make merry
And jest in a manner most rude.

"Parbleu!" said the General;
" Women and men are all
Laughing at Ferry's vile joke.
   With his second-rate wit, is an
   Insolent citizen
Fun at a *soldier* to poke ?

"No, no! in a duel
I'll give him his gruel,
At twenty-five yards, the first round :
   If we miss, we will go on
   Five nearer, and so on,
Till one of us lies on the ground."

Then Citizen Ferry
No longer looked merry.
" What ! go on till one of us falls !
   The fellow means murder !
   What *could* be absurder ?
As if we were barbarous Gauls !

" In so bloodthirsty, cruel,
And wicked a duel
I never will be a partaker ;
And so, while sincerely
Regretting, I'll merely
Reply to him, ' Not to-day, *Baker !* ' "

Jules Ferry in a public speech having alluded to General
Boulanger as a " St. Arnaud de café-concert," was challenged
by the latter. The General's seconds insisted on such unreas-
onable conditions that M. Ferry's seconds declined to accept
them, and the duel was therefore abandoned.—See *Standard,*
August 3, 1887.

WAR SYMPTOMS.

I T seems, on the whole, quite clear
That the long-threatened war is near,
For " Our Own Correspondents " are all agog :
Each day they discover fresh clouds that fog
The political atmosphere.

The statesmen protest that war
Is just what they all abhor ;
But Bismarck was yesterday seen by chance
Surreptitiously buying a map of France !
What else could he want it for ?

    *   Then General Boulanger
        Has suddenly sent away

* *Standard,* March 3.—General Boulanger has just issued a
circular to the Commanders of all French Army Corps, that for
the future officers are *not to be allowed to have any foreigner,
male or female, in their households employed as servants, &c.*
This is in consequence of General Davoust's governess turning
out to be the wife of a *Prussian officer* quartered near the French
frontier.

His valet, who hailed from the Fatherland;
And Monsieur de Blowitz, I understand,
    Says it heralds the coming fray.

  *   No one knows what the Czar is at,
    But the Petersburg Bourse is flat,
For they say that to keep up his warlike habits
His Majesty's potting his Aides like rabbits!
    Pray, what do you think of that?

  †   At Vienna and Buda-Pesth
    There's a feeling of vague unrest,
For the Emperor-King at a great Court Ball
Wouldn't take any supper, but left the hall
    Quite early, and seemed depressed.

    The Sultan, they say, last night
    Made a call on Sir William White
And wanted to borrow a five-pound note;
And you know that he always attempts to float
    A loan, when he means to fight.

    And matters at Rome look queer,
    For a War Office clerk, I hear,
Gave an order last week at a pastry-cook's
For two dozen tins of *sardines de luxe!*
    So they're laying in stores, it's clear.

---

* *Pall Mall Gazette* and other papers give currency to a report that the Czar has *shot one of his Aides-de-camp*, Major
Reutern, under the impression that the latter, who sprang up
hurriedly to receive him, was about to attack him.

† *Standard*, February 4.—*Vienna.*—At the great annual In-
dustriellen Ball the utmost eagerness was shown to learn what
the Emperor said in conversation with various persons. . . .
*Their Majesties remained only a short time in the Ball-room—
less than three-quarters of an hour, in fact—and it was the
subject of general notice that the Emperor looked very serious
during this time.*

Correspondents, you see, discern
War symptoms at every turn ;
From the veriest trifles they draw sure signs
By a process called " reading between the lines "—
It's not very hard to learn !

MARCH 6, 1887.

~~~~~~~~~~~~~~~~~~~~~~~

THE BOY-KING OF SERVIA.

I'VE never made out what papa was about
   When he gave me his crown as a present ;
But although to be King is a very fine thing,
   In some ways it's rather unpleasant.
These Regents, you know, are down on me so,
   They won't let me do what I want to.
Oh ! why did mamma have a row with papa,
   And where in the world is she gone to ?
     I want to get home my mamma, &c.

Oh ! the lessons my tu-tors compel me to do
   At the times when I ought to be playing !
They talk about Russia, and Austria, too,
   And I don't understand what they're saying.
Old Ristichs he drops on my marbles and tops,
   And declares I've more serious duties.
It was only to-day that the brute took away
   My two alley-tors—oh, such beauties !
     I want to get home my mamma, &c.

What's the use of a crown if you're always kept down
　　By a parcel of stupid old Regents ?
I'm nearly thirteen, and you bet that I mean
　　To get even some day with those three gents.
They're backed up by the dad ; I call him just as bad ;
　　But I soon shall be getting my freedom.
Old Ristichs and pa, and my subjects, ha! ha!
　　They'll see what a life I shall lead 'em.
　　　I want to get home my mamma, &c.

RECIPE FOR MILK PUNCH.

TAKE a dozen large lemons—the largest there are—
　　Peel thin to the best of your powers;
Put the rind, with a bottle of rum, in a jar,
　　And leave it for twenty-four hours.

At the end of that time put the rind and the rum
　　In a 'mug '—you can hardly mistake it;
Then squeeze out your lemons with finger and thumb,
　　Or a squeezer—but mind you don't break it.

A bottle of lemon juice thus you must get,
　　And put in four pounds of best sugar ;
And be sure that you don't begin tasting as yet
　　How nice the contents of the ' mug ' are.

Three bottles of milk measured carefully out,
　　When just ' on the boil ' you must pitch in;"
But the amateur cook will burn it, no doubt,
　　So you'd best get it boiled in the kitchen.

Five bottles of rum in the mug you must mix,
  And with three of cold water to follow.
Thus you see if you count 1, 2, 3, 4, 5, 6,
  It's half of it rum that you swallow.

Then add, most important of all,—the bouquet—
  Orange bitters—a wineglass, if handy ;
If you haven't them, put in a wineglass instead
  Of noyeau, and ditto of brandy.

The Punch is now made. You can taste if it's good,
  And you then let it stand for nine hours.
Never mind if it closely resembles the food
  That a pig with such relish devours.

As often as possible it should be stirred,
  But be careful, though, not to upset it ;
Then strain through new flannel, or, if it's preferred,
  A jelly bag—if you can get it.

Some people unhappily cannot control
  Their impatience when stirring the liquor ;
They hurry it up by inserting the bowl
  Of a spoon, and of course make it thicker.

Then bottle it, cork it, and seal it with care,
  And, if you've an artist who's able
To draw a good trade mark, a business-like air
  Is imparted by adding a label.

A dozen of Punch is concocted, you see ;
  On its side in the cellar you set it ;
And after a twelvemonth that liquor will be
  Pretty toothsome—and don't you forget it !

AN ACROSTIC AND LETTER TO FANNY ON HER ENGAGEMENT.

M Y dearest Coz, he offers you
    A *bird in*'s hand;
And in the bush that counts as two,
    You understand.

I.

All is not gold that glitters.

II.

For nine long days he wore upon his heart
This mystic word of Persian sages' art;
Then in the stream he flung the potent spell,
And waited the result—it was a sell.

III.

First of her tribe, on solitary wing,
She comes, but finds that she has not brought Spring.

IV.

His mustang o'er the New World's plains
He rides, *sans* saddle, bit, or reins;
And—pray don't let the ladies faint—
His dress is but a coat of paint.

V.

She urged this savage horde to fight
    Like Britons, and be free or die.
But when they faced the mailèd might
    Of Claudius' host, 'twas " all my eye."

VI.

Mounseer invokes "Blue Death "; the German's oath
 Is "Tausend Teufeln," "Donner," "Wetter," "Blitz."
John Bull's is rounder, more concise than both ;
 While Uncle Sam twangs slowly this——and spits.

VII.

My flesh by artisans despised,
By lords and gentlemen is prized.
My names are Legion with the "nobs."
But this I'm called by London Snobs.

I promised to send you a Valentine, cousin,
And I think this Acrostic's as long as a dozen.
If you manage to guess it, why send me the answer.
But you won't find it out—I think not, but I can't swear.
It is not quite so easy as " Troistemps " or Lancer
(You consider yourself an uncommon good dancer).

Fear not that my promise I've broken,
Of which many clasped hands were the token ;
I have not betrayed
The pledge that I made ;
Not a soul has surveyed
This sheet of cream laid,
So be not dismayed
Or the least bit afraid.
Though a fierce cannonade
Of cross-questions played
On me, yet as I've said
Your secret I never have spoken.

My firmness last Monday was splendid.
Cross-examined by all, I defended

My secret that night,
Though they bothered me quite—
Yes, they did, honour bright!
And I had such a fight;
Yet I cared not a mite.
It was really a sight,
They had hemmed me so tight
That at last I polite-
Ly took refuge in flight.
But if Fanny would write
And just free me from fright,
By saying I might
Tell her secret—all right.
My heart will be light,
And my face will be bright,
And I'll say with delight,
As friend Carl would observe, "All is ended."

Now, with love to Aunt Mary,
And Sydney and *Clary*,
To yourself and to Ada,
Not forgetting your "fader"—
Excuse all mistakes, I'm writing in bed,
And, believe me, your very affectionate FRED.

P.S.—If you shortly don't send me that photo.,
I really won't answer for where you will go to.

THE " MOIST AND JOVIAL."

To Mrs. G. M. Parker.

L ET others praise the luscious goose,
 Or turkey's tender slices;
Let others sing of Charlotte Russe,
 Or Gunter's peerless ices.
Some love the saddle or the haunch,
 While some prefer the brisket;
But be it mine my soul to launch
 In praise of thee, O Biscuit!

What snipe or duck that e'er was roast,
 What grouse that ever was born,
Can be compared with Extra-toast
 Or sweet seductive Osborne ?
If some rich uncle were to die
 And leave me wealth, I'd risk it,
And 'gainst all other dainties I
 Would back my darling Biscuit.

Some think Clicquot or Monopole
 Of ills a panacea ;
But I would urge the thirsty soul
 To try a Ratafia.
Some love the frequent S & B
 Or 'Polly' freely whiskied ;
But thirst and hunger yields with me
 To one delightful Biscuit.

At dawn I wake and always take
  A brace of Abernethies ;
An Albert then to me at ten
  Of life the very breath is.
Again at noon a Macaroon
  Revives my drooping spirits :
Some folks prefer Bath Oliver—
  That also has its merits.

At one I take an Oatmeal Cake
  To keep me in condition ;
At lunch likewise a Captain tries
  My powers of deglutition.
I like at tea a sweet Marie
  And eke an Orange Wafer ;
I take at dusk the wholesome Rusk.
  Because I find it safer.

Milk Biscuits constitute at eight
  My salutary dinner :
I frequently assimilate
  A box, as I'm a sinner !
A Cracknel then I take at ten
  And down my throat I whisk it :
From morn to eve, I do believe,
  I'm ne'er without a Biscuit.

When Ascot tempts with champagne lunch
  I feel extremely festive,
But, mindful of the morrow, munch
  The genial Digestive.
When faint and weary, hot and dry,
  As in the waltz I frisk it,
In the refreshment-room I cry
  " Give, oh, give me a Biscuit."

They tease me so, and call me "green,"
  And put me in a frenzy;
They crack their jokes at Peak and Frean,
  And laugh to scorn Mackenzie.
But I have got one sure relief,
  I care not for their follies;
In ev'ry sort of pain and grief
  A Biscuit is my solace.

Some day I'll write a ditty rare,
  A Biscuit-panegyric!
To a fair dame in Thurloe Square
  I'll dedicate my lyric;
And in dress-suit and choker white,
  And shirt superbly ironed,
I'll sing thy praise with all my might,
  Thou moist and jovial viand!

Then in a bundle I will take
  A tooth-brush and my bedding,
And on my own two feet I'll make
  A pilgrimage to Reading.
There in the church's solemn nave
  My conscience will be calmer:
I'll drop a tear on Huntley's grave,
  And breathe a prayer for Palmer

CHRISTMAS, 1884.

DIRGE OF A DISAPPOINTED MAN.

I NEVER nursed a dear gazelle—
   You'll hardly credit the assertion—
And on the whole it's just as well :
   Pets always were my pet aversion.

Gazelles, I think, were rather rare,
   Or rather dear, where I resided ;
Most people nurse them, I'm aware,
   But still I cannot say that I did.

I got on pretty well without,
   And even if my hand I'd tried,
There's not a shadow of a doubt
   The luckless creature would have died.

'Twas ever thus from childhood's hour :
   I was a most unlucky wooer :
The first I loved turned cross and sour
   When I began to cotton to her.

My next, blue-eyed and darkly lashed,
   With hair of fashionable yellow,
Just when I was completely mashed,
   Got married to another fellow !

It's always been the same with me :
   Whene'er I think I've found my Venus,
She goes to France or Italy,
   And puts a thousand miles between us.

Or else she breaks a leg or arm,
   Or catches some infectious fever,
And the fair hair that used to charm
   Begins reluctantly to leave her.

I met a girl not long ago :
   Ah ! rarely have I seen her equal !—
A girl it was a treat to know—
   I hardly need relate the sequel.

We had such charming chats together :
   She had been living in the tropics ;
And so we talked about the weather,
   And other interesting topics.

She'd read till she was nearly blind—
   Such was her studious disposition—
Whole evenings she would feed her mind
   On Shakespeare in a cheap edition.

Ah me ! I basked in smiles bewitching,
   As in the moonbeams basked Endymion ;
For she was what I find most fetching
   In women—just a shade Bohemian.

Once, if it had not been so late
   (Something occurred, of course, to baulk us)
We should have gone en *tête-à-tête*
   To tea at Charbonell and Walker's.

Too soon my misery began :
   My awful luck will never leave me :
I am a Disappointed Man !
   You may or you may not believe me.

Alas ! my grief is past concealing :
   Like all the rest, away she goes ;
And I may ne'er see A— F—
   On this side of the grave ! Who knows ?

JANUARY, 1885.

AN AFTERNOON CALL.

THROUGH Thurloe Square, without a "gamp,"
   I chanced to pass: the air was damp,
     The sky grew darker;
And when the rain began to fall,
The time seemed opportune to call
     On Mrs. Parker.

Myself and her I thought to please,
Because she thinks a lot of these
     Polite attentions.
A formal call I meant to pay,
Say, " How d'ye do ? " and get away
     To the " Inventions."

But man proposes here below,
And woman—well, of course, you know
     The common saying;
I didn't like to seem a beast,
And though I never had the least
     Design of staying,

My charming hostess pressed me so,
That really I could hardly go
     With due propriety.
She said she felt by no means fit,
And wanted waking up a bit
     By my society.

And so I tried with might and main
To strike a bright and lively vein
     Of conversation;
And every now and then, I trust,
My struggling wit emitted just
     A scintillation.

But how could I be brisk and gay,
When all my jokes were thrown away,
   Howe'er amusing?
I knew not why they fell so flat,
Until I chanced to notice that
   Madame was snoozing!

I often ask, Why has my con-
Versation this effect upon
   Her organs aural?
Have I, a thinking, breathing man,
In life no higher function than
   A dose of chloral?

I don't, for *my* part, care a fig,
But still it *does* seem *infra dig.*
   For one's humanity.
I know I talk an awful lot
Of stuff that some call "Tommy-rot,"
   And some, inanity.

Perhaps I've smoked my wits away—
My conversation, as you say,
   Is mainly drivel;
Yet though in it you cannot take
Much interest—to keep awake
   Is only civil.

But stay, Madame, though I'm a dunce,
I've got a bright idea for once—
   I haven't many;
I think I see a way to turn
My talents to account, and earn
   An honest penny.

You know, when balmy sleep has failed,
What misery and woe's entailed
    On weary mortals;
How in their beds they turn and toss,
And ever strive in vain to cross
    Sleep's blessed portals.

Now, scores and scores of remedies
Have been brought out, and yet it is
    Most strange and curious,
That no one has contrived to get
A drug that takes effect, and yet
    Is not injurious.

They patent some new cure each day,
And vaunt its virtues. Need I say
    They overstate 'em ?
A remedy that's harmless *and*
Effectual, is still the grand
    Desideratum.

'Tis surely matter for surprise
That great physicians—learned, wise,
    And scientific—
Have racked their brains and laboured much,
But vainly, to discover such
    A soporific.

Yet I—who, as you say, am dense—
Not burdened with excessive sense,
    Nor intellectual,
Have managed to devise a cure
That's easy, pleasant, safe, and sure,
    And most effectual.

So I intend to advertise
Myself a cure for aching eyes :
    It will be funny !
I feel convinced the thing will pay,
And now at length I see my way
    To making money.

I soon shall be in great demand :
I see myself in mansions grand,
    And halls baronial ;
And if a reference they crave,
I'm sure, Madame, you'll give your slave
    A testimonial.

The foe, Insomnia, I will strike
With vapid jest and twaddle, like
    A skilful fencer.
Old Morpheus shall my prowess see,
And yield his title up to me—
    The Sleep-Dispenser.

MAY 17, 1885.

RETRIBUTION.

THERE lived a youth not long ago,
    Whose fate deserves bewailing ;
Though nice enough, as people go,
    He'd one disastrous failing.

His indolence was so intense,
    He always was behind time ;
Whate'er he'd plan he ne'er began,
    Because he couldn't find time.

His debt to time he could not pay,
  Yet never ceased to borrow;
He never did a thing to-day
  That could be done to-morrow.

He never tried to cast aside
  Procrastination's fetters;
And worse than anything on earth
  He hated writing letters.

He never wrote the shortest note
  Except upon coercion.
He could not *think* of pens and ink
  Without intense aversion.

His letters they unanswered lay;
  His friends were all neglected;
And they made use of much abuse,
  As might have been expected.

'Twas useless quite for them to write
  In language strong and stronger;
Till in the end a lady-friend
  Could stand the thing no longer.

So with a frown she sat her down,
  And in her best handwriting
A letter penned, from end to end
  Replete with satire biting.

He read the cru-el letter through
  With anguish past concealing;
To tell the truth, he was a youth
  Of very tender feeling.

His heart was wrung, his nerves unstrung,
   His very soul was stricken ;
He laid his head upon his bed,
   And soon began to sicken.

Too sensitive he was to live,
   And so he faded slowly ;
But he confessed, ere laid to rest,
   It was his own fault wholly.

Some friends were found his death-bed round,
   Early one winter morning ;
And unto them at 2 a.m.
   He gave this solemn warning—

" Confess I must, my fate is just,
   But oh, my friends, do better ;
You'll come to this, if you're remiss
   In answering a letter.

Especially, if it should be
   A lady who's offended :
Be warned in time to shun my crime,
   Nor do as Pattenden did."

OCTOBER, 1885.

~~~~~~~~~~~~~~

THE BROKEN BRACELET.

Stamford Ball, 1886.

HOW happy was I when she bore me
   Away on her arm to the Ball ;
Had I known what a fate was before me
   I wouldn't have gone there at all.

I was only a foolish young bracelet,
  And the thought never entered my head
That 'twere better had I in my place let
  Some other be taken instead.

But I was so proud of adorning
  The arm where I loved to be worn,
And little I dreamt that the morning
  Would find me all broken and torn.

All golden I daintily dangled;
  To clasp the fair wrist was so sweet;
But now I'm so hopelessly mangled,
  I doubt if I'm even complete.

With the dancers we joyonsly mingled,
  And all was so happy and bright;
My links I exultingly jingled—
  My way of expressing delight.

When down on us some one came tearing,
  I cannot say who, but I think
I shall not be far wrong in declaring
  It was one of those fellows in pink.

How I wish that that colour were rarer!
  For a notion appears to prevail
That a pink coat entitles the wearer
  To romp on a magnified scale.

I was forcibly seized by the middle,
  Like the grip of a giant it seemed!
And I think that the noise of the fiddle
  Was drowned by the scream that I screamed.

It was only the work of a minute,
   An agony ran through my length,
And I felt I was simply not in it
   When it comes to a trial of strength.

It dragged all my fibres asunder;
   What the pain was I never can say;
But I now understand—and no wonder!—
   The meaning of "*Scheiden thut weh.*"

A shattered and quivering bracelet,
   All helpless I hung on her wrist;
And my owner within just an ace let
   Me tumble unnoticed, unmissed.

In the pocket of somebody's waistcoat
   The rest of that evening I lay,
And there, by the side of his dress-coat,
   I hung till the following day.

And now I must go to the jeweller—
   Most horrible prospect of all!—
To be tortured with agonies crueller
   Than those I endured at the Ball.

I remember—how well I remember!—
   The workshop wherein I was born;
It occurred in the month of December,
   About ten o'clock of the morn.

I remember the pincers and pliers,
   The blowpipe, the tongs, and the rest;
And the heat of those terrible fires
   Was like—something that's better suppressed.

I'm convinced on a calm diagnosis
  Of the tortures attending my birth,
That a more diabolical process
  Was never invented on earth.

Now back to those torments they'll take me,
  To be tugged at and twisted and torn.
Oh, why in the world did they make me?
  I wish I had never been born.

For me all life's sweetness is ended—
  Its joys are all over for me;
I shall ne'er be again, when I'm mended,
  The bracelet I once used to be.

JANUARY, 1886.

A PARTING MESSAGE.

After Edmund Waller.

G O, lovely Rose!
    Tell her, that wastes her time on me,
  That now her nose
In radiant hue resembles thee,
So bright and red it seems to be.

  Tell her its point,
That soars aloft in conscious pride,
    Is out of joint,
Because I can no more abide
A nose that looks as if 'twere dyed.

Small is the worth
Of beauty howsoe'er attired,
But—Saints on earth !—
I draw the line at noses fired
With blushes not to be admired.

Then die, that she
Each morn on rising from her bed
May learn of thee
To *dye* her nose some tint instead,
That's not so wondrous bright and red.

1886.

TCH!

A Study in pronunciation suggested by an argument on the word "Chivalry."

ONCE I dined at a charming old *Tchateau,*
A relic of *tchivalrous* times,
Looking down from a well-wooded plateau
Of poplars and beeches and limes.

The proprietor hailed from *Tchicago;*
He'd rather the look of a *tcharlatan;*
The *tchatelaine* was quite a virago
In yellow *tchenille* and pink tarlatan.

The furniture looked like veneer,
And was tarnished and soiled by the weather;
The ponderous gilt *tchandelier*
Stood in need of a good *tchamois*-leather.

The *tchef* was a simple beginner,
  And oh! the *tchampagne* was so sweet;
While the claret we drank after dinner
  Was a libel on *Tchateau* Lafitte.

The daughter, named *Tcharlotte*—a plainer I
  Have never yet seen in creation—
Tried with archness and wily *tchicanery*
  To entangle me in a flirtation.

She'd an imp of a brother, Charles Edward,
  So called from the young *Tchevalier*:
They ought to have packed him off bedward
  With an insect unnamed in his ear.

This youth, up to all kinds of devilry,
  Got behind an old dowager's chair,
And, lost to all notions of *tchivalry*,
  Pulled off the poor woman's back-hair.

The *tchagrin* of that elderly *tchaperon*,
  On seeing her *tchignon* appear,
Hung up by the young whipper-snapper on
  The top of a high *tchiffonier*!

Then they played a *tcharade*, but the crowd
  Went on talking, and never once faltered,
So I shouted out " *tch* !" very loud—
  I used to say "*sh* !" but I've altered.

I happened to stand at ten thirty
  Before a *tcheval*-glass, and found
That my shirt-front was shockingly dirty,
  So I ordered my pony-*tchaise* round.

MAY, 1886.

MY FAVOURITE PIPE.

W HAT a nuisance! Some rascally fellow
   Has collared my favourite pipe—
The one that was always so mellow,
   So fragrant and nutty and ripe.
Why on earth need the villain have chosen my
   favourite?
Hang him, whoever he is! He shall pay for it.

Without it I'm wretched and lonely,
   Distracted by sorrow and grief.
Oh, what would I give if I only
   Could manage to find out the thief!
From the County Court Judge I should certainly
   crave a writ :
" Wrongful conversion, to wit," of my Favourite.

The rascal he knew how to choose it,
   From all of the pipes lying round.
Of course he intended to use it
   For smoking himself, I'll be bound.
Oh, he must be an artful experienced knave, or it
Wouldn't have struck him to collar my Favourite.

Any other I could have forgiven—
   But my favourite pipe! It's no joke ;
To my second-best now I am driven—
   It isn't a bad one to smoke.
Though I hardly need say that for sweetness and
   flavour, it
Doesn't begin to compare with my Favourite.

How often I've smoked by the fire
  That briar—so precious to me!
That briar! Stay—was it a briar?
  Or could it have been—let me see—
'Pon my word, how absurd! I'm beginning to waver, it
Might, after all, have been meerschaum, my Favourite.

It's mouthpiece I'm positive—nearly—
  Was amber or horn, rather small;
It was curved—yes, I've now got it clearly—
  No! wasn't it straight, after all?
I remember its taste, even now I can savour it—
Odd, I've forgotten the shape of my Favourite.

My brain in a muddle is whirling—
  'Twas either a meerschaum and straight,
Or else 'twas a briar and curling;
  But which, I'm unable to state.
There's one thing, however, I safely can say for it—
Meerschaum or briar—that pipe was my Favourite.

TO MABEL.

MAID, who fillest my thoughts wheresoever I roaM,
    At breakfast, at luncheon, at 5 o'clock teA,
Be my song but the music of paper and comB,
E'en thus will I sing, and sing only of theE.
      Love I cannot conceaL:
      Let thy heart, dearest, feeL
Emotions of similar nature for mE.

TO M. G.

YOU promised, fair damsel, to give me a photo,
    But in vain have I waited full many a day;
I really can't answer for where you will go to—
    But I now know what's meant by the " Promise of
    MAY."

But at Christmas no rancour can lurk in my breast,
    Though I cannot help thinking you might have been
    kinder;
And so deep on my heart is your image impressed,
    That never, I trow, shall I need a reminder.

A RECOMMENDATION FOR A CANTON GUIDE, WONG AYEW.

IF you're wanting a guide, gentle tourist, I pray you
    To turn your attention to Mr. Wong Ayew.
He'll show you the sights of the City of Rams,
And tell you a number of innocent crams;
Discourse on the customs, the laws, and religion,
In English that's known by the epithet " pigeon ";
Show you opium dens, where the noble Celestial
Rejoices to grovel in lethargy bestial.
The Court which examines its prisoners by blows,
Or fastens them up by their thumbs and great toes—
Yes, try 'em by torture, and hit on the raw !
That's true Chinese justice and Mandarin law.

He'll rush you through streets of unspeakable odours,
To paper-shops, pawn-shops, and Chinese pagodas.
In fact, when your peregrinations are done,
You'll agree that A-yew must be reckoned A1.

CANTON, DECEMBER 8, 1882.

TO SIGNOR DATTARI

(Of Messrs. Thomas Cook and Son).

D ATTARI, mighty minstrel of the mandolinic
     measure,
A ttuning with thy magic touch our hearts to pain or
     pleasure;
T o thee, the wily hand at whist or euchre with the
     joker,
T o thee, the Checker Champion—to thee, the Prince of
     Poker!
A t ease in jolting railway car, or steamer, foul and
     tarry,
R iding in "rickshaw" Japanese, or eke Calcutta
     "gharry,"
I n ev'ry country finding home, I sing to thee, Dattari.

MOTTO FOR DATTARI.

D OES Any Traveller To A Route Incline?
     I Readily A Tour To All Define.

S.s. *Niigata Maru*, DECEMBER 1, 1882.

LINES WRITTEN IN THE AUTOGRAPH BOOK
OF MISS KOUGH.

(N.B.—Pronounced " Keogh.")

A LADY has asked me to write her an "autograph,"
So she calls it, though really I don't know the
    sort of *graph* ;
But such is my unprecedented docility,
I meekly obey with becoming humility.
Yet for nearly a week—I confess it with shame—
I've vainly endeavoured to get at her name.
And I've hitherto failed to discover a way
To articulate "cough," when it's spelt with a " K."
Can anyone anyhow give a poor wretch
A tip for pronouncing K, O, U, G, H ?
One would think at first sight it was easy enough,
By all true analogy it should be Kough ;
And I'm rather inclined to believe it, although
There's authority surely for calling it Kough.
Of course he's a hog, and should feed at a trough,
Who'll dare for a moment to speak of Miss Kough.
Perhaps after all I shall find when I'm through,
That I've been the obedient slave of Miss Kough.
But now through the roaring Atlantic we plough,
So let us be nautical, eh, Miss Kough ?
And making a rhyme with a Yeo heave yeo,
Let's finally settle your name as Kough.

White Star S.s. *Britannic*, December 7, 1883.

Verses for or to Children.

POLL PARROT.

IN Pongoland, far, far away,
  Which lies beyond the sea,
 Where all the people, strange to say,
Are black as black can be,

A tree there was, so hard to climb,
  They tried with might and main;
Some got half up, but every time
  They tumbled down again.

Of all the climbers far and near,
  Young Sambo was the best;
And he got up at last, and there
  He found a parrots' nest.

He seized a young one by the wing,
  While round him in the air
Its mother screamed and cried, poor thing;
  But Sambo did not care.

Then home he took his captive quick;
  And when it cried for food,
It got some porridge on a stick;
  And thought it very good.

Now on the strand of Pongoland
 A strange old man was seen ;
He held a necklace in his hand
 Of beads all red and green.

Now Sambo loved his Polly well,
 But beads he much preferred ;
So when the man said, " Will you sell,"
 He answered, "Take the bird."

And Poll to England sailed next week
 On board the stranger's ship.
The sailors taught her how to speak ;
 And Poll enjoyed the trip.

Then caged, and always on the move,
 They hawked her round the street.
She'd none to pet her, none to love,
 And nothing nice to eat.

Kind people bought her one fine day ;
 And so her story's done.
She's always happy, always gay,
 And talks away like fun.

TO DOLLY.

THERE was a young lady named Dolly,
 Who was troubled with great melancholy ;
   So on going to bed
   She put ice on her head
And filled up her pillow with holly.

You'd have thought the arrangement was folly;
But it very soon made her so jolly
    That she got up arrayed
    In a " chimmy," and played
With a tortoiseshell cat and a dolly.

TO RODNEY.

AN odd little fellow at Granby
    Said, " I fain would a sweet black-and-tan be."
    So he talked very gruff,
    Donned a pink and white ruff,
And said, " Now I'm like it as can be."

TO VIOLET HAMER (THE "DODO").

DODOS are quite extinct, I've heard it saiD;
    Only I hardly think it can be sO.
Do *you* believe it ?   Turn your little heaD
    One moment to the glass, and answer " nO."

CHRISTMAS, 1884.

TO MAX.

I'M sending some flowers to dear little Max—
    To get natural ones at this season is hard ;
They are cheaper and don't fade so quickly in wax,
    But the nicest of all are those painted on card.

TO GLADYS.

I SIT down to write
 On a Monday night
(I ought to have written to you before),
  At 40 Hans Place,
  In the year of grace
One thousand eight hundred and eighty-four.

  I'm writing to say,
  My darling Gay,
That I got your dear little yellow note.
  When it caught my sight,
  It surprised me quite
To see what a beautiful hand you wrote.

  And the pictures, too,
  That my Gladys drew
On the opposite page, such a smart array !
  I ne'er saw a better
  Or sweeter letter
Than that which I got from my darling Gay.

  So when I come down
  To Reigate town,
As I hope to do in a month or so,
  You'll have two or three
  Big kisses for me,
For I was always "your Fred," you know.

  And now I must say
  "Good night," my Gay,
For it's getting late, and I'm off to bed.

So with fondest love.
I remain, my dove,
Your very affectionate Uncle Fred.

P.S.—In this note
I enclose a phot-
Ograph of myself.   Get mamma to dock it,
And cut off its head—
So you'll have " your Fred "
Hanging round your neck in a silver locket.

TO GEOFFREY.

G O, sweet elf, to my dear little Geoff,
   Pitch your voice on the natural F—
At the very tip-top of the clef—
And shout in his ear till he's deaf,
A Happy New Year to you, Geoff.

TO GWENDOLEN.

G O, sweet children, far away,
   W here there dwells a sweeter;
E nter at the break of day,
N ewly waking greet her.
D rop this flower upon her head,
O ver her repeating:
L ove from loving Uncle Fred,
E very joy that Heaven can shed,
N ew Year's fondest greeting.

TO CHARLIE.

[Aged 4, with a gift of toy elephants.]

C HARLIE, little chubby boy,
  H ere's a scrubby little toy;
A ll from distant countries meeting
R un to bid you Christmas greeting.
L o ! their *trunks* they've brought and they
I n your house full many a day
E vidently mean to stay.

TO PHYLLIS.

Du bist wie eine Blume (after Heine).

O H, thou art like a flower,
  So pure and bright and fair,
That spreadeth out its tender leaves
  Unto the summer air.
And gladness steals upon my heart,
  For 'tis a goodly sight,
That nature made so sweet a thing
  So pure and fair and bright.

Yet as I gaze upon thee,
  A tear is in mine eye,
For flowers fade so fast, and youth
  Passes so swiftly by.
And I am fain to lay my hand
  Upon thy golden hair,
And pray that God may keep thee still,
  So pure and bright and fair.

1885.

TWO CHRISTMAS CARDS.

AT Christmas, cards, of course, are sent in packs,
    Brave Cupids, once so shameless, come in bags.
All kinds and qualities of flowers in sacks
  Beneath whose weight the weary postman lags.

As on us Christmas smiles from year to year
  We gobble gobblers, and our goblets quaff ;
The dotard cracks his jokes upon his beer,
  Forgets his corns, and only thinks of chaff.

Miscellaneous Verses.

AN INDIAN ALPHABET.

THERE was a young man of Assam,
  Who got drunk every night upon "cham.,"
    When told by a friend
    How such habits must end,
He answered, "I don't care a d——."

There was a young man at Bellary,
Who thought himself quite the "shikāri,"
    He determined to walk
    Twenty miles for a stalk,
But he couldn't—so chartered a "ghāri."

There was an old man at Calcutta,
Who always complained of the butter,
    So they gave him some grease,
    Which caused his decease,
And they took him away on a shutter.

There's an elderly Colonel at Delhi,
Who maketh a god of his——well, he
    Invariably eats
    Thirteen different meats.
And winds up with pudding and jelly.

19

There was a young man at Erode,
Who painted his body with woad,
   And exclaimed, " I have hit on
   A dress à la Briton,
Which shortly will be quite the mode."

There's a young man at Furruckabad,
Whose face is abnormally sad,
   " When I ask," he says, " here
   For a pint of draught beer,
I'm told that it's not to be had."

A romantic young girl at Golconda,
In poesy's paths fain would wander,
   So she tried for a time
   To make up a rhyme,
But found it completely beyond her.

There was a young lady at Humpi,
Whose form was decidedly stumpy,
   But she felt quite consoled
   When one day she was told,
That a man had described her as " dumpy."

There was a young man on the Indus
Whose heart love had burnt into cinders ;
   His poems erotic
   And odes idiotic
Were published by Chatto and Windus.

A very small lady of Jollarpet
Had made of a very large doll a pet ;
   On its failing one day
   Her commands to obey
She began most severely to wallop it.

There was a young man at Koonoor
Who said, "The life here is a bore;"
  So he wouldn't stay longer,
  But chartered a tonga,
And never came back any more.

A polite little sub. at Lucknow
Got into a deuce of a row;
  When consigned by his Colonel
  To regions infernal,
"After you," he replied, with a bow.

A certain young man of Madras,
Who strongly resembled an ass,
  Endeavoured to bray
  As he happened one day
To look at himself in the glass.

A gentleman on the Nerbudda,
Whose servant had just lost the rudder,
  Said, "You suar, what now?
  "Go in after it—jao!
And lekar ao jaldi, you gadha."

There was a young fellow at Ooty,
Who did the professional beauty,
  He wore a "terai,"
  Stuck a glass in his eye,
And said, "*I'm* the Adonis of Ooty."

There's a simple young man in the Plains,
Who ne'er of the sun's heat complains;
  For his skull is as thick
  As an average brick,
And he doesn't possess any brains.

There was a young lady of Quetta,
When the weather grew wetter and wetter.
   She didn't go out
   For a fortnight about,
And then she felt very much better.

A testy old man of Rawalpindee
Once kicked up a deuce of a shindy;
   He *blew up* his boys
   With such *blasts* and such noise
That they said, "It's exceedingly windy."

An epicure at Siliguri,
In soups would eat nothing but pureé:
   If they brought him consommé,
   He'd raise h—ll and tommy,
And throw it away in a fury.

An old woman at Trichinopoly
Used to swear at her khidmatgar properly;
   And by way of excuse
   She would ask, why the deuce
Should the men have a swearing monopoly.

A musical man at Umballa
Used to shut himself up in his parlour,
   And all the day long
   Sing that charming old song,
Whose beautiful burthen is "tra-la."

A young man at Wellington races
Was backing his horses for "places,"
   But the winning-post past
   They were always the last,
And you *should* just have seen his grimaces.

P. & O. SS. "GANGES."

List of Passengers.

Mr. and Mrs. E. Sassoon and Infant.
Mr. and Mrs. F. W. Thomson.
Major T. Blake Humfrey.
Sir Kenneth Cumming.

Mr. F. W. Pattenden.
Lieut. Smith, R.N.
Mr. Lavers.
Mr. L. Marshall.

August 29, 1882. Between Singapore and Hongkong—report that a Typhoon was coming.

Mr. and Mrs. and Baby Sassoon
   Were all in a funk of the coming Typhoon,
For Mr. and Mrs. F. W. Thomson
Declared they had reason to think it would come
   soon;
Major Humfrey, in one word the whole matter
   summing,
Affirmed with an air of conviction, "It's *Cumming.*"
The nautical Mr. F. W. Pattenden
Opined that the hatches had better be battened in;
Mr. Smith of the Navy, and young Mr. Lavers,
Were rushing around crying out, "Who shall save
   us?"
When the Baby, with judgment not wholly impartial,
Replied, to the whole ship's astonishment, "*Ma shall.*"

"WE'LL ALL GO A-HUNTING WITH REA."

*A Song descriptive of a Hunting Expedition in the Rocky
Mountains, undertaken by F. W. PATTENDEN, L. MARSHALL,
and — NICHOLLS, with G. W. REA as Guide.*

THERE once was a hunter of fame and renown,
   Who lived rather out of the way;
His log-cabin was fifty odd miles from a town,
   And his name was G. W. Rea.
      Three tourists came riding that way,
      And this was the drift of their lay:
         " We're in want of some fun,
         And we've each got a gun.
      So we'll all go a-hunting with Rea."

         CHORUS.

      " We'll all go a-hunting with Rea,
      For he's the boss hunter, they say,
         And he knows all the ground
         Where the game's to be found,
      So we'll all go a-hunting with Rea."

Now, two of the party were Britain's bold sons:
   The first was inventive and cute;
He contrived a new *Patent in* slinging up guns
   On the saddle all ready to shoot.
      The second was fat, I must say,
      But his bearing was *Martial* and gay.
         A smart Yankee the third—
         And it might be inferred
      That old *Nick'll* secure him one day.

CHORUS—They all went a-hunting with Rea, etc.

They had rifles, and shot-guns, and pistols, and knives,
  And they brought ammunition untold;
Quite sufficient to last them the rest of their lives,
  If they lived to be ninety years old.
    With such a fine outfit they came,
    They were ready for all sorts of game,
      From the elk and the moose
      To the duck and the goose,
    You had only " to give it a name."
CHORUS—They all went a-hunting with Rea, etc.

They rode with their rifles all ready for use,
  And carefully noticed the slot;
Every moment expecting an elk or a moose
  That would stand there and wait to be shot.
    Through timber and thicket and park
    They rode, but I'm bound to remark
      That not one of the lot
      Ever fired a shot,
    Though they hunted from daylight to dark.
CHORUS—But we'll all go a-hunting with Rea, etc.

Starting early each morning this hopeful young band
  Saw fresh tracks again and again;
But the game that had made them was never on hand,
  It had left by the previous train.
    Till their patience began to grow short,
    To strong language they all had resort,
      And they said, " By the Lord,
      It's a glittering fraud
    To come out to the Rockies for sport."
CHORUS—But they still went a-hunting with Rea, etc.

So for breakfast they'd nothing but bacon to eat,
  On the same bit of bacon they lunched;

And at dinner they sighed for a little fresh meat
As that weary old bacon they munched.
At their fate they began to repine,
And they cursed the salt flesh of the swine,
Till a fat deer one day
Was knocked over by Rea,
And the venison was simply divine.
CHORUS—So we'll all go a-hunting with Rea, etc.

One fine morning they came on an elk lying near,
Within thirty paces, about;
But the patent sling action was all out of gear,
And the rifle refused to come out.
Some shots by the others were fired,
But of waiting the elk became tired,
And went off P.D.Q.,
And was soon lost to view,
In a way that was greatly admired.
CHORUS—But we'll all go a-hunting with Rea, etc.

In a week the young Briton, whose form was not slim,
Had enough of the wearisome quest;
For the game didn't seem worth the candle to him,
So he thought he would "give it a rest."
For he said, "It's too much of a strain,
Twelve hours a-day to remain,
And do nothing but straddle
A beastly hard saddle;
I'll never go hunting again."
CHORUS.
"I'll never go hunting again,
Which the same I am free to maintain;
So your life you may bet it,
And don't you forget it,
I'll never go hunting again."

Soon the Yankee went, too, with his shot-gun to shoot
  The innocent sage hen and duck ;
But the Englishman called him a lazy galoot,
  And to big game right manfully stuck.
    So now both the others were gone,
    And he was left there all alone,
      Like the last of the Ten
      Little Niggers—" and then,"
    As the poet remarks, "there was one."

CHORUS.

  But *he* went on hunting with Rea,
  For he's the boss hunter, they say,
    And he knows all the ground
    Where the game's to be found,
  So he still went a-hunting with Rea.

Now, the others were hardly away when there came
  The cream of the shooting at last ;
For they very soon struck upon plenty of game,
  And forgot all the troubles they'd past.
    Dame Fortune is fickle, they say,
    And the luck isn't always one way,
      And you're certain as fate
      To find game soon or late
    When you're out with a hunter like Rea.

CHORUS—So we'll all go a-hunting with Rea, etc.

So the bears and the elk by that Briton were shot,
  And he could, if he'd liked, have shot more ;
And when after ten days he got into the train,
  He took back with him trophies galore.

And that Englishman swears to this day,
That he never has had, anyway
  (Though the time was so short),
  Such magnificent sport
As when out in the Rockies with Rea.

Chorus.

So we'll all go a-hunting with Rea,
For he's the boss hunter, we say,
  And he knows all the ground
  Where the game's to be found,
So we'll all go a-hunting with Rea.

September, 1883.

"HOW IS THAT FOR LOW?"

*Henry Ward Beecher, of Plymouth Church, Brooklyn, was one
of the principal supporters of Seth Low, Candidate for the
Mayoralty of Brooklyn, November, 1883.*

" WHEN from Plymouth the popular preacher
    Is summoned by Death to go,
Oh, Heaven will t*Hen ry-ward Beecher*
  For backing me up," *Seth* Low.

New York, November 3, 1883.

THE MELANCHOLY STRANGER'S YARN.

One of the Passengers on the "Britannic" had been on the "Arizona" when she collided with an iceberg, and was very fond of telling the yarn.

'TWAS in the smoking-room one night, I saw him
    sitting there,
An unobtrusive stranger with a close-cropped head of
    hair.
He wore a single eyeglass in his melancholy eye,
And yet beneath the glass there lurked an air of
    mystery;
Some awful secret which he longed, yet strangely
    feared to tell,
And that, no doubt, was why at first he didn't feel
    quite well.
At last I found his secret out, and felt inclined to scoff:
The man had got a yarn to spin, and couldn't get it off!
But finally he fixed on me to share his untold woes,
Because I seemed to him a patient listener, I suppose.
I would have had it otherwise, but had not any choice,
He got me in a corner once, and spoke with hollow
    voice:
" 'Twas on the *Arizona*"—thus the sombre man began,
And told me how that foolish ship into an iceberg ran;
How, in the smoking-room, they heard an awful crash,
    and how
The *Arizona* lost a large percentage of her bow.

And then he showed me photos—taken on the spot and
    dated
(I wonder where in thunder the photographer located;
Perhaps 'twas taken by the man inhabiting the moon,
Or by a passing stranger in a casual balloon).
The ice thus broken, he began to tell his dismal tale
To every one on board, until the thing was almost
    stale.

He told it to the officers, and to the captain, too;
He told it to the passengers, he told it to the crew.
He lured the unsuspecting to a dark and quiet nook;
He told it to the doctor, to the stewards and the
    cook;
Until, whene'er he entered he created quite a panic
Among the smoke-room loungers on the gallant ship
    Britannic.

He always started right away, but ere he could
    proceed
There not unfrequently occurred a general stampede;
And many a time he just began, "'Twas on the
    Arizon——"
And then he'd cease abruptly, for he found himself
    alone.
And so reduced to silence he would glare through his
    monocular,
And wither the unhappy man who ventured to be
    jocular.
A horrid notion seized him, too, that he must be the
    Jonah
For whose misdeeds the iceberg smashed the good ship
    Arizona.
So one bright day he cried aloud, "Oh, hearken, I
    implore;
You ne'er shall hear of icebergs or of *Arizona* more;

And when I sleep beneath the wave, no eye will
  moistened be,
And though I am a Jonah, there will be no *wail* for
  me."
Then with a piercing shriek, of which I can't convey a
  notion,
The frenzied wretch plunged wildly down into the
  boiling ocean ;
So finding peace at last, beneath the broad Atlantic's
  breast
The stranger and the iceberg and the *Arizona* rest.

S.S. Britannic, DECEMBER 9, 1883.

"THE LADIES' DARLING."

*A Song written on a conceited and officious passenger on
the S.S. " Zealandia," JUNE, 1883.*

Air—" I'LL STRIKE YOU WITH A FEATHER."

I'LL sing of Mr. Benjamin,
   He is the ladies' darling ;
And it would be a deadly sin
   At him to be a-snarling.
Yet all of us are jealous,
   For we can ne'er forget—
And if we did, he'd tell us—
   He is the ladies' pet.

Chorus.

"*Au revoir !* ta-ta !" you'll hear him cry
To the passengers at 'Frisco, when he bids us all
    " Good bye ; "
"I'll strike you with a feather, I'll stab you with a pin!"
Oh, the darling of the ladies is Mr. Benjamin !

There once were twelve of Jacob's sons,
    You'll all have heard about it ;
There were some very handsome ones,
    We have no cause to doubt it.
But he whose clothes were finest,
    Who always had most "tin,"
The fairest, the divinest,
    Was little Benjamin.—Chorus.

His style of wearing whiskers is
    A modified " Dundreary ";
Of gazing on his lovely " phiz "
    You never could be weary.
He'll play at nap. or poker
    Till all his money's gone ;
At euchre with the " joker "
    He is the champi-*on*.—Chorus.

He'll sing just like a nightingale—
    Oh, nothing could be finer ;
He warbles up and down the scale,
    In major or in minor.
He'll take a " G " falsetto
    Whene'er he has the whim ;
Andante—Allegretto—
    It's all the same to him.—Chorus.

At all the dances we expect
  Our Benjamin to "boss" us,
For he is not in intellect
  An absolute Colossus !
And so we always go where
  Our M.C.'s to be found ;
The Captain's simply nowhere
  When Benjamin's around.—CHORUS.

He makes us dance Quadrilles although
  We want to dance Schottisches ;
But none can murmur when they know
  It's by the M.C.'s wishes.
Upon the light fantastic
  Applause he'll ever win,
All know the step elastic
  Of Mr. Benjamin.—CHORUS.

In all the sports he has control,
  And no one could be smarter ;
He takes upon himself the *rôle*
  Of umpire, judge, and starter.
He bosses the committee,
  And lords it near and far ;
It really seems a pity
  He wasn't born a Czar.—CHORUS.

In no one else you'll ever find,
  On board of the *Zealandia*,
Such elegance and grace combined
  With majesty and grandeur.
So by express desire—
  I'm given to understand—
The Captain will retire,
  And Ben. will take command.—CHORUS.

AN INCIDENT AT HONOLULU.

M R. TYLER, the chief officer, was seen to enter the Hawaiian Hotel with a lady at 11 p.m. It may be added, to prevent misconstruction, that he left again immediately.

> I STOOD on the steps of a certain hotel,
>   In a nook that was quiet and shady,
> When there drove up a brougham containing a swell,
>   Who offered his arm to a lady.
>
> I looked at my watch—'twas eleven p.m.
>   And it struck me as rather a rare case.
> So I gazed with a curious eye upon them,
>   As they rapidly passed up the staircase.
>
> 'Twas the work of a moment, and yet I could guess
>   The name of that elegant smiler—
> Though as to the lady I'm bound to confess,
>   That I don't know by what name to *style her.*

SONG OF AN R.A.

Suggested by Mr. J. R. Herbert's Pictures in the Royal Academy Exhibition of 1886.

> O H, I'm a distinguished R.A.,
>   And though I am aging a bit,
> I still go on pegging away,
>   And I feel on the whole pretty fit,

I'm never deficient in patience,
  Nor wanting in muscle and sinew;
I've painted for two generations,
  And, please God, I mean to continue.

CHORUS.

For I'm a distinguished R.A.,
  And I don't care a straw what they say;
    They may sneer at my pictures,
    I laugh at their strictures,
  For I'm a distinguished R.A.

I know that they say it's too bad o' me
  To put in my eight on the line;
But it's lucky for them the Academy
  Has a rule against putting in nine!
For I always have thought things of beauty
  Improving to woman and man,
And I therefore esteem it my duty
  To show them as much as I can.

CHORUS.

For I'm a distinguished R.A.,
  And I'm anxious to take, while I may,
    A prominent part
    In instilling true art,
  As becomes a distinguished R.A.

These upstarts who paint now-a-days,
  And get their absurdities hung,
Think proper to sneer at R.A's.,
  And say you should paint when you're young.
But the fact is that as you grow older
  You thoroughly master the trick,
So my latter-day pictures are bolder,
  And I finish them double as quick.

20

CHORUS.

For I'm a distinguished R.A.,
And I'm painting far better to-day
Than I used to—alack!
Half a century back—
Before I became an R.A.

I've a Boar-hunt that's equal to Snyder's,
And it certainly does make me fume
When these critics declare that the riders
Are dressed up in circus costume!
Once I heard a young man, with a cursory
Half-glance at the picture, remark,
That for models I go to the nursery
And select from an old Noah's Ark.

CHORUS.

But I'm a distinguished R.A.,
So what do I care when they say,
"Just look at that shocking horse!
Why, it's a rocking-horse.
"This is as good as a play!"

Sometimes I confess that I find them
With truer perceptions of art;
For some of them say I remind them
Of poor dear old Solomon Hart.
They say I keep up his tradition,
And worthily follow his line,
And that Burlington House Exhibition
Would be dull without pictures of mine.

Chorus.

For I'm a distinguished R.A.
And there's nobody else who can play
    The peculiar part
    Of poor Solomon Hart,
That very distinguished R.A.

I laugh at these young fellows' crudities.
    Their daubs from that dreary old Venice.
Their symphonies, studies, and nudities—
    They'd much better stick to lawn-tennis!
If they're under the sober impression
    That *that's* how an artist should paint,
I can tell them—to use an expression
    Of colloquial parlance—it *aint!*

Chorus.

But I'm a distinguished R.A.,
And if they would know the right way
    Of painting, they ought
    To come here and be taught
By an old and distinguished R.A.

And in spite of their scoffs, I may mention
    That, though I am old and grey-haired,
At present I've every intention
    Of painting as long as I'm spared.
I'm as active as if I were twenty,
    And until I am on the decline,
I intend to have *(Deo volente)*
    My habitual eight on the line.

CHORUS.

For I'm a distinguished R.A.,
And nothing the critics may say
Can persuade me to stop :
I shall paint till I drop,
And I'll die as an active R.A.

JUNE, 1886.

AT SEA.

THE sea's the true-born Briton's home.
We're children of the ocean—
Though Nature's *works* are still by some
Preferred when *not in motion.*
So when we wish to celebrate
The Royal Jubilee,
It's quite superfluous to state
That we are " all at sea ! "

The great Imperial Institute
In Kensington we bury.
Our business men it could not suit
Much worse in Pondicherry !
So far away we've made the site
Of this gigantic fraud,
That London has a perfect right
To call it " all abroad " !

The Bishops, too, those Britons true
Whose home's in every *see,*
Will soon look blue as Ocean's hue
For want of £ s. d.

A great Church House for all to meet—
The Low, the Broad, the High !
To use the language of the street,
The scheme is "all my eye !"

And now, to jubilate afloat,
The gallant R.T.Y.C.,
With princely patronage promote
A yacht-race on the high sea.
Right round our coast they'll sail, it seems,
And surely you'll agree,
Whate'er you think of other schemes,
This one is " all at sea ! "

APRIL, 1887.

THE SAILOR LAD TO HIS SWEETHEART.

*Written for H. S. S., as suggested words for a song
composed by him.*

ON the dreary waste of ocean,
When the storm is brooding near,
And the undulating motion
Makes me feel a little queer ;
When my food is placed before me,
And I loathe its very sight—
Then thy spirit hovers o'er me,
And it almost sets me right.

For no matter what the weather.
What the tossing of the sea,
I am always pulled together,
Darling, by the thought of thee.

Oh, the food!   How shall I say it?
My command of language fails
Adequately to portray it—
  Salted chunk as hard as nails;
Bread that's populous with weevils,
  Armour-clad in crust of steel—
Hunger is the least of evils
  When compared with such a meal.

  And it comes across me sadly,
    Would that thou wast here to see!
  How unselfishly, how gladly
    I would share my crust with thee!

When the mighty billows roll up
  O'er the fierce Atlantic tide,
And I give my very soul up,
  Leaning o'er the good ship's side;
Then I see thee hanging over,
  In the same position, dear,
Thirty seconds out from Dover,
  When we've hardly cleared the pier.

  Then no matter what the woe, love,
    What the anguish I go through—
  It consoles me much to know, love,
    Thou hast suffered from it too.

When the skipper's dog is snarling
  Near my thinly-trousered shin,
Then I think with envy, darling,
  Of the skirts thou goest in.

Rope's end is familiar to me,
  And the cat is not unknown—
Still, on such occasions gloomy,
  Visions rise of thee, my own.
    Then the " cat " is like a feather,
      When that vision smiles on me,
    And my skin becomes as leather,
      All the time I think of thee.

When I'm crouching stiff and frozen,
  Sheltered by a dripping sail,
And I hear the brutal bo'sen
  Say, " It's coming on a gale."
When the storm is raging madly,
  And the rain is drenching me.
Then, my pet, I think how gladly
  Would I places change with thee.
    Then, no matter what the weather,
      What the tossing of the sea—
    I should never care a feather
      If it was not tossing *me.*

When at tarry ropes I'm hauling,
  Till my streaming temples throb,
And the skipper's voice is bawling—
  " Haul away, you lazy swab ! "
I recall the evening, dearest,
  Thou didst seize me by the hair,
Using in thy wrath the nearest
  Thing to oaths a lady dare.
    Then I pull myself together,
      As that scene comes back to me—
    And, in spite of wind and weather,
      Thank my stars that I'm at sea.

When I'm told to " trice the spanker,"
  " Brace the jib," or " splice the stays,"
" Reef the sheets," or " slew the anchor,"
  Till my brain is in a maze.
It's a soothing thought to me, love,
  That, if thou wert standing by—
At their jabber thou wouldst be, love,
  As completely fogged as I.

    For no matter what they cry, dear,
      What they order me to do,
    I'm as sure as fate to try, dear,
      Just the thing I oughtn't to.

Oft with envy unavailing,
  Have I thought of thee on land;
Oh, that we were only sailing
  O'er the ocean hand in hand !
If, my darling, thou wert near me,
  When the storm begins to blow—
It would comfort me and cheer me,
  In my misery to know,

    That, no matter what the weather,
      What the tossing of the sea—
    It would be, were we together,
      Worse for thee, perhaps, than me.

MARCH, 1887.

TO BRING IN THE NAMES OF CERTAIN ACTRESSES IN VERSE WITH A RHYME TO EACH NAME.

THESPIS looks down on Irving and Anderson,
And sees no lovelier daughter and no grander son'
A lordling thought to play with fair Miss Fortescue,
But failed, because he never rightly caught his cue.
Scorn not to tinge thy pallid cheeks, Miss Eastlake,
With just a touch of madder or the least lake.
Loud clap the "gods" to greet their favourite
Cameron,
The floor with heels and sticks they freely hammer on.
Last, but not least, the be-all and the end-all,
Is England's Queen of Drama, peerless Kendal,

OCTOBER 23, 1884.

ON SOME CHRISTMAS "VERSES."

SIMPLE, simple, little poet.
How l wonder if you know it :
But your verses—every word—
Are ineffably absurd.

There's already quite enough
Of such very trashy stuff;
Yet persistently you go it,
Feebly, feebly, little poet.

Nothing really could be worse
Than your childish Christmas verse :
And if you could only know it,
You'd not think yourself a poet.

Think not that it gives me pleasure
Thus to take your proper measure,
But I really feel I owe it
To my conscience, little poet.

W. E. G.

BREATHES there a man with soul so dead,
   Who never to himself hath said,
  This is my own, my native land;
Whose heart within him ne'er hath burned
For England's sake, but rather turned
  To England's foes on every strand ?
One such there is—go mark him well—
His name is B I double L.

THE POPE AND MONTE CARLO.

THOUGH they keep the plan as dark as they can,
  Yet from private enquiries we know—
That his Holiness gave him a cheque that's blank,
With imperative orders to break the bank,
  And ruin the whole Casino.

The previous Pope gave them lots of rope,
  And indulged in the vain belief:
That the sinners in time would have filled their cup,
And then they would see that the game was up,
  And come to eternal grief.

~~~~~~~~~~~~~~

AMATEUR THEATRICALS ALPHABET.

A WAS the Artist who painted the scene,
    B was the Beauty she showed as Rosine.
C was the Counter with panels below,
D the Dispute as to where it should go.
E was the Ease with which everyone played,
F was the Fuss that they none of them made.
G was the Gee-gee so proudly caprisoned,
H was the Host by which Amicus was garrisoned.
I was the Ire of De Brissac when let in,
J was the Joke Mariette couldn't get in.
K was the King who took part in the mummery—
L was the Laughter he called forth as Pomaret.
M was the Marquis in splendid attire,
N was the Niggledegee of Sophia.
O was Our Wife in a lovely costume,
P was the Pout that she couldn't assume.
Q was the Quarrel of Alsop and Flinch.
R their Retreat when it come to a pinch.
S was old Stilton who wouldn't be baulked,
T was the Tone in which Mrs. S. talked.
U was Utility played *à la mode*,
V the Vivacity Mariette showed.

W was William Montrose of Penzance,
X was the 'Xquisite tint of the pants.
Y was the Yule-night our colds were contracted,
Z was the Zeal with which every one acted.

A LETTER CONTAINING PARODIES
ON

Alas! how easily things go wrong;
A sigh too deep, or a kiss too long,
And there cometh a mist and a weeping rain,
And life is never the same again.

G. Macdonald.

March 13, 1889.

DEAR MRS. W.——,—With characteristic energy I have been assiduously prosecuting enquiries in all directions regarding the true version of "How easily things go wrong." Five friends of a literary turn have sent me their ideas on the subject, but I must confess that I entertain serious doubts whether the correct version is to be found among those that they have sent me. Indeed, I am not altogether satisfied as to the *bonâ fides* of at least one of my friends. However, I copy them out, and send them to you for what they are worth. I express no opinion upon them; and you will, I am sure, bring an unbiassed judgment to bear upon the several versions. I recollect that you were doubtful as to the authorship of the lines, and I was unable to help you. Unfortunately, there seems to be a divergence of opinion among my five correspondents on this point—"quot homines tot sententiæ,"—as Miss—— would say. I copy and send you the five versions just as received, with the names of the poets to whom my friends severally ascribe the lines. Here is the first of them :

Alas ! how easily things go wrong ;
A drop too much or a glass too strong !
And there cometh a mist, and the senses stray,
And your head is never the same next day.
Martin Toper.

I presume my friend must mean " Martin Tupper." The lines certainly suggest one phase of Proverbial Philosophy.

The next version is as follows :

Alas ! how easily things go wrong
When played at sight is your favourite song ;
And there cometh a crash and a look of pain,
And nobody asks you to sing again.
G. Sharp.

The third version runs thus :

Alas ! how easily things go wrong
When you've just half-dressed as you hear the
gong ;
And you try to sneak in without noise—in vain !
And vow you'll never be late again.

The friend who sends me this says he cannot exactly

recall the author's name, but he is under a strong impression that he has seen the lines somewhere with the initials " K.C.L." under them. I have tried my best to identify these initials without success. Perhaps you can help me.

The fourth version runs as follows:

> Alas! how easily things go wrong;
> A sneer too cutting, a word too strong.
> And there comes a fist and a stinging pain,
> And your nose is never the same again.
>
> Francis Quarrels.

My friend of course means " Francis Quarles," a minor poet of the 17th century. This version very closely approaches the one you had in your mind, though its drift is somewhat different.

The last version is one that I regard with grave suspicion. You will observe that the other four agree as to the first line, but here there is a divergence even in that.

It runs thus:

> Alas! how easily plates go wrong!
> Exposed too little, exposed too long!
> And there comes a mist and a haziness,
> And the print is never a great success.
>
> John Dryplate.

This is evidently a slip of the pen for " John Dryden," but I fail to find the lines among " Glorious John's " published works. It is possible that you may prefer this last version to the others, on the ground that it avoids the word "things," which, as you justly remarked, is eminently unpoetical.

I leave you to select from the five, merely adding that it is just within the range of possibility that none of them may be the correct version. I shall hear, I hope, when you return to Town, so that I may avail myself of your permission to call. You will then perhaps tell me which, if any, of the above suggestions meets with your approval.

Sincerely yours,

F. W. Pattenden.

A LETTER TO E. W. P.

Boston. *Tuesday.*

TRÈS CHÈRE MADAME,—I somehow am constrained to write to you to-night, though I'm inclined, Madame, to say you were not kind the other day. The Ancient One I've just begun almost to hate—too late! too late!—for he's about to cut me out. I feel and know that it is so. Too late! too late! I can descry my cruel fate with half an eye. My heart, sweet dame, is broken quite; but all the same it may come right—the pieces all, both great and small perhaps I may some future day with care collect, and I expect that I shall find some dame who'll not be disinclined to take the lot.

I'm rather down in luck to-day; from Grimsby

town I went away without a brown my fare to pay.
My abject grief is sad to see, for ne'er a brief will
come to me. And well I know, *très chère Madame*,
that when I go to Nottingham on Thursday next, the
same I'll find—I may be vexed, but never mind. And
now adieu, Madame, to you. I write, you know, sweet
dame, that so you may be brought just once again to
give a thought to

PATTENDEN.

ANOTHER LETTER TO E. W. P.

CARISSIMA *mia,*
I've got an idea
Of spending a few days at Reigate;
My business is so
Very heavy, you know,
That it's rarely a holiday *I* get.

I yearn and I burn
For your speedy return,
Your absence has filled me with sorrow:
In town for my grief
I can find no relief,
So I start for the country to-morrow.

If you're anxious to learn
When I mean to return,
It possibly may be on Saturday;
If they want me to stay
Until Monday, I may—
But I'm sure to be back on the latter day.

As you know my address,
You can hardly do less
Than send me a tender epistle ;
Though, with so many chaps
That you write to, perhaps,
For a letter I'm likely to whistle.

I hope that the air
Of the country down there
Will have made you as plump as a fattened hen;
On Monday we meet—I'm
Like clockwork at tea-time—
Yours ever,
F. W. PATTENDEN.

43, SOUTH EATON PLACE,
Wednesday, April 11, 1888.

INDEX.